# Fallen

# ANGEL

## DIANE MARTIN

To Jeanne Thanks for your support

2023

10 09 08   6 5 4 3 2 1
First Edition

Edited by Dr. William A. Martin
Printed by United Graphics Inc.
Cover and interior book layout and design by Borel Graphics
Cover photo of Jim Arbogast, Getty Images

United States ISBN Agency
ISBN 13: 978-0-9802176-3-6

Disclaimer:
The following story is completely fictional and does not depict any actual person or event; any similarities are completely coincidental.

To William, my guardian angel;
Antionio, the angel of peace;
Angelo, the angel of destiny;
Asia, the angel of grace;
A'Dante, the angel of love & video games.

Be not forgetful to entertain
strangers: for thereby some have
entertained angels unawares.

**Hebrews 13:2**

**Izrael:** Variant of Izrail and Azrael, the name of the Angel of Death, who separates the soul from the body upon death, meaning "help of God."

**Ariel:** Hebrew unisex name meaning "lion of God." It is the biblical name for the city of Jerusalem and one of the seven angels who ruled the waters.

# PROLOGUE

*B*OOM!
"Heavenly Father, who art in Heaven…"
*BOOM!*

"Damn-it," I said, "Now I have to start all over again."

*BOOM!*

"Heavenly Father, who art in Heaven…"

*BOOM!*

Frustrated, I said, "Shit, I can't even pray."

Suddenly, my sergeant walked into the barracks. "Soldier get off your knees and report to your post!" he shouted. "Right now!"

I yelled back, "Yes, sir!" When my sergeant left the room and I was sure that the coast was clear, I whispered, "Father, if you can hear me, please watch over me this day and protect all of us against forces unknown, for reasons we'll never understand. Thanking you in advance…"

My sergeant interrupted again, "Right now soldier!" he yelled, this time sounding desperate.

"Yes, sir!" I yelled again. As I collected my helmet and gun, and walked toward the door, I turned and whispered, "Amen."

As I prepared for combat, me and five others were discussing our strategy to rescue children who were barricaded in a school located in a heavy combat zone. As we were talking, I developed an urgent need to relieve myself. I excused myself, walked over, and stood behind one of the trucks.

While the other soldiers mapped out what seemed to be a simple search and rescue mission, a small child approached the soldiers who were talking among themselves. I watched the whole interaction from a distance.

"Could you help me sir? My family is hungry and haven't eaten for weeks," said the small child who looked tired and hungry.

"Where's your parents?" asked one of the soldiers.

"My father was killed. A bomb blew off both of my mother's legs and she can't work anymore. I am forced to take care of my brothers and sisters," he said in a heavy almost untranslatable accent.

"I'm sorry to hear that," said one of the soldiers. "Here take this," the soldier said, as he handed the child some currency.

Happily the child accepted. "Thank you, thank you so much," he said.

When I was done relieving himself, I zipped my pants and was walking towards them when I yelled, "Hey guys, are you ready?"

Just then the young child said, "I am so grateful sir. Please take this," he said, as he removed a small object and a piece of paper from his pocket.

The soldier reached out his hand, "Thank you. What is this?" the soldier said, as he closely inspected the object and the piece of paper handed to him by the child.

"The man in that car told me to give it to you," the child said, pointing to a man sitting in a military vehicle parked close by.

The soldiers looked at the parked vehicle where they saw the sergeant smiling and waving at them. The soldier then looked at the object and then the paper again.

"It's a note." The soldier began to read the note aloud, "Goodbye boys, I can't take it anymore." They all looked over at the car again.

Then the other soldier yelled, "Man, that's a clip to a...," Before the soldier could finish his sentence everything around us became hot.

*BOOM!* My sergeant's car blew up.

Before I knew it, I was thrown fifteen feet into the air. As my body landed onto the ground, I was bombarded by fallen pieces of flesh that once belong to my comrades. Initially, everything around me became quiet and then suddenly I heard screams. People ran and cried as shrapnel from the vehicle flew around piercing the flesh of everyone nearby.

"Help me! Help me!" someone yelled in the distance. Screams started to come from every direction.

"Run!" someone shouted. "Run!"

"Man down!" someone else shouted. "Man down!"

"Are you okay?" A woman asked as she approached me. She leaned over to try to check my injuries as I lay helplessly on the ground.

"Wha'...Wha'...?" I stuttered.

As I lay there, I could see the large hole in the ground left from the explosion. While I remained on the ground praying, something floating in the air landed near me. Instinctively, I reached over to see what it was. I picked it up holding it with my blood soaked hands. I recognized it. It was part of the final farewell letter written by my sergeant. I read the fragile letter through tearful eyes before everything around me went black.

In that moment, I had been transformed. The young man who used to run the streets of Chicago was gone. Now the only thing that's left is a walking memory of the tragedies of war.

# PROLOGUE

**|| ✶ ✶ ✶ ||**

*Ring!* The alarm clock rang. *It's time to go home soldier.*

"Turn that shit off!" a soldier yelled.

I reached over to turn it off. I sat up and placed my feet onto the cold floor. Staring at the concrete, its gray reflection staring back at me, I looked at my legs. For the first time, I didn't recognize them. As if we were meeting for the very first time, I looked at them. I took a moment to wiggle each one – one at a time becoming acquainted or re-acquainted, if you could say that. I was fascinated by their movement – by the way they took turns entertaining me. I smiled to myself, enjoying this moment.

After wiping the sleep from my eyes, I stood and walked toward the bathroom. Looking in the mirror, scratching my ass, and yawning, I looked at the reflection and thought to myself, *who am I?* As I asked that question, the obvious came to mind. I was tall with dark brown eyes, big full lips, broad nose, high cheek bones, and my body was chiseled from strenuous military exercises. Unaffected by the rays of the hot sun, I was chocolate, not a beautiful dark chocolate, but a beautiful white chocolate. As a little boy, when I asked my mother, "Why was I so light?" She would say that I was a hot cup of coffee with too much cream – that made me sweeter than everyone else. *If only she knew the truth.*

I graduated top of my class and excelled in everything I've done in life – from high school to the streets to the military. By definition, I had everything, but something was missing. As I leaned closer to the mirror, looking into my own eyes, I realized what was missing – a soul. Where did it go? When I arrived here, young and optimistic, I had one. I cared about the simple things. I once enjoyed barbeques and family reunions. I once enjoyed sitting on the front porch with my boys. I once enjoyed making-out with my girl in the backseat of my

6

daddy's car. I once dreamed of a family that consisted of a wife and a child; dreams of a job where I wore suits, carried a briefcase, sitting in an office, while making big money decisions for big money-makers, but life had something else planned for me – God had something else planned for me. Now, there was nothing left.

# CHAPTER
# 1
## MARCH 2007

When I finally awakened from a five year nightmare, I was on my way back to Chicago; a place I hadn't called home in five years. Everything looked so different now. There were large planters in the middle of the road that once held a solid yellow traffic line and the streets looked cleaner than I remembered. There were also several new additions to the Chicago's skyline. The lake looked beautiful as it rustled against the shore. It was so nice to see all of the smiling faces as they walked up and down Michigan Avenue.

For a moment, I reflected back to the look on my sergeant's face before he committed suicide. I should have known that something was wrong. I remembered the letter that said, "…I can't take this anymore." The handwriting was almost illegible and yet, the sergeant we all knew was careful, precise, and somewhat of a perfectionist – almost to a fault. He would have never written a letter like that, but it all happened so fast. We didn't have time to question it…no time to think twice.

My eyes filled with tears as I thought about how many soldiers lost their lives, died right in front of me – from suicide, to bombings, to gun fire – too many were gone too soon. *Suck it up soldier. The war isn't made for crybabies.* I thought to myself. I had to take my mind off of the bloody images. I needed a distraction so I turned to a radio station in my rental car that played soft jazz. As I was listening and enjoying the sweet sounds of Marvin Gaye, my cell-phone rang.

Looking at the caller-id, I answered and said, "Hey sweetie."

"So will you be here on time?" my wife, Ariel asked. "We can't wait to see you."

"Yeah, I'm on my way now. I'm about twenty minutes away."

"How are your parents?" she asked.

"They are fine." I was welcomed back home by my parents who arrived at the airport to pick me up.

"Are they coming to dinner?"

"No, my mother isn't feeling well," I said, lying. Honestly, my parents didn't want to have anything to do with Ariel or her family.

"That's a shame. Well, I hope that she feels better."

*She feels better already...believe me.* I thought to myself.

"Did I tell you how much I love you today?" she asked.

"No, I don't think so."

"Well, I do, and you know how good it feels to tell you that without having to wait several months for a response – praying for a response. I can't wait to hold you. Oh, you have no idea how long I've waited...I'm so excited," she said, trying to contain herself.

Almost whispering, as if I was unsure of the words coming from my mouth, I said, "I feel the same way."

"Hurry honey...I have so many plans," she said, eagerly.

*Plans.* "I can't wait," I said, exhausted from the mere mention of the word.

"Wonderful, now remember my Nana is hard of hearing. You will have to be patient when you talk to her," she said.

"Not a problem, if I'm nothing else, I am definitely patient," I said.

"Well good, I'm so glad you're home baby. I missed you so much," she said, like a woman who was madly in love.

"I missed you too baby-girl. I'll see you soon," I said, more out of consideration for her enthusiasm than anything else.

"Okay," she said, giggling.

"Bye," I said.

"Bye," she replied back.

I pushed the "end" button on my phone and looked into my rearview mirror to see the face of an outsider staring back at me. Then, I remembered the day I left my mother's home – pants sagging, white wife-beater, cornrows, and completely clueless about where my life was going. Now, I am a grown man – a soldier on my way home.

As I continued along Michigan Avenue, suddenly images of dead bodies flashed before my eyes. I became hot as my body's temperature began to rise. Next, my hands began to tremble; tremble so hard that my steering wheel began to rattle. Becoming completely overwhelmed and confused, I couldn't pull my car to safety so I hit the brakes.

*Screech!* Was the sound made by the tires on the vehicle behind me. The driver jumped out of his car and knocked on my car's window.

"Hey! What the fuck is wrong with you? We almost had an accident," he said, angrily.

Dazed, I looked up. I don't know what the driver saw on my face, but he began to walk away, apologizing.

"Look man, I'm sorry," the driver paused and while looking around him, he said, "Hey, I'm okay...you're okay...everyone's okay...okay? You have a good day."

I watched as the driver ran away. After my hands stopped shaking, I reached for my rearview mirror to check myself. What I saw was frightening. I didn't recognize myself. In the mirror was the face of a stranger...a very angry stranger.

DIANE MARTIN

■ ★ ★ ★ ■

The biggest decision of my life was made because I wanted to prove to a complete stranger that I wasn't a punk.

"Pull those damn pants up, boy," he said.

Looking at this man dressed in full military gear frightened me, but I wouldn't let on. "I got your boy," I said, grabbing myself trying to impress my friends.

"You better watch your mouth. I know that your parents raised you to respect your elders," the soldier said.

"How do you know what the fuck my parents did? You don't know me," I said, while thinking that he was right about my parents. My parents did raise me better than that.

With a piercing stare, he said, "I know that you are some...," he paused and then directed his words to the whole crowd. "All of you are some foul mouths, baggy pants, no future having, potential jail-birds...that's what you are."

"Man, you talk a lot of shit. Don't get those medals slapped off of that ugly ass jacket," one of my friends said.

Putting his finger into my friend's chest, the soldier said, "Excuse me, what were you saying?"

Now scared, my friend answered, "Umm, I'm just saying."

"You ain't saying shit. Like James Brown said, 'You talking loud and ain't saying nothing'...punk-asses," he spouted with a grimace on his face.

"Damn," we all said, directing our attention in our friend's direction. "Whatcha' gon' do now?"

Backing down, my friend said, "Nothing, I ain't 'bout to get my new "Ones" dirty over this bullshit."

Directing his attention back to me, the soldier said, "Got some shit to say?"

12

I didn't utter another word. I just looked at him and smiled. There was something powerful in making him think that his words had no impact on me.

He continued, "I didn't think so...losers. You punks walk around gunning down innocent people. I wonder what you would do if you were commissioned to stand up against a real enemy. Now, if you really want to do something with your lives, why don't you join the service? You ain't doing shit else, but taking up space reserved for people who are doing something."

His words hurt, but I knew that he was right. We weren't doing anything positive with our lives – searching for that fast money is all that we did. The things we did would only lead to jail or death. Deep down in my soul, I knew that I wasn't living up to my potential, but I didn't want to be the punk who went to college. I knew that I was breaking my mother's heart and disappointing my father. Maybe this guy was right, but the military? I had to admit that I like the way these guys humbled themselves to this man. All of them were packing heat, but it didn't matter. They respected him for standing up against them. I liked that.

I finally confirmed the decision after a conversation with my father. After his speech about the first black men who sacrificed their lives for this country and how they were treated when they returned home; how they came home to be enslaved physically, mentally, socially, economically, and emotionally. When he told me how he, my great-great grandfather, my great grandfather, and my grandfather, put their lives on the line not only for the rights of our people, but for all of the people in this country, I felt compelled to enlist and I did.

Nonetheless, it was the worst decision I've ever made. Not saying that the military is a bad thing, I'm just saying that after serving, I can truly say that it wasn't for me. I just wish that he had warned me about its long term effects and that it wasn't about my manhood or about following in the footsteps of past generations, but something other than that…something I would never understand or forget.

# CHAPTER
## 2

I was flustered and annoyed by the time I arrived at Ariel's parent's house. My first day back and I had to spend it with the most annoying people in Chicago. Her mother is a retired school teacher and her father, is a retired engineer of a railroad and a recipient of a million dollar settlement for an injury that occurred on the job. Savvy and thrifty with every penny earned, they afforded their children many luxuries like braces, limo rides to public school, and tutors to ensure good grades.

When I pulled into the driveway of their home, I immediately felt unwelcomed. If her parents had it their way, Ariel would have married a lawyer or a prince – anything other than me, not realizing that the chances of her marrying either one of them was slim-to-none. What they didn't know was Ariel needed a roughneck – a brotha who could handle her, who could hold it down for her, and protect her…and I was that man.

Before I could turn off the ignition, Ariel was running out of the house and heading towards me. Watching parts of her body bounce up and down was turning me on; made me remember what I've been missing. She was beautiful and all grown up. I became excited trying to take it all in. The girl I left behind still wore braces and pig-tails. Now a woman with the most beautiful smile and locs that draped over her sun-kissed shoulders was standing before me. The pictures that she mailed to me didn't do her justice. At that moment, I felt like a lucky man.

"What happened sweetie? Why are you late? What's wrong? Look at you. You're soaked. Do you have a fever?" she said, touching my forehead.

After spending five years taking care of myself, it was hard coming home to someone who wanted to take care of me. When I was able to get a word in edgewise, I tried answering all of her questions at once, "Nothing, I was almost in an accident, I'm okay, and no fever."

"Accident, are you okay?" she asked, looking me up and down. She paused to instruct one of the servants to get me a glass of water. "Anna, please get my baby some water."

"Right away, Miss," she replied, doing as she was told.

"I said that I was fine," I said, looking in the servant's direction. "Now stop making a fuss over me," I said, fixing my clothes.

"I'm just worried about you. You're back now, and I'm going to take care of you. Do you hear me?" she said, placing her hands on her hips and waving her finger in the air.

"Yes sir…I mean mam'," I said, saluting her.

We stopped and looked each other over like we were seeing each other for the first time. She walked up to me, placed her hand on my cheek, and then said, "You are so beautiful." She smiled and then ran her hand over my clean-shaven head. "I missed you," she said, now fighting back tears.

I smiled and said, "I missed you too."

We stood quietly staring at each other.

Breaking the romantic gaze and reflecting back to my earlier comment, she said, "I see that you brought more than your luggage back, Mr. Funnyman. You got jokes now right?"

"No, I got you," I said, placing my arms around her waist and gently kissing her on the neck.

"Cut it out, my parents might be watching. Plus, we have all of the time in the world for that," she said, trying to free herself.

"Yeah, starting in a few minutes," I said and then looked in the backseat of the car. "Daddy's been gone a long time. It wouldn't take me long, I promise. Now climb in the backseat with me."

"No, I will not," she insisted. "Now put it on ice until later. Let's get in there. You can't keep your family waiting."

I saw someone peeking through the living-room window. "I'm not up to this right now. I'm really tired. Is my family in there?"

"I'm not saying, Mr. Inquiring Minds," she teased and then continued, "Now get yourself in there…your family misses you." She gave me a hard stare. "Right now soldier," she said, nudging me in the direction of the house."

"Okay," I said, trying to resist.

Once at the door, I hesitated before I knocked. I took a moment to shake off the anxiety. When I was ready to see all of them, I placed my hand on the door. I noticed that the door was cracked. I walked in. "Hello…Hello," I said. All of a sudden, out of everywhere people began to jump out.

"Surprise!" they all yelled.

I fought back tears as they all ran up to greet me. *Suck it up soldier. The war isn't made for crybabies.* I thought to myself. I resisted the urge to cry. As I stood there surrounded by Ariel's family, I thought about my mother's arms as she held me for the first time in five years. My heart began to swell. I was happy to be home.

**‖ ☆ ☆ ☆ ‖**

Prior to this moment, I had only eaten with my brothers in the military. Now, I was breaking bread with people I barely knew.

We all gathered around a table full of food. We sat down to a twelve course meal. There was chicken, cornbread, spaghetti, greens, corn-on-the-cob, fried fish, potato salad, fresh garden salad, baked beans, ribs, burgers, and macaroni with cheese. My mouth began to water. As I envisioned making a pig of myself, I was reminded that I wasn't at home with my family with whom I could 'keep it real.'

Her mother was given the honor to say grace and then we all dug in. I couldn't get the butter on my corn-on-the-cob, before Ariel's father got started.

Sitting at the head of the table, he said, "So Izrael, now that you're back, what are your plans?"

"Well sir…" He didn't let me finish my sentence.

"Izrael, you don't have to call me sir. Call me anything just don't call me while I'm on the toilet," he said, attempting to be funny. Everyone began to laugh on queue as if it was all rehearsed. I sat stone-faced. I didn't think it was funny.

Clearing his throat and realizing that I didn't appreciate his sense of humor, he continued, "Well, you know that mama and I were thinking about you and Ariel and the fact that you left right after you guys said your 'I dos'…well, you shouldn't have to worry about finding a job right away."

I interrupted. "Sir, I want to take care of my wife."

"I understand that boy…" he said, stepping onto his high-horse.

*Did he just say 'boy'?* I thought to myself. *Bad things happen to people who call me 'boy'.*

Ariel noticed that I wasn't smiling. "Daddy, Izrael just got home.

Let him rest."

"But that's what I was trying to say if you guys give an old man enough time to get a word out."

"Daddy please," Ariel's mother pleaded.

Ariel's grandmother was sleeping quietly through the whole conversation. All of a sudden, she shouted, "Amen!" and then fell back to sleep.

*That was random.* I thought to myself.

At Ariel's request the conversation about my future ended. We proceeded with dinner. There was no noise other than the sound of spoons and forks banging against the plates. After dinner, I did everything I could to avoid Ariel's father for fear of saying or doing something disrespectful.

The rest of the night was spent playing Spades, Bid Whist, and Charades. We listened to the oldies as Ariel's parents tried to dance. I would have found it funny if it wasn't all so pathetic. Her father threw his back out trying to do his version of the "twist" and Ariel's mother's impersonation of Aretha Franklin almost made my ears bleed. As she sang, I wondered that if we sent her voice to Iraq, maybe we could put an end to the war.

After completely exhausting ourselves, we cleaned up, made some plates "to go", and then went home.

**❚❚ ✶ ✶ ✶ ❚❚**

As we drove home, I thought about the first day Ariel and I met. I recalled how I left for the military immediately after high school. When I left we had nothing, but an unrelenting dedication to one another.

It was our freshman year of high school. She was a transfer

student. Her first day at school was hell – it was like throwing fresh meat into a lion's cage. I didn't know why I felt the need to, but I appointed myself as her guardian angel.

She was a square peg trying to fit into a spot designated for a circle. She was every bit of a nerd. She had two ponytails, a mouth full of braces, glasses so thick she could see through walls, her clothes were outdated, but she was smart as hell; which wasn't cool.

One day, a bunch of girls surrounded her in the hall. I was walking pass with a bunch of my boys when I saw one of the girls slap her books from her hands. "Stuck-up bitch." I heard one of them say.

She leaned over to pick up her books when she dropped her glasses. One of the other girls stepped on them. While she was down on her knees picking up her books, another girl kicked them across the hall. The bell rang and the girls scattered to their classes. I stayed behind to help her. She was crying.

"My mother is going to be so upset," she said, spitting through her braces.

"What's your name?" I asked, handing her the broken glasses.

"It's Ariel and yours?" she asked, trying to see me through cracked lenses.

"It's Izrael," I answered.

"It's nice to meet you Izrael and thank you for helping me." She extended her hand to me thereby dropping her books again.

Picking them up and giving them to her, I said, "It's cool, Ariel. I'm sorry that happened to you. That happens to pretty girls all of the time around here," I said, trying to make her feel better.

She blushed. "You…You…You think I'm pretty?"

"The best looking girl in this school," I said, being honest and not trying to run "game" on her. She was cute in a goofy sort of way.

She wiped her face with her sleeve and then smiled.

After wiping away her tears with the back of my hand, I turned to walk away. "Stay sweet Ariel. Don't let these bitches get on your nerves. I can promise you that tomorrow everything will be better."

"You think so?" she asked, pushing her glasses off of the tip of her nose.

I turned and looked at her. "I know so. Maybe tomorrow we can have lunch together."

"You...You want to have lunch with me?"

"Sure why not." I walked back over to her and taking her books from her hands, I said, "Come on. Let me walk you to class."

"Okay."

I walked her to class. The rest of the day, I did not leave her side. We had lunch together.

At the end of the school day, the final bell rang and school was dismissed. Me and my boys were waiting at the corner when the group of girls who bullied her earlier walked pass. "Hello ladies," I said.

"Who us?" The one who looked like a possum said.

I cringed and said, "Yeah you."

"Hello," they all giggled.

Something about them had "fuck me" written all over them. I knew what I needed to do. I had a plan. My boys went along with the plan because it included getting an easy piece of ass. I told the guys earlier that I wanted these heifers to feel exactly how they made Ariel feel. We came up with a plan to do just that.

We convinced them to let us take them to the movies. We sat in the back. We were all laughing and talking until the movie started and the theater went black. I excused myself telling them that I wanted some popcorn. I left the theater, ran to the corner store, and purchased a camera. By the time I came back, my boys already had each one of them on their knees. They were sucking away when I started taking pictures.

The next day at school, the pictures were pasted all over the place. I even sent copies of them to their parents. I, anonymously, placed copies of the pictures in Ariel's locker with a note that said, "Just in case they bother you again."

The next three years would go smoothly for Ariel and me. No one messed with either one of us. As Ariel blossomed into the beautiful woman she is today, I never left her side. The day before graduation, I proposed to her. I didn't have any money for a ring, so I tied a ribbon around her finger so that she would never forget my commitment to her. We married shortly after we graduated. I was immediately shipped out to Iraq so there wasn't a honeymoon. When I left, Ariel was still a virgin.

# CHAPTER
# 3

We had been driving for about thirty minutes, when we finally parked in the driveway of a beautiful tri-level on a corner lot in one of Chicago's neighborhoods on the southside. When I left for Iraq, I was still living in the basement of my parent's home. While away, I received letters from Ariel updating me on the changes that were happening in her life – in our lives. Ariel and her family made all of the decisions for us in my absence. Now I stand in front of a building that I had no say so in acquiring and now have to call my home.

After retrieving my duffle bag from the backseat, I stood and stared at the white brick building. At the front door, Ariel handed me a key. As I fumbled with the key, I noticed a doormat that said "welcome" on the steps. For some bizarre reason, I didn't feel welcome. Once the door was opened, I hesitated to enter the house. When I entered, I was taken-aback. I was speechless. The house was "showroom" beautiful. The décor was contemporary. The house was so clean that it stunk of disinfectant.

She grabbed me by the hand and dragged me inside. "Come on in baby. Don't you like it? It's a gift from mama and daddy."

I didn't know what to say. I should have been happy – grateful even, but I felt diminished. I felt like her parents couldn't trust me to take care of their little girl.

Room by room, she took me on a tour until we ended up in the bedroom. I dropped my bag onto the floor. I grabbed a seat in the chair near the window. Ariel sat on the bed. "Come sit by me," she requested, patting the mattress. I felt weird and displaced – like I wasn't supposed to be there. "Come to me Izrael," she beckoned. I wasn't budging. Realizing that I wasn't moving, she said, "I know what you need."

*Really.* I thought to myself.

She stood and walked over to the stereo and turned on some slow music. Next, she began to slowly remove her clothes doing what looked like a strip tease. Her movements were awkward not fluid. She moved like a virgin. She shook her ass, rubbed, and then touched herself. It was cute, but it wasn't doing anything to get me in the mood. She walked over to me and whispered, "I missed you," into my ear. She kissed me hard and clumsily. She kissed my neck. She unbuttoned my shirt and kissed my chest.

"Milk does the body good," she said, licking her lips. She leaned back to admire the body that the military made.

She ran her tongue down my stomach to my navel. I placed my head back against the wall while I waited for her to unzip my pants. I closed my eyes while she stroked me. I became aroused. *Attention.* I thought to myself making a reference to my erection. She climbed on top of me. She let out a gentle moan as her virginity was lost forever. I kept my eyes closed as she rode me until we both climaxed. She let out a sound that resembled a howl more than a moan or a scream. I thought to myself, *at ease soldier,* as I became empty both physically and mentally. She didn't get up. She rested her head on my shoulder and fell asleep.

As I held her, I thought about how weird it was to make love to her – that after I've waited so long to have her – to hold her – something wasn't right. I felt like something was missing. I felt detached. I needed her and I wanted her, but something about this whole situation wasn't right. Maybe, it had something to do with all of the time we were separated, but I couldn't even feel her heartbeat as she laid against my chest – her warmth, her smell – everything about her was unattainable. The moment felt more like a dream than reality.

**‖ ✵ ✵ ✵ ‖**

At about 0300 hours, she wanted to make love again. I was awakened to gentle kisses being placed on the side of my neck. I turned my head away from her.

"Kiss me, Izrael," she begged, repeatedly.

After removing the sleep from my eyes, I stared at her. If she had asked me for this type of passion five years ago, I would be all over her, but I've done some things – seen some things – some horrible things. I wanted to embrace her, but I couldn't. My body was confused. To get through those years, I've done some things that I am now ashamed of, but my body needed it. I did what I had to do. Now, I have to forget about it and forgive myself for it…no matter how good it felt. I was home now and I had a wife who could take care of me.

As I lay there listening to her beg for what she deserved as my wife and as a woman who has waited five years to get it, I found myself wondering if she could ever forgive me for the things I've done. I wondered if she knew that she was my first and only love. I wondered if she knew how many nights I masturbated while looking at her photo and although, I did partake in things she would never understand, I wondered would it be easier to forgive me if she knew that I was never a receiver, but a giver – always a giver – willing to give my life – willing to give my body, but never willing to give anyone something that could belong only to her.

"Please daddy, kiss me. It's been so long. I missed you…I need to feel you…inside of me."

The silhouette of her body in the dark looked beautiful – as flawless as the day I left her.

"Don't you want me?" she asked, placing my hand in the warm spot between her legs.

"I do," I confirmed, feeling more indifferent than passionate for the woman who has waited faithfully for me.

"Well then make love to me again," she said, throwing herself back onto the bed and throwing her legs into the air.

I thought about Ariel and the war. The distance that the war placed between us had put my heart in an awkward position. I knew that I would have to work hard to regain those emotions that once made me want to do anything in the world to have her.

I resisted, but then I surrendered and kneeled over her. I watched as the moonlight caught the curves of her beautifully toned body – untouched by time. She teased me – sliding her body across the black satin sheets underneath me. Her body's movements were almost ghostlike. An eerie feeling came over me. I shook it off, closed my eyes, and dove into something my body and my soul has needed for a very long time.

# CHAPTER
## 4
### 0500 HOURS

I rose to complete my morning tasks. First, I prayed. Second, I relieved myself. Then I showered, and cut my hair into a low fade. I walked back into the bedroom and proceeded to clean the bed.

"Hey!" she shouted.

"Oops, sorry about that," I said, apologizing and placing the blankets back onto the bed.

I walked over to the closet retrieved a pair of jogging pants and a hoodie. I was putting the clothes on when I heard Ariel mumbling something under her breath. "Did you say something sweetie?"

She sat up in the bed, glared at me, and then laid back down pulling the blankets over her head.

*Okay,* I thought to myself. After putting on my gym shoes, I said, "I'll be back in a little bit."

She mumbled again.

I went out into the front yard and began a series of calisthenics. After a five mile run, I returned home to a cranky wife. She was slamming things around when I walked in.

"Good morning, sweetie," I said, trying to diffuse the ticking time-bomb.

"Morning," she grunted.

She walked over to the table and slammed a cup of hot coffee on it thereby spilling part of the contents on the floor.

Standing to retrieve some paper towels, I said, "Is the honeymoon over?" I was hoping to make her smile.

She scowled.

Feeling a chill, I said, "Someone woke up on the wrong side of the bed."

Seizing the opportunity to say something, she said, "Izrael, who the hell gets up at 5:00am to do chores?"

"I'm really sorry about that Ariel…"

"Sorry!" she screamed.

Thinking that this was something related to her hormones, I said, "Would you like for me to get you something for that?"

"For 'that' what?" she asked, with a crazed look in her eyes.

Stepping away from the anger that was rising inside of me, I said, "Look, I don't know what happened, but whatever I did, I'm sorry."

"Since you don't seem to know what you did, let me explain it to you. You woke me up out of the best sleep I've had since the day you left. I thought that once you came home, I would be at peace, but noooooooo you decide that you want to do chores at 5 o'clock in the damn morning."

Scratching my head, I said, "I'm confused…are you happy that I'm home or not?" I asked, frustrated and ready to walk out of the door.

For a moment, she didn't say anything. Suddenly as if someone served her a "chill-pill," she responded, "I'm sorry sweetie. I was just so tired. Of course, I am glad that you are home. I just wasn't expecting you to get up so early…that's all." She kissed me on the forehead.

*What the hell?* Looking at her suspiciously, I said, "Are you okay?"

"I'm fine honey. Why do you ask?"

"Why do I ask? Are you serious?"

"Yes baby, I'm fine. I said that I was sorry," she said.

I paused as if to say something, but decided against it. Not wanting to deal with it, I decided to let it go. "I'm going to take a shower."

Waving at me as I walked down the hall, she said, "Okay baby, I'll be right here when you come out."

*I hope not.* Looking back at her, I thought to myself.

**‖ ✷ ✷ ✷ ‖**

Since I've been home, I have been experiencing some extremely painful headaches so I made an appointment to see my VA doctor to make sure that everything was okay.

After examining me, the doctor said, "Looking at your chart, I see that you were prescribed painkillers."

"Yes, doc' I've been taking them, but I'm still having the headaches."

"Is there any particular time of the day or a particular activity that causes you to get a headache?"

"No…it just happens. Sometimes, I have these thoughts. They are really bad dreams that happen randomly throughout the day and night. I can't even tell you if I'm sleeping when it happens…it just happens…then suddenly my head would begin to hurt."

"Interesting." He took notes and then said, "What are these bad dreams about?"

"People dying…people dying all of the time," I said, wringing my hands.

"That's expected. You just returned home from the war. Is there anything else?" he asked.

"Sometimes I lose periods of time. Like I could be in my car, check my clock and it would say 1:00pm…I'm sitting at a stop sign, the next thing I know, car horns are blowing. I look at the clock again and it says 1:15pm. I have no idea what I was doing for fifteen minutes."

"What about trouble with concentrating, irritability, and anger?"

"Let me see…trouble concentrating? Yes, I do have a lot on my mind. Irritability? I can't really say. Maybe I am, sometimes. Angry? I guess that could apply."

"Why are you angry?" he asked.

"How much time do you have?"

Ignoring what he thought was sarcasm, the doctor continued, "Are you seeing things? Are you hearing voices?"

I didn't respond, but smiled instead.

"Are you having any difficulty eating or sleeping?" he asked.

"No, not really," I said.

"I see," the doctor said, taking notes. "Have you spoken with your wife about these bad dreams?"

"No, I don't want to worry her," I said, buttoning up my shirt.

"It sounds like Post Traumatic Stress Disorder," he said, beginning to diagnose my condition.

"Look, I don't have a "disorder". I just need some well-deserved sleep and some more painkillers," I said, stuffing my shirt into my pants.

The doctor tore a piece of paper from his prescription pad, handed it to me, and then walked over to the sink to wash his hands. Disagreeing with me, he said, "Look, I recommend that you see a psychiatrist. There are plenty of them out your way. I've written a few of their names on that sheet of paper. I want you to make an appointment as soon as possible so that they can help you deal with all those inner thoughts and dreams. To be honest, I don't think that you will ever be able to get rid of them all together, but I'm sure with the right amount of counseling you can get them under control. In the interim, I've written you a prescription for your headaches."

"Look, I don't need a "shrink". I just need something for the headaches," I said, taking the papers from his hand and hopping off of the table.

"Look, it's okay to see a "shrink". It doesn't mean that you're crazy or anything. It just means that you need help finding answers or help finding meaning to some of the things you're dealing with," he said, opening the observation room door.

"I don't need a shrink," I said again, this time with conviction.

"You came to see me because you thought something was wrong. I didn't call you and force you to come in, you did that yourself. Now, I can only tell you what I see. PTSD is common among vets or among people who has experienced a traumatic event. You witnessed a lot. Probably more than any normal human being could handle."

"I can handle it," I said.

"I'm not saying that you can't." He paused, removed his glasses, rubbed his forehead, and then said, "I don't understand why they send children to fight wars. Their minds are not capable of handling such tragedies. An adult can't handle it. I know that I couldn't, but I guess that if you can make and have babies, drink, drive, and vote...I guess you can go to war. It just doesn't make it right." He paused again and then continued, "I apologize. You came here for treatment not my feelings about sending young folks to war."

"Look doc, it's no problem. What many people don't know is most of us who live in urban communities have either killed, seen someone get killed, or know of someone who has been killed. The war over there is no different than the war over here. We are fighting for the same thing...respect. That's really what it boils down to. Think about it. There are a lot of people in the ground because somebody disrespected somebody. Sad thing is, a lot of innocent people get caught up in other people's bullshit. Lies are told to get everybody on the ban-wagon; people get shot, blown-up, and then what? After we clear all of the debris and bury our dead, we find out that the war is all about the fact that somebody disrespected some-body's daddy and folks had to die because of it."

"There wasn't a draft. Why did you go?" he asked.

"In the beginning, I thought it was cool. I wanted to make my father proud. I did it to keep from being one of those brothas with no purpose. I could have gone to college, but there was something cool about being paid to kill people." I chuckled. "I know that sounds bad, but it's the truth. You see pictures of them carrying guns and then when you see them in the video games carrying guns and blowing up shit, you say to yourself, Why not? I can do that." I paused and then said, "Don't get me wrong. We saved a lot of people too."

He looked uncomfortable. "That's good to hear." He paused and then said, "Have you ever killed anyone?"

I looked at him. For a minute, neither one of us said anything. Finally, I broke the silence. I smiled and patted the doctor on his shoulder. "I like you doc. Thanks for the 'script'."

"You are welcome and I will see you in two weeks."

"Two weeks," I confirmed, shaking his hand out of habit. Not letting go of his hand, I looked at him again. He tried to get out of my grip, but couldn't. There was another moment of silence. When I saw the bead of sweat roll down his face, I let go. I smiled and said, "Have a good day doctor."

"You…You too," he stammered. "Please call the psychiatrist."

I didn't respond.

I walked out of the office holding the list of psychiatrists that the doctor gave to me. I randomly picked one and called them on my cell-phone. When the receptionist at the doctor's office answered, I hit the "end" button on the phone. *I can do this. I don't need a "shrink".* I thought to myself. *I'm going to get through this.* I balled the paper up and threw it in a nearby garbage can. *Heavenly Father, which art in Heaven,* I repeated to myself as I walked across the parking lot to my car. Once inside, I continued my prayer as I started the ignition. *BOOM!* The sound rang in my head. I closed my eyes and waited for the heat to surround me, but nothing happened. I mumbled to myself, "You will get through this soldier." When I opened my eyes, I realized that I was okay. I looked up at the sky and whispered the words, *Thank you.* I buckled my seatbelt and slowly exited the parking lot.

# CHAPTER
# 5

Exhausted, I laid on my back looking into the darkness. The drum beating in my head wouldn't allow me to sleep. I looked over at Ariel to find her resting peacefully. I envied her. I tried closing my eyes in an attempt to will away the headache, but I was unsuccessful. Realizing that I wasn't going to win the fight against the pain, I quietly got out of bed to search for some relief. I walked into the bathroom, opened the medicine cabinet to find some painkillers only to be disappointed by the bottles of Midol, vitamins, a few bottles of prescription medicines with no labels on them, toothpaste, and an empty bottle of Tylenol. *That is so annoying.* I thought to myself.

I splashed some cold water on my face, removed a towel from the holder, and patted my face dry. Frustrated, I decided to watch some television. I turned the bathroom light off and proceeded to go to the living room, when I felt the grain of the hardwood floor under my feet. It felt liberating to be free of concrete. I was embracing the joy of deliverance when a light flashed into the room. Just as I looked into the direction of the light, there was a loud crackle that followed and then suddenly a loud *Boom!*

My heart began to beat rapidly. I was out of breath. It felt like someone was choking me. I began to feel dizzy and sick to my stomach. I thought that I was going to die – or maybe I was just going crazy. Each time the sound hit the house, images of buildings flashed before my eyes. I could see them – people being blown to pieces, bodies on fire, everyone screaming and trying to find cover. *No!* I thought, grabbing my head and trying to shake the images from my head. I ran to the bedroom, jumped into the bed, and covered my head with the blankets thereby causing Ariel to stir. She mumbled something, reached over, placed her arm around my waist, and then she gently kissed the back of my head. Shaking, I tried to understand my fear of the thunder. I couldn't understand why something that excited me as a child now held me captive. I turned over to find protection in Ariel's arms. "Are you okay, sweetie?" she mumbled, sleepily. I didn't reply. Trying to find solace in the depths of her bosom, I prayed for the storm to end.

**❚❚ ✶ ✶ ✶ ❚❚**

The next morning, the sun embraced me as if apologizing for the unwelcome visit of my enemy the night before. I looked over to find that I was alone and instead of waking up to the face of my wife it was replaced with a note on her pillow that said:

> *I'm going to work-out. After that, I'm going shopping with mother. I love you. See you soon.*

I placed the note back on her pillow and raised my arms to stretch. My body felt like it had been run over by a truck. I grimaced in pain. Sitting up, I surveyed the room. It suddenly looked different. The first time I entered this room, I remembered the walls were painted white, but now they seemed tan; affecting my mood.

*I need to exercise. Maybe that's what I need.*

I proceeded to complete my morning requirements: make my bed, relieve myself, shower, shave, and dress. Clothed in my fatigues,

I left for a run. The morning air felt good against my face. I had run four miles and was coming around a corner when I ran into someone completely knocking him onto the ground.

Reaching out to him, I said, "Damn man, I'm sorry."

He began to yell and scream. "Get away from me!"

Still trying to help him standup, I continued to reach out to him.

"Get away from me!" Pointing, he continued, "I know you. They sent you, didn't they?" Afraid, he stood up and began to back away from me.

"Who and what are you talking about?" I asked.

"So you finally found me. It's that chip that you planted in my head," he said, pointing his finger at the back of his neck.

Confused, I said, "What chip? What are you talking about?"

With a crazed look on his face, he said, "Don't act like you don't know what I'm talking about. I eluded you for years, but now you have found me. You won't take me, you hear me?" He began to claw at his face drawing blood. "You tell them that they won't get me! You tell them that they won't get me!"

I didn't know what to do. "Sir, please don't do that." I reached for his hands trying to stop him from hurting himself.

"Get away from me," he said, running away, laughing, and shouting, "You won't get me!"

For a minute, I was paralyzed trying to figure out what had just transpired. Not able to make sense of anything that happened, I was left feeling disconnected. I didn't continue my run, but turned around and walked all the way home.

**|| ☆ ☆ ☆ ||**

When I walked in, Ariel was standing in the kitchen. "Hey, you're home," she said, emptying the dishwasher.

I didn't respond. I was walking down the hall when she approached me from behind. "Are you okay?"

I turned to look at her. She read the look on my face and retreated back down the hall. I entered the bedroom, removed all of my clothing, and then walked into the bathroom. While waiting for the tub to fill with water, I bowed down on my knees on the side of the tub and began to pray for the man that I had run into earlier. As my eyes were closed and I whispered the *Lord's Prayer,* visions of the transient came to me. His skin was dirty. All of the hair on his face and head was matted. His teeth were yellowed and he smelled like he hadn't bathe in years. His clothing hung loosely from his broken frame. His wardrobe consisted of old military clothing. His coat was embellished with metals including a Purple Heart. I finished my prayer for the stranger, turned off the water, and slid into the tub. I continued to think about the stranger; wondered what happened to him, and then I thought about myself. In a moment of weakness, I began to cry. Suddenly a voice in my head said, "This war ain't for babies." Since the death of my brother, I never felt close enough to anything to shed tears over it. I listened to the voice, filled the palms of my hands with some of the water from the tub, and splashed water on my face in an attempt to wash away this moment and the memory of the fallen brother.

# CHAPTER
# 6

The next morning, I woke up to find Ariel lying on top of me. I rolled her over, yawned, and arched my body in an attempt to remove the kinks. I stood, removed my pajama pants and walked across the floor to the bathroom. After relieving myself, I jumped into the shower. I was enjoying the warmth of the running water when Ariel entered the bathroom. She mumbled, "Good Morning," and proceeded to use the toilet. She flushed the toilet causing a sudden change in the water's temperature. "Shit," I said under my breath. Suddenly the shower curtain opened, Ariel undressed and entered the shower. She squeezed passed me and placed her head under the running water. I enjoyed watching the water run over her skin accentuating every curve and dimple on her body. I became aroused as the water ran down the arch of her back into the darkness of her beautiful round behind. As I watched her, I remembered the bodies of the male soldiers I've showered with over the last five years. I immediately became turned-off. I left the shower, wrapped a towel around my waist, and then went back into the bedroom. As I lie in bed, allowing the cool air of the room to dry my skin I thought again of the men, the acts performed in the showers, the "kiss and don't tell" policies, and I wondered how many of them remembered not to tell.

My thoughts were interrupted when the door to the bathroom opened. The bedroom was suddenly engulfed in steam. Through the steam she walked in like something out of a dream – body still wet from her shower. She crawled into the bed gently placing kisses from my feet, to my calves, to my thighs, and then finally on the place she has dreamed about for the past five years. I closed my eyes. When she felt that I was ready to receive her, she climbed on top. I flipped her over onto her back and begged for her forgiveness with each stroke; forgiveness for leaving her, and forgiveness for the things I did in her absence to fight against the loneliness.

**❚❚ ✫ ✫ ✫ ❚❚**

The next day, I thought that it would be nice to take a drive down Lake Shore Drive. I love the Chicago skyline. I remembered as a kid, how we spoke of downtown like it was on the other side of the world. I remembered thinking that the city was a place built and set aside for the wealthy. I was always fascinated by how you could see the Sears Tower from the Dan Ryan Expressway. I used to have dreams of taking the elevator all the way to the top.

It was graduation night when that dream finally came true. Me and a few of my boys from the neighborhood decided to take a trip downtown. We were all drunk from celebrating and willing to do almost anything; at least that's what I thought. My boys talked shit all night long about how they were going all the way to the top, but once we arrived I found that I was the only one willing to ride the elevator of one of the tallest buildings in the world. Once inside of the elevator, my friends waved good-bye to me. I stood with my back against the wall of the elevator. I watched as the number to each floor lit up. At about the 60th floor, my head began to spin and my stomach felt queasy. So determined to make it to the top, I did every-thing to fight back the urge to vomit, but I couldn't contain it. By the time I reached the top, I was completely empty, begging God to stop the pain. When the elevator arrived at the bottom floor, I was on my knees begging for death to arrive and take the pain away. When the door opened, my boys saw me on my knees and in a drunken stupor began to laugh as if they were watching something on Comedy Central. When I was able to catch my breath, I told them all to kiss my ass.

**‖ ✶ ✶ ✶ ‖**

Ariel loved being downtown. After a trip to Macy's, Garrett's Popcorn, and every other store on State Street, we strolled to the Congress Parkway. We were enjoying each other's company when we were accosted by a homeless woman requesting some change. Ariel reached into her purse and removed a fifty. She gave it to the woman without thinking twice. "Thank you so much…Oh thank you Jesus. I am so grateful. Now, I can feed my baby." While she spoke, my eyes drifted into the direction of her protruding belly that was being hidden by several layers of dirty clothing. Ariel saw it too. Her eyes widened. She covered her mouth with her hands and began to cry. Suddenly, she reached into her purse and removed several large bills and handed it to the lady. "Oh Ms., thank you so much. God is so good." She reached for Ariel's hand and began to kiss the back of it. "God bless you," she repeated. "God bless you." She walked away. We both stood there watching the woman rejoice as if she had just won the lottery. I was so proud of Ariel at that moment. I wrapped my arms around her in an attempt to redirect her attention back to the matter-at-hand. We walked until we finally found ourselves at the

Buckingham Fountain. Ariel didn't speak all the way there. Abruptly, the silence was broken when she began to cry again.

"What's wrong Ariel?" I asked.

"Why do you think God does that?" she asked.

"Does what?" I asked, searching my pockets for some change to throw into the pool of water to make a wish.

"Why do you think he gives some more than others?"

"I don't know why He does that. You are asking the wrong person that question. I've seen some things on the other side of the world that would break your heart...People killing each other for food...just crazy. Then I come home and I see fools dying in the streets for a pair of Nikes. It's nuts."

She didn't say anything. I assumed everything was okay when she took my hand and led me toward Lakeshore Drive.

She stared into the traffic. "Sometimes I get so tired of this. The world is so screwed up."

"Ariel, where are we going?"

Ignoring my question, she said, "Izrael, I missed you so much when you were gone."

"Okay...but I'm home now," I said, as the wind from the speeding vehicles made my eyes water. "Look, let's turn around and go home."

Crying, she said, "I was so lonely. That woman had nothing and I have so much..."

The bags in my hands were becoming heavy. I placed them down at my feet. "Look Ariel, I'm tired. Let's go home."

She looked down, grabbed two of the bags, and then slung them into the street. I did a double-take. "What the hell is wrong with you?" Cars began to swerve to avoid the flying pair of shoes and handbag. "Ariel, what are you thinking?" I said, waiting for the traffic to stop so that I could retrieve the items.

"I don't deserve any of this."

I ran into the streets waving my hands in an attempt to stop traffic. Once I gathered everything, and my feet were on the curb away from traffic, I grabbed the bags, snatched her by the arm and dragged her all the way back to the car. I ignored the cursing drivers and the whispering onlookers all the way there. I was so furious, I was going to snap. My heart was beating so fast, I thought that I was going to have a heart attack. She was trying to explain her actions when I blew my top. Locking the doors, I leaned over to the passenger side of the vehicle where she was sitting. I was so close that I could smell the breakfast on her breath. Sticking my finger into her chest, I said, "Do that dumb shit again and I'm going to kill you. I don't mean that I'm going to hurt you. No, I am going to sling your ass into traffic like you did those shoes."

Shaking, she said, "I'm sorry."

Looking her deeply into her eyes, I said, "The next time you feel like making a political statement, write a fucking check and send it to the NAACP. Do you understand?"

"But…"

Through tight lips I said, "You better evaluate this moment carefully. Now, if you think I'm playing, finish that sentence with the following words, "good-bye world" because seconds after you say it, I'm going to fucking kill you." I looked at her and she became quiet. She threw her hands across her chest. She didn't mumble or say another word. She sat quietly and looked out of the window all of the way home.

When we pulled into the driveway, she was careful not to slam the car doors for fear of setting me off. That night, we didn't sleep together. I was pissed. If she only knew how close I came to hurting her. Drained, I dozed off in the recliner in the living room. A few hours had passed when I was awakened by a swift change in the temperature of the room. It became hot. I felt like I had a fever. Sweat began to spill from my pores like someone had left a water faucet running. I stood to check the thermostat. The heat wasn't on. Confused and exhausted, I blamed it on the early summer months in Chicago. I removed my t-shirt and walked back to the recliner. Closing my eyes, I drifted into a deep sleep. I began to dream. I found myself standing in the middle of the desert dressed in heavy fatigues, carrying a loaded backpack, and a semi-automatic. The sun was beaming down on me. I was alone and as I searched for other forms of life, it became hotter. Sweltering, the sun was relentless. I looked up. The glare from the sun was blinding. The sweat above my brow began to roll like a stream down my face. I wiped my eyes, but the salt in the sweat began to sting them. I removed my canteen and poured it over my face, but water did not come from the bottle. Through blurred vision, I could see that the contents of the bottle were red – blood red. I wiped my face with my hand. I saw the fluid and began to panic. I removed my jacket and started to wipe my face and hands with it. The wind began to blow, picking up the sand, hitting it against my body like hot coals. The sand began to burn through my clothing. Welts began to form on my body. I pleaded for it to stop. I shielded my exposed skin from the blows of the winds. All of a sudden, it stopped.

Now able to survey my surroundings, I could see the heat rising off of the sand. Unable to bear the heat, I began to remove my clothing until I stood in nothing, but my boots to protect my feet. I stood there helpless with no sense of direction. My skin began to burn, my lips and hands became so chapped that they began to bleed, and I was becoming dehydrated and delusional. I began to pray. At some point, I realized that God was too busy dealing with other things in the world then to stop and save one man so I reached out to His arch enemy. I told him that I would do anything if he could save me – told him that I would give my soul if he would take me away from this, alive. I fell to the ground, no longer able to cope, I began to cry, but there were no tears. Suddenly in the distance, I could see someone approaching. At my feet, he stopped. "You rang," he said.

I couldn't speak and the glare from the sun kept me from seeing the face of my visitor. "You rang," he said, again. I gasped, searching for breath, I couldn't speak. "Poor thing," he said, "Look at you…out here all alone. Tsk, Tsk, Tsk," he said, shaking his head. He began to touch me. I screamed as he began to dig his nails into the blisters on my body. "Where is He? Did He forget about you Izrael?" As if he read my mind, he said, "Yes, I do know you? You are one of His favorites and look at how He repays you for all of your hard work…left alone to die. Here," he said, handing me a canteen full of ice water. I began to drink it. "Thank you," I whispered. He placed his hands on my body and all of the wounds began to heal. "Thank you," I said, weakened from the event.

"Don't thank me now. We have all the time in the world for you to thank me." He began to walk away. He turned and walked back towards me. He kneeled down and placed his hand on the lower part of my back. "Awwww!!!!" I screamed as my flesh began to burn.

"Just in case you forget," he said, standing and walking away.

Feeling a hand on my shoulder, I awakened gasping for air. "What…Where am I?"

Standing over me, Ariel said, "You are home with me."

I reached for her hand. I grimaced in pain. "Argh, what the fuck?"

"How did that happen?" she said, looking in the direction of something terrible. She stood there with her mouth open, I became afraid. Running to the washroom, I stood with my back to the mirror, and there it was – the permanent reminder.

# CHAPTER
# 7

I was so confused and pissed, that I left at daybreak. I exercised, took myself to breakfast, and went to the park to avoid her. I started to suspect that all wasn't right with Ariel. I couldn't understand what was going on, but nothing was right. I placed my hand over the spot where the bandage was. I couldn't help but wonder if she tried to hurt me while I slept. Why would she do something like that? But where else could the wound have come from? I didn't like what I was thinking because I knew that if I thought that she would intentionally hurt me, there would be consequences.

My thoughts began to take me to a very dark place in my mind. I shook away the thoughts and tried to block out the voices in my head that were fueling my anger. I took a few deep breaths. I glanced at my watch and then my cell-phone. *No missed calls.* I hadn't heard from Ariel all day.

Nothing was the way I thought it would be. Guys don't usually expect their marriage to be something out of a fairy tale; that's a girl's fantasy, but I definitely didn't expect this. Maybe, we were too young to make the decision to commit the rest of our lies together. Sitting on the park bench, I thought about how many nights I yearned for her love – for her touch. Could we be that different than the two young lovers in high school? I had to admit that we both did a lot of growing up since I left, but I was starting to question this arrangement.

When I returned home, she was waiting for me at the door. "What happened at the doctor's office?" she asked, handing me a cool glass of lemonade.

"He said that I was fine," I said, lying because I didn't want to hear her mouth in addition to the fact that I didn't think it was her business.

Squinting her eyes, she said, "So everything's okay."

"Yes," I said, with finality.

On my heels and ignoring my desire to end the conversation, she said, "What did he say that was?" She pointed at my back.

"He said that he didn't really know what it was. He gave me some cream to keep it from getting infected," I said, still lying.

"So everything is okay?" she asked, with a look that indicated that she was up to something.

"That's what he said," I said, becoming annoyed because I didn't feel like playing games. "What's up, Ariel?"

"What do you mean?" she asked.

"You have that look on your face," I said.

"Well, I was thinking…"

Hearing her start a conversation with those words made me want to run and take cover.

She continued, "Now we can start talking about babies. I'm thinking that we should start out with one and then wait a year or two before we get pregnant again. When do you want to start?" she asked, happily.

Thinking about her erratic behavior lately, I exhaled noisily. "Let's put a pause on that until I get re-acclimated," I said, sipping from my glass.

"Re-acclimated to what Izrael? To being back home, to me, to us, to what?" she asked, placing her hands on her hips.

"Just let me get settled in before we start talking about kids," I said, thinking about my earlier episode.

She walked over and wrapped her arms around my neck and began to nibble my ear. "Come on baby. I'm not getting any younger." She took my hand and placed it over her belly. "Don't you want to put something in there?"

Trying to distract her, I kissed her on her neck and said, "I plan to put something in there later on...I promise."

Clarifying herself, "I meant a little boy or girl."

Pushing away from her, I said, "I know what you meant Ariel. I'm a lot of things...stupid ain't one of them."

"Well come on, my parents want a grandbaby," she said, trying to lead me to the bedroom.

Resisting, I said, "Look, I'm going to keep it real...I'm not ready to be anybody's father. I'm still trying to get use to being someone's husband."

Rolling her neck, she said, "This 'someone' has a name."

"Bring it down a notch, okay. I'm just saying that right now is not a good time."

"What's the problem?" she asked, letting go reluctantly.

Staring at her, I noticed how beautiful she was. I didn't want to hurt her feelings, but I couldn't say 'yes'. "How about we have this same conversation in a year, okay?"

Folding her arms and pouting, she said, "Why a year?"

"That should be enough time for me to get some things in order?"

"What things?" she asked.

"Will you please stop asking me so many damn questions? I'm

not ready to be a father," I said, standing to leave the room.

"Why not?" she asked, standing her ground.

"Cause I said so," I said, adamantly.

"You can't just say 'no'. We're married. Married people have babies."

"Right now, I'm not interested. This world is too fucked up to bring babies into it."

"Well, I want a baby."

"Well, I want a million dollars. I don't see either one of them happening anytime soon," I said, feeling an overwhelming urge to leave. I thought to myself. *I love my wife. I love my wife. I love my wife.*

"When you left, you were a sweetheart...now you're an asshole," she said.

*This is getting ugly.* Tired of having this conversation, I said, "I'm done talking about this." She grabbed my arm.

"I'm not done talking Izrael," she stated, defiantly.

Without thinking, I balled my hand into a fist and punched the wall behind Ariel's head so hard that plaster flew into Ariel's face.

Dusting plaster out of her hair and face, she said, "What is wrong with you?"

I removed my hand from the wall. "I said that I don't want any damn kids. Do you understand?"

There was a moment of silence. I stared deeply into her eyes. Suddenly, a bead of sweat rolled down the side of her face.

"I do," she said. She grabbed my hand to look at it. "I do."

**❚❚ ✷ ✷ ✷ ❚❚**

That evening at dinner, we barely spoke to each other. I hated what happened between us earlier, but she wasn't taking 'no' for an answer.

Ariel went through a lot of trouble to make the evening romantic. The room was semi-dark. She lit candles and made a special meal of spinach lasagna, salad, and garlic bread. There was classical music playing in the background. It was nice, but I really couldn't appreciate it due to the migraine headache and the throbbing pain in my hand. I swallowed two of the painkillers that the doctor prescribed with a glass of wine. I was watching her do everything to avoid eye-contact. I made up my mind that I wasn't going to apologize, but I didn't want to spend another night sleeping in the living room so I decided to break the silence.

"Dinner is delicious. Thank you," I said, watching to see her reaction.

"You're welcome," she mumbled through a mouth full of food.

We fell silent again.

I spoke to break the tension. "I'll fix the wall."

"Okay," she said, tearing a piece of garlic bread and wiping some of the marinara sauce from her plate.

"Look Ariel, it's all too much too fast…everything…this house…you…the kids…"

"Me?" she asked.

I sighed. "I don't know…maybe, it's me."

Again, we fell silent.

She spoke. "I was only saying Izrael that it would be nice to have a little one running around the house."

"You just don't get it do you? It would also be nice to be able to take care of it and you."

"We will be fine Izrael."

"You say that…all I ask is that you give me a little time to get myself together and then we can talk about having a baby."

"We can talk about it?" she asked, looking for more.

"Yeah, we can talk about it," I said, telling her what she wanted to hear to get her off of my back.

Happy with my answer, she ran to my side of the table. "Okay," she said, wrapping her arms around me and kissing me. Suddenly, she bit my bottom lip.

"Ouch!" I said, grabbing my lip.

She giggled playfully.

I looked at her. Not reacting, I sat still.

"Come on baby," she begged.

Giving in to her advances, I stood and walked toward her.

"Let's see what you got," she said, grabbing me by my belt buckle and dragging me down the hall to our bedroom.

Once inside of the bedroom, she pushed me onto the bed. I laid motionless staring into the ceiling while she took what she needed because at that moment my mind wouldn't let me give it to her.

**‖ ✫ ✫ ✫ ‖**

The pain woke me from my sleep. "Argh!" I said, screaming and grabbing my stomach. I tossed the comforters onto the floor and ran into the bathroom buckled over. I fell to my knees and placed my head over the toilet.

"What's wrong?" she asked, groggily and turning on the bedroom light.

"My fucking stomach...Argh!" I threw up contents from tonight's dinner. "What the hell, Ariel?" I said, trying to catch my breath.

"What do you mean, 'what the hell'?"

With my head still dangling over the toilet, I said, "What the hell did you put in that food?"

"Oh no you didn't...Excuse me? It must be something else because

I didn't put anything in your food…not even salt and pepper because I know how funny you are…Wait a minute, are you accusing me of something?" she stood with her hand on hip, twisting her neck with her mouth poked out.

"Argh!" I said, throwing up some more. When I caught my breath, I said, "I was fine until dinner."

"Well, it wasn't my cooking. I can tell you that. You must have taken something that upset your stomach. Did you have anything else?"

Remembering that I had taken some painkillers earlier, I said, "It must be the medication that the doctor prescribed," I said, leaning over the toilet.

Rolling her neck and giving me a look of "I told you so," she said, "I thought that you said that he said everything was fine."

"He did, but he put me on something…Argh!" I grabbed my stomach and buckled over. "He gave me something to help me with the headaches."

"What headaches?" she asked, taking a face towel from the towel rack, running it under cold water, and placing it onto my neck.

"Argh!" I screamed as I continued to throw-up Ariel's romantic dinner.

Rubbing my back sympathetically, she said, "Izrael, what do you want me to do?"

Pushing her away, I said, "Right now just leave me alone." Heaving, I moaned, "My fucking stomach…my fucking head. Argh!"

"Humph," she said, folding my arms, "I'm just trying to help. Since you're going to act that way, I'll leave you along with your pain. I'll be in the other room." She stumped out of the bathroom.

Ignoring her, I kept my head over the toilet until nothing was coming out, but air. While resting my head on my arm on the toilet seat, I decided that I was never taking that medication again.

# CHAPTER
# 8

The next morning, I awakened to find Ariel staring blindly out of the bedroom window. I stretched, whispered *Thank you* because I was grateful for another day. I looked at Ariel. She didn't acknowledge my presence. She continued to stare out of the window. I walked over to her. I looked out of the window to see what she was staring at. Other than the beautiful scenery, there was nothing there.

"Good Morning," I said.

She mumbled, "Good Morning," never looking at me. "I placed a glass of orange juice on the nightstand." She pointed to where the glass was sitting.

"Thank you," I said, looking in the direction of the cold glass. I walked back to the bed, picked up the glass, and began to drink from it. "Is everything okay?" I asked, sipping from the glass.

Still not looking at me, she said, "Everything's fine. Why do you ask?"

I began to pick-up a strange vibe from her. I figured that she was angry so I left the topic of "how she was feeling" alone. When I reached over to place the glass back onto the nightstand, I noticed that there was a ring of water on it. I stood to walk toward the bathroom to retrieve a towel. The room began to spin. I fell back onto the bed. I closed my eyes to rest my head. Suddenly, everything was black.

**|| ✶ ✶ ✶ ||**

When I finally opened my eyes, it was dark out. My head hurt so bad that it felt like I had been kicked in it. I rubbed my eyes to regain focus. I noticed that the house was unusually quiet. I assumed that Ariel was out. I stood to go to the bathroom. When I looked to my left, I saw a shadow. Not clear what it was, I turned on the light. Ariel was sitting in the same spot that she was in earlier that morning; still staring out of the window.

Carefully, I approached her. "Ariel, are you okay?"

"I'm fine," she said, standing. "Are you hungry?"

"Sure," I paused and then said, "Have you been sitting there all day?"

"No silly. That would be crazy." She stood and walked slowly pass me looking me up and down. "I'll meet you in the kitchen." She walked quietly down the hall.

As weird as that moment was, I didn't focus on it. Instead, I sat on the edge of the bed trying to fill in the gaps of lost time. I couldn't piece things together. Frustrated, I gave up.

Ariel came back to the room. Standing in the doorway, she said, "Are you coming?"

I stood to follow her down the hall. She sashayed seductively. Feeling dizzy, I held onto the wall until I made it to a chair in the kitchen. "Man, I don't feel good."

"You just need something to eat," she said, walking toward me with a plate in her hand.

The smell of the food was making me sick again. "I think I'm going to pass. I don't feel good."

"Okay," she said, unresponsive to my current need.

I dragged myself back to the bed. Diagnosing my condition as fatigue, I turned over and went back to sleep.

# CHAPTER
# 9

The next morning, I awoke feeling completely rested. As I lay there trying to remember the past couple of days, I kept coming up blank. The more I thought about it the more it caused me pain. I felt the tension growing in my temples. I decided to shake it off. There were other things to think about. Promising myself that I wouldn't dwell on it, I focused my attention on today. I looked over to find Ariel sleeping peacefully.

I decided that I wouldn't follow my regular routine today. Instead, I made breakfast and began to do a job search in the local newspaper. Later, Ariel walked into the room, poured herself a cup of coffee, and sat down next to me at the kitchen table.

"What are you doing?" she asked.

"I'm looking for a job."

"Daddy said…"

I gave her a look that indicated that I didn't want to hear what her daddy said.

She suddenly changed her tone. "Well, if you must insist, I hope you find one soon."

Ignoring her comment, I said, "I fought for my country. You think it would be easy for a brotha' to get a job?"

"A lot has happened since you left…The employment market is scarce. People are losing their jobs, but the positions aren't being refilled with qualified workers. Instead, companies are shutting down and moving to countries where the labor is cheaper."

"All of that bloodshed and what do we have to show for it? Higher gas and food prices, a crappy-ass housing market, high-ass taxes, and no jobs; the shit doesn't add up and still people are dying."

"I think it's ridiculous that you would pass up an opportunity…"

I looked at her.

"I'm just saying. We have a chance to enjoy our lives…," she paused and suddenly her tone changed again, "Let's not talk about this. You're home now," she said, rubbing my shoulders to relax me.

The change in her demeanor made me suspicious. Removing her hands from my shoulders, I said, "I don't want to work for your daddy. I would stand in a welfare line before I take another penny from your family."

"Damn, it wouldn't be that bad. Daddy would take care of you."

*I knew that she was up to something.* "That's the damn problem, I don't need your daddy to take care of me. I am a grown man," I said pissed.

Trying to calm me down, she said, "I didn't say that you wasn't." She began to rub my shoulders again. "How about we calm down?"

Agitated, that she was trying to emasculate me, I said, "How about you get off a brotha's back? It's too early for this shit." I looked at her. She was pouting. "I need to be able to take care of my wife."

"Baby, we'll be okay. You know that my family has money. You never have to work."

"Why are you trying to force this shit down my throat? You

see…I have to work for mine's. It hurts that after all I've been through I'm forced to come home to nothing and it doesn't help that you constantly flaunt your family's money in my face reminding me of what I don't have."

"You still have me."

Turning up my mouth, I said, "You know what I mean." Not wanting to be around her at that moment, I said, "Look, I think I'm going to get with some of my boys today. I have to get my mind on something else."

"If you're looking for a distraction, I got what you need," she said, opening her rode exposing her naked body and breasts that were standing at attention.

*Here we go again.* I thought to myself. "Ariel, sex isn't going to fix everything. It isn't going to put food on the table and it isn't going to pay the bills."

Grabbing my hand, she said, "Let's not worry about that now. I need you."

I snatched my hand away. "Ariel, I know that you might feel the need to get caught up, but…"

She interrupted me with a passionate kiss. "Please don't leave me. I'll be good and I promise that I won't bring up daddy and his wonderful proposal."

I looked at her. *This motherfucker never gives up.*

She dragged me to the bedroom. Pushing me back onto the bed, she landed on top of me like a lion about to feast on its latest victim.

She was ravenous, scratching, and clawing at me. She bit and pulled at my bottom lip. "Shit," I cringed. "That hurts."

"Stop acting like a bitch, soldier. Man up and fuck the shit out of me."

"Bitch?" I asked.

"That's what I called you," she challenged.

Not appreciating being called a 'bitch', I said, "So I'm a bitch. Is that what I am?"

She giggled. "Yeah, with your punk-ass," she said, tugging at my pants.

If she thought that this was foreplay, she had another thing coming. "So now I'm a punk-ass too." I pulled my pants off and exposed myself to her. "Does this look like something that belongs to some bitch?"

Not quite understanding the magnitude of the situation, she continued to antagonize me. She reached up and slapped me so hard that it made my ears ring. She laughed.

Without thinking, I flipped her onto her back. I threw her legs into the air and began to prove to her that no man deserves to be disrespected. Before the night was over, I had earned mine.

The next day, she limped pass me. We didn't say anything to each other. That day, she didn't work out. As a matter of fact, she didn't work out for the entire week. That day, she and I developed an understanding.

**❙❙ ✮ ✮ ✮ ❙❙**

"Man down! Man down!" I shouted, but no one came to my aid. As I watched the blood squirt from the soldier's wound, I pleaded, "Hold on soldier, help is on the way." The soldier tried to speak, but nothing came out. He grabbed my hand. He made every effort to speak, but nothing came out. "Hold on soldier just a little longer." The soldier began to squeeze my hand. He coughed and blood oozed down the side of his face. Acknowledging his distress, I said,

"Soldier, pray with me. As I began, the soldier choked, took his last breath, and then his hand eased gently away from mine. "Man down!" I screamed. "Man down!"

In the distance, I heard someone say, "Baby, wake up."

"Man down!" I screamed again.

"Izrael, please wake up," she said, as she gently nudged me.

Startled and disoriented, I reached out to her, "Baby, save me," I pleaded as I fell helplessly into her arms.

Kissing my forehead, she said, "It's gonna be okay. I promise you."

I panted heavily as if I had just run a marathon. She stroked my head. "I had a bad dream."

"Yes," she said, confirming that.

Shaken by my dream, I said, "Ariel, do you believe in God?"

With a confused look on her face, she said, "That came out of nowhere. Why do you ask?"

"Because I want to know," I said, disoriented.

She paused for a moment, looking for the right thing to say. "Well, I would rather live my life as though there is one than to act an ass and have to find out the hard way."

I thought about what she said. "I've seen a lot of bad things in my life...done a lot of things...a lot of terrible things. I know that it is because of Him that I am able to lie in your arms tonight, but I often question how He could sit back and watch what we do to one another."

She looked at me. "Izrael, you have to believe that it's all part of His plan. He would have never allowed things to go on this long. I have to believe that He has something great in store for all of us who do right and live right."

"Do you think that He would ever forgive me for what I've done?"

"Izrael, whatever you've done, you did to protect your country and your family."

"So you think that it's okay to shed the blood of another to protect…"

She placed her finger to my mouth. "Hush and try to rest. You have questions that no one, but you have answers to. I can't help you understand what's going on with you…only you understand that."

Her fingers felt cold. Her whole body was cold. An eerie feeling came over me. I shook it off and wrapped my arms tightly around her waist to warm her. She rocked me in her arms until I fell back to sleep. In her arms, I slept soundly. For the rest of the night, I didn't have anymore dreams.

# CHAPTER
## 10

I awoke the next morning determined to find employment. I didn't know what to expect. I went into the military as a child. I received some training, a degree, but my job was to 'serve and protect.' It was the only thing I knew and understood, but I wasn't going to let that hinder me. So I got up early, got dressed, grabbed a cup of coffee to go, and hit the streets of Chicago. I walked up and down State Street and Michigan Avenue to a point where my feet began to swell in my Stacy Adams. My feet weren't accustomed to the narrow tips of my civilian footwear – they missed the round toe of my military shoes.

I wandered into a building seeking relief from the throbbing pain coming from the soles of my feet when I noticed a glass door leading into an office. I limped in. I figured, what did I have to lose? I approached the desk. There was a young lady on the phone.

"Gurl, did you see what that heifer had on?" she said, into the receiver.

I cleared my voice to acknowledge my presence.

She looked up, rested the receiver on her shoulder, smiled, and said in a flirtatious manner, "Oh my...Can I help you?" She licked her lips.

I ignored her advances. I was talking when she spotted the ring on my finger. She turned up her mouth, rolled her eyes, and then said, "Gurl, let me call you back." Turning her attention back to me, she said, "How can I help you?"

I looked at her and then suddenly a vision of her body in flames appeared. I shook my head to erase the image and then said, "Are you hiring?"

With all of the attitude she could muster, she reached for a binder that was sitting behind her desk and then handed it to me.

"These are all of the open positions. Here's an application. Fill it out and then return it to me."

I took the materials and walked to a seat located in the corner of the office. My butt hadn't hit the chair before she was on the phone again.

"Gurl, let me tell you..."

I shook my head and began to look through the binder carefully. There was a position for a Sales Representative. I looked the application over. I began to fill it out. There were so many questions that it made my head spin. Where it asked for 'job experience' on the application, I entered "soldier". In the section where it asked for 'specific duties performed', I was tempted to write "killer", but decided against it. I was stumped. I was trained to keep what we've done as soldiers confidential. I contemplated this for what seemed like forever and then I finally decided to embellish and filled in the blanks with the following:

✔ *Business-oriented professional skilled in meeting day-to-day challenges in a fast-paced industry.*

✔ *Solid ability in juggling multiple priorities thereby delivering consistent dependable results.*

✔ *Flexible and analytical with a keen eye for details, skilled in synthesizing and evaluating information to achieve overall objectives.*

✔ *Accustomed to applying diplomacy when dealing with extremely confidential information.*

✔ *Dependable and dedicated to seeing each task completed to the fullest. Willing to do whatever is necessary to get the job done.*

*That's about right.* I thought to myself. I handed the application to the secretary and waited. She stepped away from the desk with the application. Shortly, she returned with a gentleman who was now holding and reviewing the application.

He walked up to me and with his hand extended, he said, "Sir, my name is Mr. James."

"It's nice to meet you, Mr. James," I said, cringing from the pain of standing up.

Walking toward a room down the hall, he said, "Follow me so that we can discuss your application and see if we have anything for you."

"Sure," I said, thinking that having to take another step in these shoes was "cruel and usual punishment."

Once inside of the room, he offered me a seat across from him. There was complete silence while he looked over the application. Suddenly, he spoke. "Sir..."

I interrupted, "Sir, I went to the war right after graduation. While in the service, I received training in various fields, and..."

"Look, I don't mean to cut you off..." The resource manager paused and then said, "We are so grateful that you served your country and that you returned home alive...and safe, but I regret that you don't have the qualifications we're looking for."

*Why do I want to snap this man's neck?* I thought. "You can't be serious."

"Excuse me?" he said, pushing a pair of thick-framed glasses from the tip of his nose.

"I said that you can't be serious," I repeated with an extremely serious look on my face.

There was a moment of silence. As if stumped by my statement, he began to look for something to say. He adjusted his tie nervously, "I was just saying that we are only considering candidates with several years of sales experience."

Frustrated, I stared directly into his eyes, I stood, leaned over the desk, grabbed him by the tie, and pulled it tightly. "I would have several years of sales experience if I wasn't on the other side of the world fighting for your fucking freedom."

His eyes began to bulge out of his head as he fought to breathe. I thought about how undeserving he was — how easy it would be to kill him and the knuckle-head answering the phones wouldn't have a clue. Reluctantly, I let him go.

He screamed, "Get out!"

Snatching my application from his desk, which was proof that I had been there, I stood and left slamming the door behind me. On my way out, the "bitchy" secretary looked at me.

I looked at her and said, "You might want to hold all of his calls."

**|| ☆ ☆ ☆ ||**

After six interviews, and having no luck, I arrived home to a wife who had been shopping all day.

"Hey honey," Ariel said, placing six bags containing twelve pair of new shoes on the sofa. "How was your day?"

"Crappy…I didn't get a job," I said, looking into the refrigerator for something cold to drink. Grabbing a soda, and pouring it into a glass, I said, "You went shopping?"

"Yes…I caught a sale," she said, trying on a pair of shoes.

Looking over the glass, I said, "So how much did you spend?"

Admiring the shoes, she said, "About six hundred, give or take a few. Who's keeping count?"

"Sweetie, you know that I'm not working and my benefits haven't kicked in."

"What does that have to do with me, sweetie?" she said, admiring the shoes.

"Well, we can't afford to blow our savings."

"We talked about this already...my family is wealthy. We don't have anything to worry about."

"I didn't marry your family. I married you and I want to be able to take care of my wife. I can't do that if you spend every dime that I've sent home on shoes."

Looking at her feet, she said, "If it makes you feel any better, I didn't use any of the money that you sent home. I brought these myself."

"I know that I've been gone a long time and you've been taking care of yourself in my absence, but I'm home now. Also, it's not *my* money or *your* money anymore. We're married so it's *our* money that you're spending on shoes."

Removing the shoes, she said, "I'm sorry, I'll take them back."

Feeling bad, I said, "Look, I'm sorry...you keep them. You deserve them. I just feel like crap."

Putting the shoes back on her feet without thinking twice, she said, "Why?"

"I fought for this country and no one respects what we've done. So many people have died and this is what we come home to...unemployment. All of my boys are going through the same thing. Then they tell me that I'm not qualified...I served in the armed forces…I've saved lives for God's sake!" I said, becoming frustrated and throwing the glass against the wall and shattering it.

She walked over to me and said, "Baby, calm down. It's going to be okay."

"No, it's not. I can't take care of you. I'm a man. I'm supposed to be able to take care of you."

"You're strong, smart, and you have me…we will get through this."

Looking at her, I said, "You'll never understand."

She stroked my back. "I can't begin to tell you that I understand because I don't, but I promise that we will get through this…together."

Uninterested in her words of encouragement, I began to pick up the shattered glass.

"I love you," she said.

I didn't respond.

**‖ ✯ ✯ ✯ ‖**

The next morning, I awakened to find her standing over me. Frightened, I jumped up, almost knocking her onto the floor. "What the hell is wrong with you?" I asked, frightened by her.

She didn't say anything. She just stood there with a troubled look on her face.

"Ariel, don't do that," I said.

She snapped out of her trance. "I was just watching you sleep."

Crawling over to the other side of the bed, I said, "You have to let a brotha know when you want to watch him sleep."

She crawled into the bed beside me. "Then you wouldn't be able to sleep because you would know that I was watching you."

I crawled back to the other side of the bed. "Ariel, you scared the shit out of me."

She followed me. "I'm sorry," she purred.

To keep me from running away again, she threw herself on top of me. "Did I tell you I love you today?"

Confused, I said, "What's up Ariel?"

Kissing me on my chest, she replied, "Nothing." She began to undress me with her teeth.

When I stood to get away from her, I became aware of the boner that my pants were trying to restrain. Ariel noticed it too. She pulled the string to my pajama pants causing them to fall to the floor.

"Hello," she said, before greeting "him" with a kiss.

I watched as she took care of "him". As she took care of "him", the following thought came to me, *Is she crazy?* Suddenly, my thoughts drifted back to the warm lips on my body. I moaned and threw my head back to focus on the ceiling. It felt so good. I closed my eyes. I grabbed the back of her head to control the rhythm. My thoughts drifted back to my time in the military and to all of the beautiful exotic women who threw themselves at us. *How young they were and how obedient they were.* I thought to myself. No matter what you did, they loved you for it. *That's it bitch...Take all of it. You love this American dick...Oh shit, that feels good.* Her lips felt warm around my shaft. "Yes," I moaned. "Yes." *They were all so beautiful. We could have whoever we wanted. They desired us. All we had to do was open our mouths. English...Broken English...It didn't matter. We were their ticket overseas..."to the land of the free and to the home of the brave." They read about our culture...our history, but what they wanted they couldn't get from a book.* "Yes," I moaned. I released and she swallowed every drop. I stroked the top of her head to indicate that she had done well. I looked up again until every drop had been released. I opened my eyes, looked down to find Ariel looking up at me. My knees began to buckle. I sat down on the bed. Closing my eyes, I waited for the blood to rush back to my head. When I opened them again, it wasn't Ariel's face that I saw. "Did that feel good?" she asked. Horrified, I stood and ran out of the room.

Running closely behind me, she said, "Izrael."

I turned so abruptly that she ran into me. "Ariel?" I asked

"Yes, it's me," she confirmed.

Grabbing her by the face, I kissed her on the forehead, and then said, "It's you. It's you."

# CHAPTER
# 11

"Sweetie, I'm going to go visit one of my friends who just returned home," I said, not sure how she was going to react. "That's fine, honey. I have plans myself."

"Cool," I said, grabbing my keys and heading for the door.

Clearing her throat, she said, "Don't you want to know where I'm going?"

Dropping my head and doing an "about face", I answered, "No...I mean, yes. I'm sorry. What are you doing today?"

"Me and a few of my friends are going to the spa." The smile on her face was so big that it looked like it hurt.

Leaning to kiss her on the cheek, I said, "That's good...well okay, I'll see you later." I turned to walk toward the door.

Clearing her throat again, she said, "Ummm, did you forget something?"

Dropping my head again and doing an "about face", I said, "What did I forget?"

"You forgot to tell me that you love me."

Trying to refrain from choking her, I said, "I love you."

She kissed me. "I love you too."

Before she could say anything else, I was running toward the door.

I jumped into the car and sped out of the driveway as fast as I could. I had no idea where I was going. Being at home with Ariel felt like I was being buried alive. *What the hell is going on?* I didn't know who she was or what was going on. Everyday was a coin toss – heads or tails – sane or crazy.

# CHAPTER
# 12

The next day, I was sitting in the kitchen when the telephone rang. I answered it. There was no "hello".

"Man, my wife left me," Eddie said, sobbing into the phone.

Eddie and I served in the same unit. Since we returned home, we've tried to keep in touch with one another.

"What happened?" I asked, sipping from a cup of coffee, head deep into the classifieds.

"She was fucking around on me while I was in the service and got pregnant by the motherfucker."

"How do you know that she was fucking around?"

"She got pregnant," he said.

"And it wasn't yours?" I asked.

"Hell naw! How can she get pregnant by me when my penis was still attached to my ass overseas?"

"You have a point."

"She would have been able to fool a brotha if the baby didn't come out "light" as hell."

"Light? You felt that the baby wasn't yours because he was light-skinned?"

"Light with blue eyes," he clarified.

"Ah damn man, that's messed up."

"Yeah, that shit is messed up. I loved that woman."

"I'm really sorry to hear that, man."

"You say that shit like she's dead...although it would be easier to deal with it if she was."

"Man, I don't know what to say."

"Shit happens...I just wish that it hadn't happened to me."

"Yeah, that's pretty fucked up. What are you going to do now?"

"I haven't really thought about it. I didn't expect to come home to this." He started to cry into the phone.

*The war ain't for crybabies.* I thought to myself. "Man, crying and shit ain't gonna make it better."

"This shit is messed up. I go through all of that mess and then come home to this."

Agreeing with him and thinking about my own situation, I said, "I know."

"This shit hurts like hell, man...to go through all of that and then come home to nothing."

"I know what you mean."

He sighed, "You can't possibly know what I mean. I did this for her and the skank cheated on me."

"You are right...Not about the skank part." I paused and then thought about it for a second. "Well, I guess you are right about that part too...You know what, let me shut-up."

"See, that's what I'm saying. I could have died over there and her ass is back here getting her freak on," he said.

"Well, what are you going to do about that skank?" I asked, reiterating what he said.

"I am going to move on, shit...starting today. Forget her ass. I can get another woman."

"Good for you," I said, sounding more like a cheerleader than his "boy."

"What are you getting into this afternoon?" he asked, trying to change the subject.

"I was gonna go over to the hospital to see our boy, Greg. You remember Greg, don't you?"

"Yeah, I remember him. That guy was funny as hell – had me laughing all of the time. Where is he at?"

"He's at the VA hospital. He lost both of his legs trying to save a little girl?"

"Damn, here I am complaining about that bitch. He lost his legs. I can get another girl..."

"Yeah," I agreed.

"You don't mind if I tag along."

"Naw man, it'll be nice to have you along for the ride. I'll pick you up in thirty."

"Thanks man for letting me ride with you...I'll be ready."

"Cool...bye," I said, hanging up the phone.

I ran a bath and then I jumped into the tub. The water surrounded me. I washed myself. I grabbed the bottle of shampoo sitting near the tub. I lathered the soap onto my head. When I was done, I slid down into the large body of water to rinse my hair. Under the water, everything went silent. I held my breath. It was quiet – peaceful. I remained there. I closed my eyes and continued to hold my breath. After a while, my chest began to hurt, but I didn't want to come back up. I slowly began to release air through my mouth. I thought about how easy it would be to remain under...how quickly the noises would stop, but then I remembered my wife trying on those shoes. She needed me. I jumped up gasping for air. *Not this time soldier...Not this time.*

# CHAPTER
# 13

The building reeked of disinfectant and death. At first appearance, it looked like every other hospital, but what made it different was that these hospital beds held the bodies of many displaced men and women whose memories kept captive images of indescribable horrors.

As we slowly walked down the halls that led to his room, I thought about what I would say to him. I was lost for words. What do you say to someone who has lost his ability to walk forever doing something as noble as protecting his country? I had no idea. At his door, I paused and promised myself that I would smile and that I would not let on that I was angry about what has happened to him. I knew that deep inside that would be easier said than done.

When we walked in, he was asleep. I stood at the foot of his bed and looked at the empty spot that would have once been his legs. He had a pained look on his face. We sat down at his bedside. Eddie turned on the television and began to watch sports while I sat silently looking at my friend. I wondered why God decided that it should be him and not me who lost his legs that day. I should have been glad that the only thing he lost that day was his legs, but why would that be okay. So many young men joined the service with high hopes only to be returned home in body bags and wheelchairs and for what, I asked myself over and over again...for what?

I touched his hand. He awakened. "Hey, what's going on?" he asked, groggily.

Holding in my anger, I said, "Hey man, how are you?" *That was a dumbass question.*

"I'm good...as good as I can be. Who is that over there?" He sat up and tried to look around. "Eddie? Is that you?" he asked, trying to sit up.

Not looking at him, Eddie replied, "It's me man."

"Come over here man and let me see you," Greg requested.

Eddie walked over keeping his eyes on the floor.

"Damn man, you letting yourself go. Look at that gut."

Eddie smiled and said, "Yeah man, I have a personal relationship going on with fast food and my TV."

"Man, you need to end that relationship. It ain't healthy. Where's the wife? You should be at home sweating some of that off."

We both looked down.

"My wife decided to get her "sweat" on with somebody else," Eddie said.

"That's fucked up," Greg said.

I shook and dropped my head. I couldn't believe that he would bring that up.

Greg continued. "Dude, you too... that shit seems to be going around."

The room went silent.

"Your woman left you too?" I asked.

"On the first thing smoking," Greg joked.

"Damn," Eddie and I said at the same time.

Again, we all became silent.

I broke the silence by changing the subject. "How long are you going to be in here?"

"Well, they said that it's going to take awhile before they can release me. I guess you can't lose your legs and expect your life to be normal again. They said that I have some other issues that need to be addressed before they will release me."

"What other issues?" I asked.

"Well, it seems that during one of our tours I contracted HIV."

"Damn!" Eddie said. "That is so fucked up." Looking like someone had kicked him in the chest, he walked back over to the chair to catch his breath. He removed a bottle from his pants pocket, removed two pills and swallowed them down dry.

"You think?" Greg said.

"HIV? Man, I am so sorry to hear that," I said, sympathetically.

"Hey, it is what it is. Who would have thought?"

"Damn, nobody mentioned that shit," Eddie said, angrily.

"Is that why your wife left?" I asked.

"She left me when she found out that I lost my legs. It was too much for her to deal with. She doesn't know anything about the HIV. It's better that she doesn't know."

"Man, you guys were married. You have a duty to tell her."

"I'm sure I would if she was around. When I say that bitch left, she left; changed the phone number and everything."

*Damn.* I began to wonder if Ariel would have left me alone like Greg's wife left him if something bad had happened to me while I was over there.

"Well, when they release you, let me know. You can come stay with me," Eddie said.

"What and become a burden to you? I'm good man. I still have family, but thanks for the offer."

"I am so sorry that all of this has happened to you. You don't deserve this shit," he said, fighting back tears.

Looking at Greg, I said, "You have to forgive Eddie. He's a little emotional today."

"It's okay...I've come to terms with this. The way that I see it, nothing happens unless it's supposed to. Obviously, He has a plan for me. I've decided that once I'm released – if I'm released, I will share my stories with others...let them know that when you think that your life sucks just know that I'm a living example that things could be a lot worst." He laughed to himself. Next, he began to cry. Then Eddie began to cry. I decided that there would be no tears for me so I stood stoned-faced until they were done. Then he shouted, "Attention!" Eddie and I stood straight up with our hands to our forehead. Then he said, "There is no room for crybabies in this war. Now suck it up." He paused and then said, "At ease, soldiers." They wiped their tears, Eddie smiled unwillingly, and I promised him that we would visit him everyday.

On the ride home, Eddie and I didn't speak. As Eddie looked out of the window, he removed the bottle of pills from his pocket, took two of them, and proceeded to swallow them dry. I focused my eyes on the car in front of me to try to take my mind off of things.

**‖ ✯ ✯ ✯ ‖**

I was sitting in the bay window of our bedroom thinking when Ariel walked in. She approached me from behind and began to rub my shoulders.

"What's wrong?" she asked.

"I went to see my boy in the hospital," I said, drawing away from her touch.

"How is he?" she asked.

"He lost his legs and he's HIV positive."

She didn't say anything for a long time. Suddenly, she began to cry.

I forgot that hearing that someone was suffering would be a cause for her to cry. "I'm sorry. I shouldn't have told you."

Looking for something to blow her nose on, she said, "That could have easily been you, Izrael. I'm so grateful to God that you are here with me safe and unharmed."

*Safe and unharmed, I don't know about all of that.* I thought to myself. "That's sweet."

She wiped the tears from her face. "Izrael, don't do that."

"Don't do what?"

"You are trivializing my emotions."

"I didn't get this far being no chump. I appreciate what you have said, but I can't sit around crying about shit that I have no control over. The shit is what it is."

She stepped back. "Izrael, that was insensitive."

"I didn't mean for it to come out that way. I've just learned that shit happens for a reason...that's all." I paused and then inhaled deeply. "Do you smell that?"

"Oh no!" she screamed. "I'm burning dinner!" She went running from the room.

I remained in the room thinking about Greg's plight. As I remembered how helpless he looked lying there, the memory of the strong smell of disinfectant came to mind. It was so strong that I could smell it now – taste it now as if I was still there. The memory made my head spin.

# CHAPTER
## 14

The next day, I barely got out of bed. I was staring at the ceiling when the memory of Greg's tragedy came to me. The memory replayed itself like a movie in 3D. I remember the day that it happened like it was yesterday. He was trying to save a little girl from enemy fire and then there was an explosion. People were screaming and running everywhere. At first everything was red, orange, and yellow. Then everything around us turned black and gray. There was debris and pieces of flesh coming from the sky like raindrops. When the smoke cleared, there was nothing, but chaos. I remembered seeing him lying on the ground, with the remains of a vehicle crushing his legs. He cried in pain as three of us worked to free him before the enemy had another chance to strike.

In boot camp, he was always the person lending a helping hand…always going beyond the call of duty to get the job done and now he was going to die of AIDS.

I was deep in thought when Ariel entered the room from the bathroom, naked and bringing the scent from her shower with her. The room was engulfed with the scent of tangerines. "Honey, are you leaving out today?" asked Ariel, as she put on a sexy lace camisole and matching panties. I remember thinking how beautiful her locs were as they draped her face.

"I don't know. Yesterday took a toll on me mentally." I sat up on one arm to watch her dress.

"I hate that happened to your friend," she said, as she rubbed oil on her skin.

"Yeah, his wife left him too. Can you believe that?"

Shocked, she said, "I can't believe that. Why would she do something so cold? He needs her more now than ever before."

"I know...tramp could have stuck around to see him through this."

"There had to be a reason she left...he does have HIV."

"So?" I asked.

"So, how did he get it?" she asked, bending over to rub oil on her legs.

"Does it matter?"

"Yes, it matters."

"Are you saying that he cheated on her?"

"I'm not saying anything. I do know that he would get more sympathy if he got it trying to save his life or the life of another then to get it fucking some dirty piece of ass."

I couldn't say anything because in a weird way it made sense.

"He was...I mean, he is a stand-up guy. I think that he contracted it through a blood transfusion. He lost both of his legs trying to save a little girl."

"You see, a woman can respect that, but if he was out there hoeing then his dick should fall off."

"I honestly can't say that I know for sure what he did or didn't do. I saw some wild shit in the service."

"What do you mean, 'wild shit'?"

"I don't want to talk about it."

Looking at me, she said, "Did you cheat on me Izrael?"

*Define cheating.* "Look, I never loved anyone, but you and that's all you need to know."

She pulled her locs off of her face and said, "So you cheated on me?" she asked, innocently.

"Look, don't ask me questions you don't want the answers to. I've been gone five years."

Her eyes began to fill with tears.

I decided that I would spare her the ugly truth about what men did to get by, so I said, not telling the whole truth, "I masturbated a lot, okay."

"So you cheated on me with your hand?"

"Yeah, sure," I agreed, telling her what she wanted to hear.

Happy with my answer, she ran over and jumped into the bed on the side of me. She smiled and snuggled under me. She smelled good…a hell of a lot better than the people I shared a barrack with. Her body felt good against mine. I rubbed her arms and gently kissed her neck. She cooed. She sounded so sweet. I held her tight as we both drifted to sleep.

## ▌ ✯ ✯ ✯ ▌

I awakened to the smell of steamed broccoli and baked salmon.

"I can't believe we slept all-day. What time is it?" I asked, stretching.

"It's not late. It's only 3:00 in the afternoon."

I walked over to the stove to watch her as she stirred the brown rice. "That's good. I didn't miss my reruns of *Law and Order.*"

"Why do you watch that stuff? There are so many other things you could be doing," she said.

"I like "who done it" shows. I like watching them try to catch the killer."

"You find that interesting?"

"Yes, I do," I said, walking over to the table.

Placing a plate of food in front of me, she said, "Watching movies with dead bodies…You would think that you would do everything to avoid seeing more blood and gore."

"That doesn't bother me. It's a part of life – people live and people die."

"I worry about you," she said, sitting at the table across from me.

"There's no need to worry about me. Everything's fine. Believe me."

After dinner, I went into the living room to watch TV. I wasn't sitting there five minutes before Ariel was all over me.

She grabbed me between my legs. "Do you want dessert?"

Pushing her hand away, I said, "I would love to watch TV."

"Come on," she pleaded.

"Ariel, I love you, but you got a brotha working double duty. Let me get with you a little later. At least let me digest my dinner."

Feeling jilted, she said, "Okay," and walked away.

Sometimes it was hard to feel anything for her. Sometimes I wanted her and then other times the thought of her left me cold. I thought about the nights I spent away from her – lying awake at night needing her. I would lay there wondering what she was doing – wondering if she was missing me.

At times, my thoughts of her were often interrupted by the sounds of men jagging off and when jagging off wasn't enough, whether straight or not, it didn't matter, some of them sought comfort in the arms of another man.

One particular night, while I was jagging off, while looking at a photo of Ariel, one of the guys asked me if he could 'top it off.' At first, I hesitated, but then I told him to get the fuck away from me before he got hurt. I told him that no matter what, I don't swing that way. That shit just ain't for me. He called himself getting pissed off, rolled his eyes, and walked his sweet ass back to where he came from with his mouth stuck out. I couldn't even climax after that shit. I turned over and forced myself to sleep through the sounds of moans echoing through the halls.

# CHAPTER
## 15

The next day, I left for my follow-up checkup at the doctor's office. It was warm out and the breeze coming through the window felt good against my skin. I really didn't feel like going to see the doctor so I decided to play hooky. Without thinking twice, I pulled over and parked my car on 55th Street, walked over to the lake, sat among the rocks and spent the rest of the afternoon watching as the waves danced against the shore.

It was beautiful and serene out. I watched as couples held hands and walked along the path, people rode their bikes, and young people enjoyed a game of basketball. It felt good to be home. All of a sudden, everything changed.

*Pop! Pop! Pop!* I ran and ducked behind the rocks. *Pop! Pop! Pop!* I closed my eyes. Someone screamed. I covered my ears. In an instant, everything around me turned black.

A voice said, "Man down! Man down!"

"Wha…Wha…?" I asked, looking around.

"Soldier, what the hell are you doing? Get the hell out there and save him!" someone shouted.

Taking my orders to save the wounded soldier, I went running into the crowd. "I'm coming soldier…I'm coming!" I shouted. When I awakened from my trance, I found myself standing in the middle of a crowd of people looking into the sky at fireworks. Immediately, I remembered where I was, and feeling overwhelmed, I ran to my car.

84

Behind the wheel, I worked to regain my composure. When my breathing leveled itself, I started my car. I rolled the window down to dry the sweat above my brow.

"Everything is going to be okay." I told myself. "It's going to be okay."

**‖ ✠ ✠ ✠ ‖**

My concept of time was off. I didn't know that it was a holiday. I guess the waving flags, fireworks, and the smell of burning flesh on almost every grill in the city should have been obvious clues, but my head wasn't right. I needed to collect my thoughts; piece some things together. Today would be the perfect day to sit at home and sort things out, but Ariel would be there. I had enough stuff going on. I just didn't want to deal with her at that moment, so I drove around until it was dark.

When I pulled into the driveway, I noticed that the only light on in the entire house was in the kitchen. I parked my vehicle and turned the ignition off. As I approached the door, I noticed that it was cracked. The aroma coming from the inside embraced my senses. I knew that wasn't Ariel because her cooking didn't have that affect on me. Only one woman's cooking smelled that good.

I walked in slowly. "Mama?"

"Hey baby," she said. "Daddy, he's here."

Flushing the toilet, my father exited the washroom and then entered the room. "Hey son, where have you been?"

Confused, I said, "Mama, where's Ariel? How did you get in here?"

They gave each other a look. "Boy, don't start with me and you should know better than to leave your doors unlocked. Have you heard of crime? Well, there's plenty of it everywhere. You need to listen to the news," she said.

Glad that Ariel wasn't home, I said, "Mama, what are you

doing?" I walked over to look into the pots. "My goodness...everything smells so good. Somebody really loves me."

"Somebody does," she said. "Now get out of this kitchen and let me do what I do."

"Okay mama," I said, excited to see the both of them.

After dinner, we watched some TV. After developing a bad case of "i-tis", my parents went home. Sitting in front of the TV, I fell asleep. Later, I was awakened by the sound of keys at the door. Ariel walked in with ten shopping bags.

"Hi sweetie," she said, kissing me on the forehead. "How was your day?"

"My parents stopped by. My mother cooked me dinner."

"So she did?" she said, sarcastically.

"Yes, she did," I said, feeling some BS coming.

"You know that your mother doesn't like me," she said, as a matter of fact.

"That's not true, she doesn't really know you."

"Why doesn't she want to know me? I'm her daughter-in-law. I'm the woman that her son is going to spend the rest of his life with. Who does she think is going to have her grandbabies? Me damnit."

I sighed.

She continued, "We always seem to conveniently miss each other. Have you noticed that?"

"Don't do this Ariel..."

She interrupted, "And she didn't even leave me any food."

I searched the kitchen and she was right. There were no leftovers and everything was cleaned and put away eliminating any trace evidence that she was there. I defended my mother. "She came to see me. She just wanted to cook dinner for me..."

"Well, the most decent thing to do would have been to save a plate for me, but I shouldn't expect a lot from someone who hates my guts."

Walking up to her and kissing her on the mouth, I said, "She doesn't hate you. Anyway if you're hungry, I can go out and get you something to eat."

"That's okay, I'm not really that hungry."

Scratching my head, I said, "Then why did we just have a ten minute discussion about some damn food? You know what? Just forget it." I threw my hands into the air.

"Yes, we've spent too much time talking about this. Anyway, I caught a fantastic sale at Neiman's. Come darling, I want to show you what I've purchased." She dragged me down the hall to the bedroom. I sat quietly as she tried on everything for me.

**‖ ✶ ✶ ✶ ‖**

Later that night…

"That was so good baby…I swear that I don't deserve you," she said, wiping sweat from her forehead. "It was so good…I'm not going to be able to walk for a week."

I didn't say anything.

She continued, "I like the way you kept screaming 'at ease, soldier'. That was kinky."

*Did I do that? I don't remember doing that.*

"You are a tiger," she said, jumping up from the bed. "I'm hungry. You want something?"

"We just ate," I said.

"That was a few hours ago," she said, heading for the door.

I stopped her. "I'll do it. You want a sandwich?"

Walking back over to the bed, she said, "A sandwich would be good. Could you add some chips and a soda?"

"Sure, I'll be right back."

I left the bedroom. Ariel rested quietly.

Looking in the refrigerator, I grabbed the smoked turkey, lettuce, tomatoes, bread, and mayo. I removed a knife from the cabinet drawer. I was slicing the lettuce when a sharp pain struck me right between the eyes.

"Ahhhhh!" I screamed. Stumbling backward, I fell on the floor. "Ahhhhh!" I screamed again.

Ariel came running into the kitchen. "What's wrong? Give me that," she said, reaching for the knife that was still in my hand.

I clutched it tightly.

"Let it go," she said, reaching for the blade again trying not to cut herself.

Not realizing that I was still clutching the knife, I began to swing it at her.

"Izrael, what are you doing?" she said, dodging the blade.

"Get away from me," I said, stabbing at her.

"Izrael, it's me. Stop this, I'm begging you." She reached for the blade and accidentally cut her hand.

"Throw down your weapon!" I shouted.

"Sweetie, what are you talking about? What weapon? I'm not trying to hurt you," she said, slowly backing away.

"I'm not going to ask you again...Throw down your weapon!" I said, walking toward her.

"What are you talking about?" she said, stumbling onto the floor.

I lunged at her. Placing the blade at her throat, I looked at her. She was shaking.

Snapping out of my trance, I said, "Oh my God, what have I done?" I dropped the blade. There was blood on my hands and on the blade. "What have I done?" I ran and snatched the dish towel from the sink.

I walked over to Ariel who was cowering against the refrigerator. I walked toward her.

"Get away from me!" she screamed.

"Ariel, let me help you. I'm sorry," I said, reaching out to her.

Scurrying backward out of my reach, she said, "Get your crazy ass away from me!"

*Crazy?* Walking toward her, I said, "I'm sorry. Please let me put this on your hand to stop the bleeding."

"Fuck you," she said, running down the hall. I heard the bedroom door slam.

I followed her. *Crazy?* I thought to myself. *Interesting.* I tried the knob, but the door was locked. I knocked on the door. There was no answer. "Ariel, open the door."

There was no answer.

"Ariel, I'm going to ask you one more time. Please open the door."

Suddenly, I heard the door unlock. I walked in, the room was dark. "Ariel, I'm sorry," I said, searching the darkness for her.

At first, I couldn't find her. I turned on the light to find her crying in the chair next to the bed.

I walked over to her.

"Izrael, I don't know what the hell that was, but...you need some help." As she spoke, she waved her hand in my face to emphasize her point. The smell of astringent engulfed the air. The smell irritated my senses.

I knew that what I did was wrong, but I was really in no mood to hear her mouth. The pain in my head was relentless. Ignoring her suggestion, I said, "Ariel, let me look at your hand?"

Looking at me through frightened eyes, she hesitated and then said, "Sure."

After taking care of her wound, I said, "I'm sorry."

For a moment there was silence. She allowed me to lift her from the chair and carry her to the bed. I tucked her in. Neither one of us fell asleep.

# CHAPTER
## 16

At the breakfast table, we didn't speak. The only sound in the room came from the clanking of our spoons and forks against our plates. When we walked down the hallway and we bumped into each other neither one of us said 'excuse me'. No 'good-byes' were exchanged when she left for the gym.

When she finally came home that night, she climbed into bed without even saying 'goodnight'. I couldn't sleep. I tried watching television, but it wasn't helping. I decided to get dressed and go for a walk. It was beautiful outside. The streets were quiet, there was a full moon, and the stars were bright. As I strolled down the street enjoying the night air, I noticed a lady on the side of the road with what seemed to be car trouble. I approached her. "Are you okay?"

"My car won't start," she said, looking under the hood.

"What do you think is wrong?" I asked, walking over to the other side of the car to look under the hood.

"I think it's the battery. Do you have any cables?"

"No, I'm not driving."

"Oh," she said, looking over her shoulder.

"Let me take a look."

Handing me the flashlight, she said, "Sure."

As I leaned over to look under the hood, I felt a blow to the back of my head. As blood streamed down the side of my face, everything around me went black.

**|| ✶ ✶ ✶ ||**

"Ouch," I said, reaching for the back of my head.

"Oh sweetie, I'm so glad that you're okay. I acted foolishly. I should have known better. What were you doing out tonight?" Ariel said, frantically.

"Shit, my head hurts. What the hell happened?" Looking around the hospital room, I noticed that we weren't alone. "What's going on?"

"Someone found you on the ground, unconscious…you were robbed," the officer said.

"Robbed?" I asked, grimacing in pain.

"Yeah robbed, your wallet was gone," Ariel reiterated.

"That bitch stole my wallet after I tried to help her?"

"It was a woman?" Ariel asked, whispering trying not to cause me anymore pain.

"It was a scam," the officer said in a normal voice causing my head to throb.

"A scam?" I asked.

"Yes, that happens all of the time. Some hot chick pretends she's having car trouble and some unsuspecting sucker…I mean…some guy comes to her aid. The scam usually consists of two people – One to lure the sucker in…I mean…guy in and another to take him out. Did you see anyone else?" he asked as he took notes.

I looked at him. I didn't like being called a 'sucker'. I was going to "check" his ass, but figured now was not the time. I made a mental note to take care of it later. "No, I didn't see anyone else."

Looking me up and down, he said, "So you served in the military?"

"Yeah, why do you ask?" I asked, becoming annoyed by not only his questions, but his mere presence.

"Your cute little wife told us," he said, now looking Ariel up and down. He continued, "I ask because you would think that you would know better than to fall for that bullshit." Turning his attention to Ariel, he said, "Sorry about that Ms."

*So he was a smartass. There's ways to deal with smartasses.*

Ariel frowned. Directing her attention to me, she said, "Sweetie you have to be careful…things have changed a lot since you've been gone. You can't just go around helping people…unfortunately, you can't trust everyone."

"My job was to serve and protect…I should have seen it coming. Damn, how could I have not seen that?"

"What did she look like?" asked the officer.

"What are you implying?" I asked.

"I'm not implying anything, but we will need a description in order to catch her."

"I can't tell you what she looked like. It was dark."

"You didn't see anything?" she asked, stroking my hand to comfort me.

"I saw stars after she hit me," I said, getting sick of the both of them.

The officer laughed causing his belly to jump.

"Look officer, I'm going to have to ask you to leave. My husband needs his rest."

Removing a card from his pocket, he said, "Well, if he remembers anything tell him to give me a call."

"Sure officer," she said, taking the card before escorting him out.

After they were gone, she sat in the chair near the hospital bed and said, "She could have killed you."

"Yeah, she could have," I said.

"Please don't leave out again without letting me know where you're going. I was worried sick about you."

"I'm a big boy. I can take care of myself," I said, turning my back to her.

She dragged the chair to the other side of the bed to face me. The noise almost sent me over the edge.

"Damn, will you cut that shit out?!" I shouted.

"I'm sorry," she said and then continued, "I almost lost you tonight. I don't think it's too much to ask."

Not wanting to argue because my head was killing me, I said, "Okay...Ariel." I was hoping that she would let it go.

She stood and said, "Now get some rest. I'll be right out here if you need me." She walked toward the door.

"Okay...thank you..."

When she exited the room, she turned off the lights. Lying in the dark, I thought about the attack. I let my guard down. I couldn't believe it. I assumed that since I was at home, I was safe because the enemy was on the other side of the world. So I thought.

**‖ ✵ ✵ ✵ ‖**

Although, I was given something to help me relax, I couldn't sleep. I tossed and turned in an attempt to exhaust myself, but it didn't work. The faint throbbing in the back of my head was unyielding. I turned on the television, I pressed the "mute" button, but even muted it was too loud. I searched for the "call" button on the side of my bed to call the nurse to request some painkillers, but there wasn't one. Finding this odd, I sat up and searched the bed and the wall behind it; still there was nothing. Confused, I decided to walk to the nurse's station to retrieve one of them. There was no one there. I wandered through the halls to find one. There was no one. I was all alone. Suddenly, I felt a chill. The floors were ice cold underneath my bare feet. I grabbed my hospital gown tightly to ward off the draft that was wafting from behind.

A low howl filled the dark halls. I followed the sound to an empty hospital room. I stood in the doorway, looked around, and as I turned to leave, I heard someone whisper, "Help me."

"Who's there?" I asked, still standing in the doorway.

There was no response. I turned to leave the room. Again, the voice whispered, "Help me."

I walked into the room, looked around, finding nothing, I turned to leave the room again when I heard it again, "Help me."

I looked behind the hospital room door. There was a door adjacent to it. There was a light coming from underneath. I walked over to inspect it and found another door leading to another room. "Help me," I heard the voice again. I touched the knob. It was covered in ice. The sharp edges of the ice cut my hand. I looked around the room for something to use to open the door. Removing one of the pillowcases from one of the beds, I wrapped it around my hand to open the door. When I opened it a burst of cold air greeted me. I couldn't see so I blinked to regain my focus. Freezing, I wrapped the pillowcase around my shoulders for warmth. I walked in. The floor was covered in ice. My feet stuck to the floor causing them to bleed with every step. As I struggled to walk inside of the room, in the distance, I saw a form – a shadow of something hanging from the ceiling. "Help me," I heard, no longer in a whisper. I walked closer.

Shaking, I reached out. Now able to see what was hanging from the ceiling, I stood speechless. It was the body of a young woman. Her head hung lifeless over her chest hiding her face. Her body swung back and forth. I stood facing her – terrified, when suddenly her head began to rise. Now we were looking at each other. With a rope around her neck, she said, "Izrael, why?" She reached out to me.

"Ariel! Noooooooo!" I stumbled backward falling onto the floor. "Ariel! No!" I screamed. I stood and left running down the hall to my hospital room. I jumped in the bed and covered my head with my covers.

Shaking me, I heard, "Sir, I'm here to check your vitals."

"What...where's Ariel? Where's my wife?" I asked, breathless.

Placing her fingers on my wrist, she said, "She went home after you fell asleep. Now lie still while I check your pulse."

"She's dead," I said.

"She looked very much alive when she left," she said, listening for my heartbeat.

When she was done, I lifted the bed sheets to check my injured feet, but there were no wounds, no blood, and no scars. I reached over to the phone lying next to the bed. I frantically dialed my home phone number.

She answered on the third ring. "Hello."

"Ariel?" I asked, confused.

"Izrael?" she asked, sleepily. "Baby, what are you doing awake? You need to get your rest."

I didn't respond. I hung up the phone, closed my eyes, and began to pray for peace.

**‖ ★ ★ ★ ‖**

When Ariel came to pick me up from the hospital, I was already dressed and standing at the door. I couldn't wait to get the hell out of that place. I walked up to Ariel to embrace her. I was so happy to see her. I held her so tight, she was begging for me to let her go.

"Izrael, I can't breathe."

I released her. "Ariel, let's go home."

# CHAPTER
## 17

The next morning, I was awakened by the smell of coffee brewing. I attempted to lift my head, but the pain caused me to lie back down.

Ariel walked over holding two little white pills and a glass of water. "Here take this."

I took what I thought were painkillers from her hand, placed them in my mouth, and washed them down with the water.

"I'm so sorry...sorry about everything," I said.

"It's okay. Get some rest."

"Look Ariel..." I tried sitting up again. The room began to spin. "I...I...Whew, what did you give me?" I said, lying back down.

"I gave you something to help you relax. Let me make you something to eat." The telephone rang. "Let me get that. You rest," she insisted.

My eyelids became heavy. I drifted off to sleep.

**|| ✶ ✶ ✶ ||**

As I pulled the blankets back to get out of bed, I noticed that my wrists were burning. I looked at them to find that they were both red. I ran out of the room to look for Ariel. After running through the entire house, I found her in the bathroom taking a bubble bath.

"Ariel, look at my arms," I said, sticking my hands in her face.

"Calm down, Izrael. Let's take a look," she said, reaching out to touch them.

The soapy water burned the wounds on my skin. I drew my arms back. "Ouch! Did the officer put handcuffs on me?"

"What officer, Izrael?" she said, playing with the bubbles.

"The officer who took the report after the incident," I said.

"What incident?" she asked, still playing with the water.

"Are you serious? The robbery...the other night, my wallet got stolen...the lump on my head?" I reached back to the spot where the lump was and noticed that there was nothing there. My eyes widened. "What the hell is going on? What the hell was that shit you gave me," I said, making a reference to the two white pills that she gave me earlier.

"You were having an episode. You told me that when you get that way to give you two of those pills. I did. You calmed down and you went to sleep." She stood. With a body covered in bubbles, she said, "Now be a sweetie and hand me my towel."

I grabbed her hand. I saw the scar. "So *that* did happen?"

"Yes and I forgave you for it a week ago. Now can we move on?" she asked, drying herself.

"A week ago?"

"Yes sweetie, a week ago," she said, handing me the towel. "Now can you hand me my robe?"

Confused, I said, "Sure."

"Go lie down, Izrael. I'll bring you your dinner in a little while. Also, your mom called while you were resting."

"Um...okay." I walked back into the room. I picked up the phone. I held it and looked at the date on the caller-id. I dialed my mother's phone number, but hung up before she had a chance to answer. I couldn't talk to her. I was confused and disjointed. My sense of time was off. *A week ago? That can't be.* I had to regain my footing before I called her or she would worry to death about me.

**‖ ✯ ✯ ✯ ‖**

"How long has this been going on Izrael?"

"How long has what been going on?"

She waved her scarred hand in the air.

"I don't know what the hell is going on...let alone the shit you're talking about."

"You pulled a knife on me. I asked you to make me a sandwich and you tried to kill me. If you didn't want to make the sandwich, you should have told me."

"Okay, there's some shit missing. You said that happened a week ago."

"That's right," she said.

"Then where have I been?"

"Izrael, what are you talking about?"

"I'm talking about this shit...What the hell is going on Ariel?"

"I don't understand."

"I don't understand either." I was becoming frustrated. "Forget it...I can't explain it."

"You need to figure out how to explain it before somebody in this house gets hurt."

"There's nothing wrong with me. I just...I just..."

"You just what? And what exactly are those pills for?"

"I have no idea. They weren't painkillers and I don't remember giving them to you or even instructing you to give them to me."

"Then where did I get them from?"

I tilted my head to the side. I raised my brow and said, "Exactly...that's a damn good question. Where did you get the pills from?"

She tilted her head and raised her brow. "Izrael, are you having another moment? Of course, you gave them to me."

Thinking about what she said earlier, I said, "Episode?"

She waved her hand in the air.

"Look, don't be slipping me anything."

She gave me a strange look. "My parents told me..."

I walked over to her. Standing face to face, I said, "What did your parents tell you? What did they have to say about Izrael?"

She stepped back. "Are WE talking in third person, I-z-r-a-e-l? And for the record, they warned me. They told me what to expect."

"And what are you expecting?"

With piercing eyes, she said, "You know what, I'm going to be nice because I know that you've been trying to get adjusted, but here's the plan..."

I interrupted her. "Before you say something and I do something that we both will regret, I'm going to leave."

"Good idea," she said, turning up her mouth and folding her arms. "In the meantime, I will pray for you."

"Do whatever the hell you want," I said under my breath. I grabbed my car keys and left slamming the door.

I was pissed, annoyed, and had the worst headache I've had in a very long time. I jumped into my car and rolled down the windows to allow the air to put out the fire brewing inside of me. With no idea where I was going, I drove around until I found an area on the "low-end" of Chicago. Circling the block, I ended up on the road that led straight to Hell. Looking around, I noticed that this block contained everything a person needed to dull their senses. There were street-walkers, drug-dealers, strip clubs, churches, and liquor stores.

I was driving when the light turned red. Sitting at the light, I began to rub my temples. Suddenly, a voice came out of nowhere, "Hey brotha, I got what cha' need."

I looked up to find a young man standing near my car. "Son of a bitch!" I shouted. "You scared the shit out of me. What the fuck is wrong with you? I could have killed you."

"Sorry about that man...anyway, you need anything?"

Trying to catch my breath, I said, "Naw man, I'm cool." He walked away. The light turned green and I pulled off. Further down the road, I could hear the "click-clacking" of the heels of a woman's shoes marching up and down the pavement. I slowed down. The scene reminded me of some of the towns I visited overseas. I was driving down the block, when someone shouted, "Hey!" I looked in the direction the voice was coming from. I pulled over. A young lady approached the car. "Hey big daddy, what cha' doing in this part of town?"

I didn't say anything.

"You want some company?" she asked.

I didn't say anything.

She leaned into my car window, opening her coat, and exposing a beautiful set of 34DDs. The cool evening air made her nipples hard.

I didn't say anything.

Standing and closing her jacket, she said, "You don't want nothing. Sorry to have bothered you."

Not saying anything, I grabbed her hand before she walked away. She looked at me. I don't know what made me do it. There was no logic behind my decision to take this woman – to take this stranger up on her offer, but I needed something. What? I didn't know. Suddenly, without thinking, I pointed to the passenger side of my car. Taking the hint, she walked around to the other side of the car and got in. I pulled off. She was talking. When she realized that I wasn't interested in her conversation, she became quiet. I drove around until I found an alley. I didn't know what I was doing and I didn't care. Once she placed her head between my legs, the pain in my head subsided. When she was done, I paid her, took her back to the spot where I picked her up and then went home to my wife.

## ❚❚ ✶ ✶ ✶ ❚❚

"Where have you been?" Ariel said, when I walked through the door. She was yelling and screaming, when I turned around and walked back out of the door.

"Where are you going?!" she yelled.

I didn't answer. I got back into my car and drove off. I drove for about thirty minutes. I pulled in front of Eddie's house. I rang the doorbell. After about five minutes, Eddie answered the door.

"What's going on man? What time is it?"

I walked passed him without saying a word.

Eddie said, "Oh okay man, you don't feel like talking…we can do this in the morning."

I walked over to the couch, laid my head down, and went to sleep.

## ❚❚ ✶ ✶ ✶ ❚❚

My cell-phone vibrated all night. Becoming frustrated, I finally answered it.

"Izrael, I'm sorry," Ariel said, not giving me a chance to say 'hello'.

"I know that you are concerned and you have every right to be, but I'm a grown ass man. Anyway, you have nothing to worry about. I actually feel better."

"I was so worried about you. I'm so sorry. Lately, I've acted like such an ass."

"It's okay. Look, I'm tired let me go back to…"

She interrupted, "Do you want to talk about what's been going on?"

"I just said that I feel better. Why would you want to mess that up?"

"One day, you will have to talk about what's going on with you. You would hate for your memories to manifest themselves into something else," she said.

"That's good advice. Thanks. They won't."

She didn't say anything.

I broke the silence. "I'm going to take a nap."

"When will you be home?"

"In the morning," I said.

"Could you come home now? I miss you. I need you."

"I'll be there in the morning," I said.

"Okay love, I'll wait up for you."

I closed my eyes. I lied there for what seemed like an hour. When I awakened, the room was dark. I looked around the room. I jumped up. *What the hell?! How did I get here? What is going on?* I was at home. *I'm losing my freakin' mind.* I thought to myself. I rubbed my eyes to make sure that I wasn't seeing things. I stood and ran through the house to make sure that I wasn't losing my mind. I suddenly realized the feel of the floor underneath my bare feet. I went into the bathroom to splash some cold water on my face. Rattled, I walked back to the bedroom and climbed into bed. I laid there staring at the ceiling. Looking out of the skylight that was positioned over our bed, I tried to put things together. Nothing was making sense. I closed my eyes again to see where I would end up. I was still at home. *It must have all been a dream,* I told myself. I tried to calm down.

I continued to stare up at the sky trying to piece things together. It reminded me of the nights spent sleeping under the stars as a soldier. It was one of the things I loved because it reminded me of the many nights I spent camping with my father. I could hear him now yelling at me about over-cooking the smores. As a soldier, I would always try to remember those moments shared with my father. Suddenly, a sense of peace came over me. I took a deep breath, sighed, and turned over to find Ariel's body curled into a ball. I rubbed her legs. She purred. I nuzzled my nose into her hair and then I fell back to sleep.

# CHAPTER
## 18

The morning sun embraced me. The moment I opened my eyes, I felt grateful, grateful to be alive, and grateful for what seemed like a sane moment. I rolled onto my back and smiled as I reflected on my life. I thought about where I had been and how far I'd come. For the first time in a long time, I didn't dream about the war – I didn't dream about anything – I rested. I was going to go downstairs, but decided to spend a little time looking out of my bedroom window. As I stared out into the backyard, a sudden level of peace came over me. I could have sat there all day, but the rumbling in my stomach dictated something else. I heard the front door open. Ariel had just come in from the gym. I continued to look out of the window while Ariel showered.

When she came out drying her hair, she said, "How are you...today?"

"I'm good...That was the best sleep I've had in a long time. So, what time is service?"

"Izrael, what day do you think it is?"

"It's Sunday, now get ready because I want to get back in time for the game."

"Honey, today is Tuesday," she clarified.

"No, it's not," I said, pointing at the calendar on the wall.

Snatching it from its place, sending thumb tacks flying across the room, and realizing that I was wrong, I said, "You are kidding me. Where have I been?"

"You've been asleep for the past couple of days."

Shocked, I said, "Why would I be sleep that long? Who the hell sleeps that long other than Sleeping Beauty?"

"Obviously you...Sleeping Beauty," she snorted.

Rattled, I said, "Hold on. Let me get this straight. For no apparent reason whatsoever I climbed into this bed and slept for two days and no one fucking questioned that?"

"You told me not to bother you because you were tired. I checked on you and by all indications, you looked fine."

"I don't believe you."

"Believe it."

"Damn, that must have been some blow to my head."

She didn't say anything.

"About that night..."

Looking frustrated, she said, "I don't know what that shit is you are taking, but the shit you are about to talk about, happened a while ago." Plopping down into the chair, she continued, "Izrael, I don't have time for this. I'm exhausted. I haven't been feeling well lately and trying to take care of you has been more than a notion." She stood and walked over to the door. "I've been so tired. I am so hungry all of the time and no matter how many sit-ups I do, I can't seem to get rid of this stomach. It's hard trying to take care of the both of us."

"I didn't come back home to be a burden to you."

"Don't start feeling sorry for yourself. It isn't attractive and it's not who you are."

Baffled, I said, "And who am I?"

Frustrated, she said, "I don't have time for this. When you find out *who* the hell is Izrael, tell him to come downstairs. I brought food home." She stomped out of the room.

I began to talk to myself. When I noticed that I was doing that, I began to panic. I took a few deep breaths to regain my composure. When I knew that I had it somewhat together, I stood and left the room.

"I'm famished. What you got?" I said, trying to deflect my attention to something else.

"Well, we have pork barbequed ribs, greens, string beans, spaghetti, potato salad, and corn bread."

"Man, that's a lot of food, but you know that I don't eat pork."

"Yes, you do. We had pork chops the other day and you loved them," she said, sitting the plate down in front of me.

The ribs soaked in barbeque sauce looked liked someone's rib cage after it had been ripped from their chest. Pushing the plate away, I said, "Get that away from me...I couldn't have eaten pork. I can't have it...never have and never will."

"Whatever," she said. She retrieved the plate. "Okay, okay...make up your mind. One day, you eat pork and anything with legs, including me," she smiled at her attempt to make me laugh. "Then the next day, you're freakin' out."

Uncomfortable, I said, "Don't play games, Ariel. You know that I don't eat that shit."

She frowned attempting to express her frustration.

"What else do you have?" I asked.

"I got some catfish."

"That shit is filthy too."

Again, she frowned. "Take it or leave it."

Too hungry to fight, I said, "I'll take some of that."

Taking a bite out of the ribs, she said, "You don't know what you are missing." She licked the sauce from her fingers.

"You're going to eat all of that?"

"Yes…I can't explain it, but lately, I've had such a tapeworm."

"That worm is really hungry. That's enough food to feed a small village."

"Whatever… if you're looking for me I will be standing over the stove eating straight from the containers."

"No, you're not."

"Watch me and I'd advised you to stay clear until I leave the kitchen," she said, keeping her word. It was a mess. Sauce was flying all over the place. Every once in a while she would lift her head to breathe and lick her fingers. There was something unsexy about watching her eat like that. This was unlike the young lady I married who was raised by a family with money. She acted like she hadn't eaten in years. It was crazy. I couldn't watch it. I grabbed my plate of food and went into the living room away from the carnage.

# CHAPTER
# 19

I was sitting on the toilet when I noticed it. My wife was doing her makeup over the bathroom sink, when I saw a small bump that now stood in the place of what use to be Ariel's perfectly toned abs. I didn't say anything at first until I looked up to find a pair of big full breasts that replaced what was once just a mouth full.

Wiping myself and flushing the toilet, I said, "When was the last time you had a period?"

"Why do you ask?" she said.

"Not trying to be mean, but you've gained a little weight."

Scowling, she said, "Why would you say something like that?"

"Look at your stomach...your breasts. You've been eating a lot lately."

"I'm eating because I'm stressed out...that's all."

"Are you sure that's all there is to it?"

"Are you a medical doctor?"

"No," I said, picking up on her attitude.

"Then back up," she said, pushing pass me.

Her approach to this conversation was abrasive and warranted an ass-whooping, but I reminded myself that you don't hurt the people you love. I took two deep breaths and was in the process of following her when the door was slammed in my face. I closed my eyes, took a couple of deep breaths to regain my composure, and then turned the knob to open it.

"I didn't mean to imply that you're getting fat or anything."

"Whatever," she said, stomping down the hall, and slamming the bedroom door.

Feeling the tension rising within, I began to clinch my fists. I closed my eyes and repeated to myself, "I love this woman. I love this woman. I love this woman." I took another deep breath and walked down the hall. I could hear her sobbing from the other side of the door.

I walked in to find her sprawled across the bed crying.

Sitting on the bed beside her, I said, "That was wrong of me. I shouldn't have said anything. Please forgive me."

Crying, she said, "I've just been so stressed out...that knife incident...you being sick...watching you constantly sleep and praying that you will wake up okay...you've only been home for six months and..."

"Six months...that's all?"

"Yes...Izrael, don't start."

Embracing her and placing her head on my shoulder, I said, "It's going to be okay..."

"Izrael, I don't know what is going on. I don't know if I'm capable of dealing with this."

Pushing her away from me, I said, "Are you talking about leaving me?"

"What are you talking about? I didn't say that. I just said that it's been hard. I don't want to spend the rest of my life dealing with this."

"Are you saying that you're leaving me?" Without emotion, I looked at her and awaited her response.

She looked at me. "I...I...don't know what I'm saying," she stammered.

*Good answer.* I thought to myself. I embraced her to assure her that everything would be okay.

**II ✭ ✭ ✭ II**

The next day, I made every effort to make things right between us. She wanted to go to the mall. The day almost went by without a hitch…almost. Ariel decided to wear a low-cut top that accentuated her "new" breasts and she wore some jeans that was once a little loose, but was now fitting her ass like a second skin.

We were getting some smoothies when she walked away to look into the window of a jewelry store. I was paying for the drinks when I noticed a young man approach her. I watched the interaction from a distance. From where I stood, I could tell that she was trying to be polite and not wanting to cause a scene. I moved in closer to hear what was being said. Suddenly, the young man snatched her purse and ran. She screamed. Something inside of me snapped. I didn't take off after him. I sat the drinks down and watched as he disappeared around the corner. I calmly walked around the corner to find that there was nothing in that area other than the men's washroom. A sudden sense of satisfaction came over me. I entered the men's washroom and locked the door. I tip-toed pass each stall looking underneath to find the thief.

At the last stall, I could hear him – see him emptying the contents of Ariel's purse onto the floor. Without thinking, I pushed the door open with such force that it threw the assailant against the wall. He was disoriented. I grabbed him by the collar and said, "You like women's purses? Huh, are you a woman? Let's see how much of a woman you are." He didn't answer my question. He just stood with a dazed look on his face. I leaned over to find Ariel's lipstick on the floor. I picked it up, opened it, and smeared it all over his face. "Oooo, look how pretty you are." He tried to scream. I tightened the grip around his neck, looked at him, and then looked at the purse. "You stole my wife's purse. She hasn't been feeling well lately. All she wanted to do was spend a day with her man and then yo' dumbass decided to spoil it because you got a thang for women's purses. She's never done anything to you and now her life will be profoundly affected by your decision to be an asshole. When I took the vow to love her, I also took the vow to protect her from people like you." I sighed. I hated what I was going to do next, but I did take a vow. "So you want to be a woman. Is that your wish?" I looked on the floor to find a pocket knife I had given to her for protection. I picked it up and began to admire it. "So you want to be a woman." Loosening my grip around his neck, I said, "Is there anything you would like to say?"

Trying to catch his breath, he said, "Yes, man, I'm sorry...I'm really sorry."

"I'll be sure to tell her." I flipped him around and forced his head into the toilet. I took my foot and placed it on the back of his neck to keep his head emerged in the water. I unbuckled his pants, pulled them down, and used the knife to grant the man's wish. I plunged the blade between his scrotum and his rectum. With a quick jerk, he was no longer a man. After about a few minutes of struggling, he stopped moving. I retrieved all of the contents of the purse from the floor. I checked myself in the mirror to make sure that everything was okay and then I left the bathroom.

Coming around the corner, I ran into Ariel.

"Are you okay? You have my purse," she said, excitedly.

I handed her the purse. "I'm fine."

"What happened? Where's the guy who took my purse?"

"When I caught up with him, he explained that it was a misunderstanding and that he apologizes." I paused and then said, "Oh, remind me to buy you a new pocket knife."

Disappointed, she said, "Baby, you gave me that as a gift. Did you beat him up? I hope you didn't." She looked at me suspiciously.

Smiling, I said, "Now baby, why would I do that?"

# CHAPTER
## 20

The next day, at Ariel's request, I went to see my doctor. As I waited for the nurse to call my name, I decided to browse through some magazines that were sitting on the table in front of me. A woman walked into the doctor's office, scanned the room, and chose a seat next to me. I thought that this was strange considering that there were about fifteen other chairs in the room, and we were the only two people sitting in the waiting area. She walked passed me dressed in a mini skirt, a tight knit sweater, and a pair of stiletto sandals. When she sat down, she crossed her legs bringing attention to the tattoo on her inner thighs. I tried to keep my eyes focused on the magazine. She introduced herself.

"I'm Candy," she said, extending her hand.

"Hi," I said, never taking my eyes off of the magazine.

A few minutes had passed. She was getting anxious. I could tell by the way she bounced back and forth in her seat. She stood to get a magazine. She bent over in front of me exposing the red thong that she was wearing. I looked away before she could catch me staring. A few more minutes had passed before the nurse finally came to the waiting room and called, "Mr. Thompson. Is there a Benny Thompson out here?"

We looked at each other and shrugged our shoulders.

When no one answered, she looked at me and said, "What's your name?"

"It's Izrael."

She walked away and when she came back, she said, "I can't seem to find your folder. Could you fill these out?" She handed me some documents.

"Again," I asked, frustrated.

"I'm sorry sir, but we can't seem to find your record."

"Damn." I took the papers from her.

The woman sitting next to me didn't say anything.

I answered all of the questions. *Does my family have any history of diabetes?* No. *Does my family have any history of high blood pressure?* No. *Does my family have any history of mental illness?* I was about to check the "no" box when the nurse came out.

"The doctor will see you now," she said.

I handed her the papers. I stood and placed the magazine back onto the table. I was walking away when the woman purred, "Have a good day."

I kept walking. Shaking my head, I thought to myself how friendly women can be if a brotha looks good enough.

*If only it was another place and time…I would have given her what she wanted.*

## ‖ ★ ★ ★ ‖

After having every orifice of my body looked into, I said, "So what's the diagnosis, doctor?"

"I'm a little concerned about the excessive sleeping. There's no medical explanation for it…all of your tests are clear." He took notes and then said, "Are you depressed?"

Confused, I said, "Why do you ask that?"

"Because sleeping a lot is one of the symptoms of depression," he affirmed.

"I have a lot going on, but I don't think I'm depressed," I said.

"You could be depressed and not even know it."

"Really?" I asked, putting on my shirt.

"Do you have any feelings of helplessness or hopelessness?"

"Do I look helpless or hopeless?"

Ignoring my question, he said, "What about your appetite? Has there been any change in it?"

"Not really," I said, buttoning up my shirt.

"What about self-loathing, aches and pains, or irritability?"

"Maybe some aches and pains."

"Where?" he asked.

"Mostly, just headaches…and then there's this scar." I said, pointing to an area on my back. "I told the other doctor all about this."

"What other doctor?" he asked.

"The other doctor that works out of this office," I said.

"I'm the only one here. I've been the only one here for a year."

"No, that's not true. There was another doctor here…I can't remember his name…It was something Jewish…and has a 'ski' on the end."

"Do you mean, Dr. Majeski?"

"Yeah, that's his name."

"You couldn't have seen him. He has been dead for years."

"Look, I don't know what is going on, but I've been here before."

"If you say so, but I can assure you that I've been the only one here."

I began to rub my temples.

"You want to talk about it?" he asked.

"I'm trying to forget all about it."

"That won't make it go away."

Thinking about it, I said, "You're probably right."

"I know that I'm right. Now do you want me to write you a prescription?" Maybe I should write you a referral to see…"

I interrupted, "He asked me the same thing."

115

The doctor shook his head.

"I'm telling you...I've been here before."

The doctor began to write on a piece of paper. I grabbed his hand. "If it's okay, I would rather talk to you."

"Well, my schedule is free for the rest of the afternoon. Go ahead, I'm listening."

"You see Doc, it all happened when..." As I began to talk, the doctor sat quietly and listened. During my descriptions of some of the things I saw and experienced as a soldier, you could see the expression on his face turn from worry to fear. When I left, he was still sitting there speechless with his mouth hanging open.

**II ✯ ✯ ✯ II**

That night at the dinner table, I said, "That felt good. I'm glad that I went to see the doctor."

"Me too," Ariel said, licking gravy from her fingers.

Watching her choke down the food, I said, "Maybe you should make an appointment to see the doctor too."

Smacking her lips, she said, "Why do I need to do that? I feel fine."

Frowning I said, "Something's not right. If only you could see the way you're licking that gravy from your fingers."

"What do you mean?"

"I mean it's scary."

"What do you mean?" she asked again.

"I mean that it's scary...even unattractive." Before I knew it, as if I had called her the B-word, she stood up and went stumping down the hall. I was watching her when she turned around, stomped back, grabbed two drumsticks, two slices of bread, a glass of soda, and then went stumping back down the hall.

# CHAPTER
## 21

"I hear that the school district is hiring substitute teachers. If you must do something, why don't you do that? You could work without being committed," Ariel said, the next morning obviously forgiving me for the night before.

Looking through the classifieds again, I said, "Substituting? I never thought about that."

"It doesn't pay a lot, but it will keep you busy."

"It's something to consider."

"You should think about the affect you could have on the lives of young men? You've seen the world...you've done things that others could only dream about. They need to hear your story."

"I'm trying to get pass that part of my life."

"Why? You're home baby. I know that you're dealing with some things, but you're home. Your story is one of survival...if nothing else. These kids complain about not having new shoes or a pair of two hundred dollar jeans...selfish bastards...and kids in other parts of the world wish they had food and clean drinking water...not all of them, but enough of them. It makes me sick when I hear that a child lost their life over a jacket, a cell-phone, or some sneakers. The shit that's going on here in this country is ridiculous. The shit they take for granted...I've never heard of anyone in this country being killed over food. Can you imagine being killed over a pair of shoes? Where did we go wrong?"

I sat quietly as she ranted. She was right. I've seen some terrible things...children being blown to pieces for something they don't even understand when instead they should be playing with their dolls, playing hopscotch, baseball, or jumping rope. I remember the swollen bellies of children who hadn't had a meal in days...sometimes weeks. Then I remembered the child who delivered the suicide note. I never found out if he survived the explosion. I was daydreaming about that day when suddenly I was snapped out of it by the sound of someone vomiting.

"What's wrong?" I said, running towards her.

"I don't know," she said, heaving and grabbing her stomach. "Help...me." She fell to her knees.

I tried lifting her. "Can you stand?"

She tried to stand, but fell back on her knees. I ran to retrieve some towels from the bathroom, I ran cold water on them, and then ran back to the place were she was kneeling to place them on the back of her neck. I grabbed her hand. I buckled to my knees when she began to squeeze so hard that it cut the circulation off in my fingers. She screamed, squeezed my hand, and then threw up. She continued until she was empty. Then she became quiet, her breathing slowed down, and then she released my hand. She collapsed into my arms. I picked her up and carried her to the bedroom. I laid her on the bed, brushed her hair from her face, and noticed that she had vomit in her hair. I ran into the bathroom to grab a towel and some soap water. When I reentered the room, she was resting quietly. I took the towel and wiped her face, hands, and hair. She grabbed my hand, kissed my fingers, turned over, and fell asleep. I walked back into the kitchen to clean up the mess that was all over the floor. I retrieved the mop bucket from the utility closet and filled it with bleach and hot water. As I cleaned up the mess, my suspicions were confirmed. She's pregnant.

# CHAPTER
## 22

fter I went through what would seem like an application for a position with the CIA, I was given my first assignment at a school on the Southside of Chicago. After I parked my car, I stood in front of the building staring at it hoping that I was lost. Suddenly, someone approached me, placed their hand on my shoulder and said, "The bell is going to ring in a minute."

I looked at the person with a glazed look in my eyes and said, "Thanks."

Just as I struggled to get through the crowd of teenagers waiting at the door, the bell rang. Next, I found myself sandwiched between them. I had this overwhelming urge to tell them to get off of me, but I resisted. I just followed the wave of students until I found myself standing in the halls, lost, and confused.

The students hurried pass me. "Excuse me could you tell me...excuse me...excuse me." They all gave me a strange look and kept walking.

"Excuse me!" I yelled, becoming aggravated. The police officer standing at the door asked, "How can I help you?"

Annoyed, I said, "Could you please tell me where the main office is?"

"Why are you here?" he asked.

"I'm here to substitute. This is my first day."

The officer snickered and then said, pointing down the hall,

"Down there to the left."

Giving the officer a strange look, I said, "Um thanks...I guess."

He snickered again and then walked away. Suddenly he turned and said, "You try to have a good day."

"You too," I said, feeling uneasy.

When I walked into the office every seat was filled with a student. At the counter, stood a woman who looked like she had been there for hours when the day had just started. Frowning, she looked at me and said, "Why are you in here? Go to class."

"I'm sorry Miss, but I'm the sub."

She looked me up and down and then said, "Take this badge, hallway pass, and report to room 219."

"That's it...just report to the class?" I asked, confused.

"Yeah, it's up the stairs and down the hall."

I stood there looking at her.

"What?" she asked, frustrated.

Looking dumbfounded, I said, "There's no manual?"

Everyone, including the students, started laughing.

Wiping tears from her eyes from laughing so hard, she said, "You just made my day. That was funny. For that, I'm going to give you my direct extension. You call me when and if a fight breaks out." She looked at me and then said, "Good looking and funny...You take care of yourself."

Not saying anything, I grabbed the items she gave me and carried them to the class. As I approached the classroom, I could hear the student's loud voices in the hall. When I entered the classroom, they didn't even acknowledge my presence. I sat the materials on the desk and then said, "Good morning class."

No one said anything. I tried it again. "Good morning class." Still no one said anything instead they became louder. I walked over to the classroom door, opened it, and then slammed it as hard as I could.

The students stop talking. "Now let's try this again...Good morning."

Like a choir, they all said, "Good morning."

One student looked at one of the other students and said, "Oooo gurl, he looks good." The other young lady nodded her head in agreement.

I ignored them. "My name is Corporal...I mean, it's Izrael, but you will call me Sir and I am your sub today. I don't know what you are accustomed to, but here's how this is going to work. You respect me and I will respect you."

"Fuck you," mumbled a student under his breath.

"Excuse me, who said that?" I asked.

No one answered.

"So no one knows who said it...interesting," I said, walking around the classroom. "Okay, now I'm going to have to make an example out of someone." Pointing at a female student, I said, "You don't know who did it?"

"No," she said, popping gum.

"Get out," I instructed.

"What?" she said, looking confused.

"I said, get out."

"I'm calling my mama," she said, grabbing her books and leaving the room.

Looking around the room, I said, "Who's next? Let's see...you," I said, pointing at a kid with a pair of headphones on.

"What?" he asked.

"Who said it?"

"Said what?" he asked, looking confused.

"So you don't know what I'm talking about?"

"No," he said, bobbing his head and tapping his feet to the music that he wasn't supposed to be listening to.

"Get out."

"What did I do?" he asked, dumbfounded.

"I said, get out."

"Damn, I hate this school," he said, on his way out.

Looking around the room, I said, "Who's next? Let's see."

Suddenly a hand went up. "How can I help you?" I asked.

"I said it," the young man said.

"So you said it…why? You know what, I don't care why…Get out."

The student didn't say anything. He just followed my finger that was pointing to the door.

Looking at the class, I said, "Does anyone else have something to say?"

No one said anything.

"Good, now, let's get to work."

After my first day, I developed the reputation of being someone tough and able to deal with the students. Soon, I was getting calls to fill-in almost everyday. Being busy kept my demons away…at least for now.

# CHAPTER
## 23

After getting a positive reading on one of those pregnancy tests from the pharmacy, I took Ariel to the doctor to confirm something I had suspected for a while. I have to admit that when the doctor told us that we were expecting a child, initially, I wasn't happy. I thought that it was too convenient that after I insisted that we don't have children that she ended up pregnant anyway. I know that it takes two to make a baby, but I can't help but feel trapped.

"How are you feeling today?"

"I'm good," she said, sipping orange juice instead of her regular cup of coffee. She walked over and sat next to me.

She was rambling on and on about things related to babies, when I said, "I thought that we were going to hold off on that?"

"How off on what, sweetie?"

*Don't sweetie me.* "Don't play Ariel...I thought that we agreed that we wouldn't do this for a year."

"Do *this?* This, what? Have sex or have a baby?"

*Now she's playing with me.* "Have a baby."

With her hands on her hips, she said, "What are you implying, Izrael?"

"My fault, I should just say what's on my mind," I paused and then said, "I think it's real fucking convenient that a brotha says that

124

he doesn't want any babies and then all of a sudden you come up pregnant."

Rolling her neck, she said, "Ummm, Let me think...hold on, don't say anything..." She tapped her finger on her chin pretending to remember something. "You know what? I can't remember raping you. You don't remember being raped, do you?"

"Don't play with me Ariel...motherfuckers have gotten hurt for less."

"Excuse me."

"I'm just saying that if you knew where my head was at on this issue, you should have taken certain precautions."

"Are you serious? First thing, Mr. Man, it takes two to make a baby. Second, contraceptives are made for both men and women. Third, we can flip this shit around on you..."

"What do you mean?" I asked.

"You are walking around here thinking that I deceived you when it could have been you trying to trap a sistha."

"Is that what you think?"

"I'm not thinking anything...I will say this, I'm pregnant and neither one of us can change that."

"Yes, we can."

Sitting back in her chair and folding her arms, she said, "What do you mean, 'yes, we can'? If there's something on your mind just say it."

I stood to walk out of the room, but before leaving, I said, "What's done is done. I'm going to love and take care of mine." I leaned close to her and continued, "But in the future, be extra careful about how you do things. I don't like mistakes...people get killed that way."

# CHAPTER
## 24

The next day, after changing the bandage on my back, I was exiting the bathroom to find Ariel on the telephone. She was so engrossed in the conversation that she didn't even hear me walking towards her. She had her hand over the receiver and was whispering when I approached.

Hurriedly, she said, "Look mother, I have to go." She hung up the phone. Standing to throw her arms around my neck, she said, "Hey sweetie."

Pushing her away from me, I said, "Who was that on the phone?"

She hesitated as if she was looking for a lie to tell. Not being able to come up with one, she said, "Why do you want to know?"

With one eyebrow raised, I said, "So is that where we are now?"

"What do you mean?" she said, nervously.

"We've talked about this," I reminded her.

Twisting her hands and looking down, she confessed, "It was mom."

"Why couldn't you tell me that?"

"Well, she's a little worried about you."

"Why is she worried about me?"

"Well, I might have mentioned some of the things you've been going through."

"You might have?"

"I did." Looking around the room, she said, "You've been acting a little different...strange even."

"Of course, I'm different. I've been gone for five years. The man you see standing in front of you isn't the boy you knew back then."

"Well, I know, but..."

"So you're telling your family our business...my business?" I asked, interrupting her.

Rubbing my arm, she said, "No Izrael, I would never do that."

"Then what the hell are you telling them?"

She stepped back. She threw her hands on her hips. "Don't take that tone with me."

Stepping toward her, I said, "I asked you, what the hell have you been telling them?"

Folding her arms, she said, "You know what Mr. Man, when you change that tone you can come talk to me, but right now I'm not trying to hear..." She turned to leave the room.

I snatched her by the arm and spun her around to face me. "Let's try this one more time."

She pulled her arm away from me. We were at a stand-off. She wanted to prove something, but she had no idea who she was fucking with. This stand-off went on for five minutes before she walked up to me and began to kiss me. I stood my ground. She tried forcing her tongue into my mouth, but I wouldn't give in. She reached between my legs and began to stroke me, but there was no response. She became frustrated. She kept trying, but she was unsuccessful. She stopped and looked into my eyes. I didn't flinch.

Standing my ground, again I asked, "What the hell did you tell your mother?"

"Awwwww!" she screamed in defeat. She stomped out of the room slamming the door behind her.

I opened the door and followed her down the hall. "I didn't

receive my answer. Why are you stalling?"

She stopped, turned, and said, "There's something wrong with you, but you are in denial."

"Let's see…" I said, pretending to examine myself. "Everything seems good to me."

"You think this shit is funny, but it isn't. You are not the same man I fell in love with. Something about you is wrong…cold."

"I've done a lot of things…seen a lot of shit…"

"You have to talk about it, Izrael."

"Look, in the military, we were trained that you hold your tongue…no matter what…people may ask, but you never tell. I'm a grown man. You don't go to your mama when there's something wrong with you and me. You come to me." I walked up to her and placed my hands onto her shoulders and looked her straight in the eyes. I began to rub her shoulders – gently at first, but then I began to apply some pressure. "Do we have an understanding…sweetie?"

"Yes," she said, nervously.

"I love you Ariel," I said as though I was reading from a script.

"I…I…love you too," she stuttered.

# CHAPTER
## 25

The next day, I was called in to "sub" for a teacher suspected of having a nervous breakdown. Lately, I'd received a lot of calls to "sub". I guess it was hard being a teacher – having the responsibility to educate tomorrow's leaders, having to deal with the bureaucracy, and on top of that having to dodge bullets outside and inside of the classroom. I guess the concept of war could exist in every aspect of our lives – you don't have to enlist to fight or be forced to.

After taking attendance, I said, "Your teacher has left several assignments for you to work on. Let's get busy," I said, writing the assignments on the chalkboard.

"Damn," said one of the male students.

Looking in the back of the classroom where the comment came from, I said, "Excuse me."

"You're excused, punk," he said, trying to hide behind the student sitting in front of him.

I spotted him and laughed. "Punk, huh? You must be lost. Don't curse in my class."

"Naw man, *you* must be lost...for a minute you thought that you had a class," the student said laughing and looking around hoping that the other students would laugh with him.

Walking to the back of the classroom, I stood over the student. "So you thought that was funny?" I asked, without any sign of emotion.

"Hell yeah, I'm sorry that "subs" don't have a sense of humor. Is it because you have no life? Or is it because you're forced to do this for a living 'cause you can't get a real job? You do not have to answer that because you are a loser," he said, laughing again.

His words struck a nerve. Suddenly, I had the student by the collar and dragged him kicking and screaming into the hallway. Once we were outside of the classroom, I said, "Look motherfucker, I'm in no mood for your shit. You don't know me and you don't want to know me, but what you do want to do is sit your ass in that chair, do your fucking assignment, and shut the hell up before I do something to you that would leave a permanent scar." When I knew that we had an understanding, I let go of his collar. "For the record, you shouldn't mess with a "sub"…we don't have shit to lose – nothing. I could stuff your sorry ass in one of those lockers and not give a shit about them firing me and do you think those motherfuckers you were trying to make laugh would help you? No, they wouldn't because they wouldn't want the same thing happening to them." I looked into his eyes and said, "Do we have an understanding?"

The boy looked terrified. "I'm sorry, I'll do my work," he said, running into the classroom.

Turning to walk back into the classroom, I caught a glimpse of myself in the glass by the door. I had a crazed look in my eyes…so crazed that it frightened even me. I took a couple of deep breaths, forced a smile on my face, and went back to work.

**‖ ✫ ✫ ✫ ‖**

On the way home from work, I was exhausted both physically and mentally. Putting kids in their place was a lot of work. I needed to unwind. I was coasting down State Street, when I had an urge to visit a bar. When I entered, I noticed that the bar was unusually crowded for that time of the day. There were people still in work attire, laughing, talking, and trying to drink their cares away.

There were televisions surrounding the bar. I sat down on one of the stools and ordered a glass of water. The bartender handed me a menu so I ordered some appetizers and became engrossed in one of the games.

Some guys sitting across from the bar at a table were cheering, laughing, and drinking beers. I looked over at them. One of them signaled for me to sit with them. I ignored him and turned my attention back to the game.

"Hey you, come on over and join us," one of them said.

To be sure that they were talking about me, I pointed at myself and one of them nodded 'yes'.

"Naw man, I'm good," I replied.

"Come on man, we won't bite."

At first, I hesitated, but I didn't want to seem off-standish. I walked over, shook all of their hands, and then sat down.

"Hey man, what 'cha drinking?" one of them asked.

"Just water for me," I said, sipping from the glass.

"You can do better than that," one of them said.

"No really, I'm good," I said, realizing that this was the first time I had been to a bar since my return home.

"Come on," he insisted, signaling for the waitress.

"Well, I guess I could have a beer."

"Good, cause you were looking like a real nerd with that glass of water in your hand." When the waitress approached the table, he ordered for me, "Get my friend a beer."

"Sure," the waitress said, walking away.

One of the guys turned to me and said, "So what's your name?"

"It's Izrael and yours?" They all took turns telling me their names.

"So do you guys come here all of the time?" I asked, trying to be friendly.

"Everyday, it's a tradition," one of them said, sipping from their drink glass.

The waitress approached the table, "Here you go." She placed the beer and appetizers on the table.

"Thanks." I tipped her. I held the glass in my hand, but didn't drink.

"Something wrong with your drink?" she asked.

"Naw, it's good," I said.

Patting me on the arm, one of the men said, "Look man, we come here to have a good time. We laugh, we talk, we talk shit, and we get drunk as hell. If we're lucky enough, we can get so drunk that those hags we call our wives will miraculously turn 'fine' like Eva Longoria."

Everyone at the table began to laugh…everyone except me.

One of the other guys spoke up, "I don't know what the hell you are drinking, but I've never been able to make that happen. My wife still looks the same whether I'm drunk or sober."

"Stop drinking those sissy-ass drinks…how the hell you gon' get drunk sipping on margaritas all night?"

Defending himself, he said, "Margaritas are strong…I don't know what you thought," he said, sipping from his glass.

They all started laughing again.

We continued to watch the game. The guys at the table were buying drinks one after another. I was still holding the same glass that

I started out with. They laughed and talked about everything; from politics to blow jobs and the lack there of.

I decided that I had enough "hanging-out" for one evening, so I decided to leave. "Okay guys, I'm leaving. I'll talk to you later."

"Not a problem. We will be here again tomorrow. We will save a place for you."

"That won't be necessary, but thanks for looking out."

"Well, if you change your mind…"

"Alright," I said, leaving.

# CHAPTER
## 26

When I walked in, Ariel was waiting for me at the door; foot tapping, arms folded, mouth turned up, and ready to argue. I was really in no mood for whatever she had to say. "Where have you been?" she asked.

"I've had a long day. I needed to relax a little so I went to a bar. Met some guys..."

"So you hung out with some guys you didn't know instead of coming home to be with me?"

"It's no big deal...doesn't have anything to do with you."

"Izrael, I'm pregnant."

"I know..."

"Well if you know then why am I standing here reminding you?"

Remembering that she was carrying my child, I decided to be nice. "I'm sorry..."

"You've been gone for five years...that's long enough."

I was getting annoyed. Before the military, I took orders from my mama. I didn't get married to get a new mama, but I knew that diplomacy must be applied in situations like these. "I heard you," I said, through clinched teeth.

She continued, "I'm not going to do this alone."

"I don't expect you to." I grabbed her hand and led her to the couch. "Let me rub your feet." Removing her slipper, I began to massage her calves, "I didn't mean to upset you."

She looked at me and then said, "Okay, as long as it doesn't get out of hand."

I didn't respond. After diffusing another potential explosive situation, I gave her a little TLC and she began to get sleepy, I took her to bed and tucked her in.

That night, I couldn't fall asleep. On the other hand, Ariel had no problem at all. She was out cold as soon as her head hit the pillow. I watched her as she slept. She didn't have a care in the world and was completely unaware of the storm brewing next to her.

# CHAPTER
## 27

"Look who's here guys," one of the guys at the table said. The next day, I decided to stop by the bar again. "Hey what's up?"

"Hey man, grab a seat…what 'cha drinking?" he said, signaling for the waitress.

The waitress approached the table.

"I'll have a glass of water…this time let me get a slice of lemon."

"Not that shit again…get the man a beer," one of the guys said, slapping me on the back.

"Who are you?" one of the guys asked.

"What do you mean?" I responded, being thrown off-guard by his question.

"I mean, what man comes to a bar and don't drink…unless he's a cop. Are you a cop?"

"Naw man, I'm ex-military. I just don't drink. I've seen what it can do to people. A lot of people got killed drinking and running around with a gun. Plus, the smell of it makes me sick. I'm good. I just need to keep my wits about myself. You know how it is?"

"So you're a soldier?"

"Not now, I've done my time."

All of the men at the table raised their glasses. "A toast to one of our heroes." They clicked their glasses together and then drank from them.

"Thanks guys," I said.

"Man, what was it like over there?"

I thought about it for a second; remembered the "code". I wasn't comfortable with sharing, but maybe Ariel was right. I needed to talk about it and who better to share it with than a bunch of strangers. I started out by talking about the death of my brother and then ended with stories of the war. The men at the table hung on to my every word. There were moments when they laughed and then there were moments when the men were wiping tears from their eyes. I talked until it was closing time.

# CHAPTER
## 28

The next day, they called me in to "sub" for a Science teacher. They pre-warned me that the students in this class would be challenging and that this particular teacher called off often claiming to need a mental health day.

Walking through the halls of the building often reminded me of a game show. I often imagined someone standing in an office spinning a wheel and as I walked through the halls whatever the wheel landed on was the crap I'll get to see before arriving at my class. On this particular day, the wheel must have landed on a student giving another student a "bj" in the boy's bathroom because that's exactly what happened.

I don't know what made me use the student's washroom that particular day. I usually use the bathroom that's intended for the teachers, but I had drunk one too many cups of coffee that morning. Some students walked in. I was on the toilet when I looked down and saw two sets of feet in the next stall. At first, I thought that I was mistaken, so I leaned over to verify it. Still looking, I heard someone's pants unzip and then I saw someone get on their knees. I didn't say anything because it really wasn't any of my business. So I continued to finish what I came in there to do.

*Shit.* There was no toilet paper. "Excuse me, can I get some toilet paper?" I asked.

There was no response. Instead there were muffled moaning sounds.

I asked again, "Could I get some toilet paper?"

Suddenly, there was some banging against the wall. I could see the student's leg shaking and then there was nothing, but silence. Finally, a hand appeared out of nowhere holding a wad of paper. I took it, wiped my ass, got up, flushed, and exited the stall. I was washing my hands when the door to the other stall opened up. I watched through the reflection in the mirror. A boy student ran out of the washroom. I waited to see the young lady who would allow some boy to disrespect her in the boy's washroom, but that didn't happen. The door swung open again. Standing before me, was not a young lady, but a young man and not just any young man. This young man was the star player of the school's football team. He froze when he saw me. We stood there looking at each other. The moment was interrupted when the bell rang.

As I walked to get to my class, I couldn't stop thinking about what had happened. I was entering the class when right behind me entered the football player. We looked at each other. He grabbed a seat toward the back of the class. I took attendance, gave the students their assignment, and spent the rest of the hour trying to erase the memory from my head.

# CHAPTER
## 29

I stopped by the bar, but decided to leave early to be with Ariel. Since we found out that she was pregnant, she had become more emotional than usual. Being with her often felt like being on a rollercoaster ride – not knowing from day-to-day where we were going to end up.

"How was your day?" she asked, kissing me on the cheek.

I didn't want to tell her about the incident that happened in the boy's bathroom, so I said, "It was good and yours?"

"Well, I went to visit mama today, I got my hair done, and I did a little shopping," she paused and then said, "You didn't notice my hair?"

"I just got home. Give me a minute, I would have noticed it."

Folding her arms and patting her feet, she said, "I'm waiting."

"Waiting for what?" I asked, plopping down on the living room sofa.

"A compliment," she said.

*Are you serious?* Not wanting to argue, I said, "I really like it. It's pretty."

"Well, I hate it," she insisted.

Rubbing my forehead, I said, "Then why did you ask me…"

"You don't love me," she interrupted.

*Here we go.* "Huh?" I asked.

"You don't love me because I'm fat and ugly," she said, with her mouth stuck out.

I walked over to comfort her. She pulled away.

"I know what you're thinking," she said.

"Ariel, let's not do this. I really have no idea what we're talking about. I don't think that you're fat, and I love your hair because I love you...okay," I gave her a look that meant "I surrender."

Calming down, she said, "You mean it?"

"Yes, I mean it," I said, kissing her.

"Okay," she said, returning the kiss.

"Now finish telling me about your day," I said, tired of the hair conversation.

"Well, I stopped at the Cheesecake Factory on the way home."

Excited, I walked over to the refrigerator. "You brought cheesecake? I haven't had cheesecake in a long time." I looked around, but there wasn't any. "Where's the cheesecake?"

"I ate it," she said, rubbing her stomach.

"You didn't save me any?" I asked.

"No," she said, smiling.

I didn't say anything.

Pouting, she said, "So you *do* think I'm fat."

I dropped my head into my hands. I tried to imagine the sound of grenades going off to help drown out the sound of her voice.

# CHAPTER
## 30

The next day, I awakened to a pounding headache. I didn't sleep well because I spent the entire night watching my wife try on everything in the closet to prove to me that she was still sexy – that she wasn't fat. It was both funny and frightening watching her try to squeeze her new ass into an old pair of jeans.

I was asked to "sub" the same class that day. It would seem that the teacher had become mysteriously ill and wouldn't be returning for the rest of the school year, so until they found a replacement I would be keeping the seat warm.

The teachers were placed on high-alert because of the recent shootings involving teens in the neighborhood. The school was placed on lock-down and the students weren't allowed to leave the classroom unless there was an extreme emergency.

On this particular day, the air conditioner in the classroom decided to malfunction. The kids in the classroom began to whine and complain about the heat.

"Mr. Sub, what's up with the AC? This classroom is hot as hell…literally," one of the students said.

Accustomed to extreme heat, I said, "I know it's hot, but it's almost over."

"What's almost over? Those motherfuckers in that main office are trying to cook us alive? I bet their asses got "air"," said another agitated student.

142

"Okay, I know it's hot, but we need to keep the language under control," I instructed.

"Man, whatever. It's too damn hot to try to be polite," said another student.

All of a sudden, all of the students began to complain at the same time. I tried to quiet them, but the heat and the inability to leave the classroom was starting to spark a riot.

"I'm getting the fuck up out of here," said a student, standing and attempting to leave the classroom.

Trying to calm their tempers, I said, "The bell is going to ring in a few minutes..."

"I'm not going to last that long," said one of the other students.

"I'm going to have to ask you to sit down," I said to the student trying to leave the room.

"It's too hot in here...suspend me, but I'm getting the hell out of here." A couple of the other students began to grab their things to follow him.

"I said, sit down," I insisted.

"Bye," the student said, waving at us.

Before I knew it, I rose from my seat grabbed the student by the arm and threw him into a chair. "I SAID, SIT YO" ASS DOWN!" The entire classroom fell silent. The other students that were standing froze in their tracks. With a wide-eyed look on my face, I said, "We are all going to calm down, shut the hell up, get our work done, and try to get through the last few minutes of class without somebody getting hurt. Do we all understand?"

"Yes," they all said in unison.

"Very good," I said, returning to my seat.

Sitting there, I began to stare at my hands. They began to shake and I began to sweat uncontrollably. As I looked around the room, I thought about how many lives were taken by these hands. Suddenly, everything around me went black. I fell into a trance. I could see myself back in Iraq holding a gun shooting into the window of a storefront. We were told that the enemy held meetings in there only to find out later that it was a building being used as a school. We didn't know. We were given the wrong information, but it didn't matter. Within minutes, the teachers and all of the students were gone in a blaze of bullets.

*Ring!!!!!!*

When I awakened from my trance, my clothes were soaked. The students for my next class were coming in. I could hear them commenting on my frazzled condition.

"What's wrong? Are you okay?" asked a student.

I didn't say anything. I stared aimlessly around the room.

When they were all in their seats, they looked at me waiting for my instructions.

I didn't say anything. The students watched as I walked over to the window to look out into the school yard. Suspecting that something was wrong, the students worked independently as with all of the rest of my classes that day.

# CHAPTER
## 31

After another night of restless sleep, I prepared for another long day at work. I was driving, half asleep, when I heard the news broadcast over the car radio indicating that there was a shooting at a school on the Southside. I was pulling around the corner near the school where I was assigned when I saw police cars and people standing everywhere. I slowed down. Beyond the crowd, you could see a body lying on the ground. I didn't stop. I grabbed my cell-phone, called the school, and informed them that I wasn't coming in.

I drove to the bar. None of the guys were there, but it did not matter because I would rather be by myself. I didn't order my regular. This occasion required something stronger. Instead, I ordered a beer. I looked at the glass for a long time questioning myself, but I needed something to numb what I was feeling inside. No longer hesitating, I put the glass to my mouth. The taste was bitter at first, but after the third one I was use to it and enjoying its affect on me. I became really relaxed. I was on my fifth drink when I noticed a beautiful young lady sitting at the other end of the bar watching me. I smiled. She smiled back. She waved. I waved back. She walked over and introduced herself. We talked, laughed, and drank for several hours. Before long, I had graduated from beer to Jack D. The smell of the "Jack" was a lot stronger than the beer. It was so strong that it burned my throat and my chest as it went down.

"Has anyone told you how good-looking you are?" she asked, seductively.

"That's what people tell me," I said, unaffected by her attempt to flirt.

"Why haven't some woman snatched you up yet?" she asked, moving closer.

"Why are you in my business?" I said, sipping from my glass.

"S-o-r-r-y...I didn't mean to get in your business," she said, poking out her mouth and throwing her hair back.

I didn't say anything.

She continued to flirt. "What cha' got planned for the evening?"

"I plan to go home and you?" I responded.

She giggled. "You're funny and fine, but I'm serious. You want to hang out?"

"You don't even know me."

"Do I need to know you? It's not like I'm asking for your hand in marriage. Plus, you look good enough to eat."

"So that's all you require...a brotha who looks good enough to eat?"

"Doesn't every woman? It could be worst. You could look like that gorilla at the other end of the bar," she said, pointing and laughing.

We both looked down at the end of the bar to find a man grinning from ear to ear with a mouth full of gold teeth. I had to look away to keep the glare coming from his mouth from blinding me.

She reached for my thigh. I stopped her hand. "You don't want none of this."

"Let me be the judge of that," she said, placing her other hand between my thighs.

Removing her other hand, I said, "Believe me. You don't want none of this."

She leaned close to me and placed her wet tongue into my ear.

"I'm a big girl. I can handle whatever you have to give."

I knew that she was a "working girl". I could tell by her assertiveness, so I said, "How much is this going to cost me?"

"Let's play the evening by ear," she said.

The affects of the alcohol began to take over. Her warm breath against my neck caused my "nature" to rise. I looked at her and wondered why would a woman who could have so much, would be willing to risk everything on a complete stranger. Suddenly, the alcohol stripped away any rational for any decisions made for the rest of the evening. When she asked me to go home with her, I didn't say 'no'. I needed what she had to offer. I needed to forget the terrible memories that plagued me. I needed to forget that I hated my job. I needed to erase the memory of that young boy who was shot dead on the street; even if it was just for a moment – I needed to forget.

I allowed her to leave the bar first. I followed closely behind her. When we arrived at her apartment, without thinking, I ripped her clothes off. Naked, I dragged her to the sofa, pushed her down, and unzipped my pants. She began to touch herself, moaning while she waited for me to enter her. I threw her legs into the air and entered her roughly. I took her, forcefully.

At first, she was really into it then she complained that it hurt. I ignored her. She screamed and begged. I slapped her. She began to claw at me. She reached under my shirt and dug her nails into my back accidentally digging them into the existing wound on my back. I slapped her again. Blood ran from her bottom lip.

I needed to release. I jumped out of her, grabbed her by the head and climaxed. I let her go. I looked at her. She wiped her face with her hand.

"That will be two hundred dollars," she said, licking her fingers.

*Cheap.* I looked at her. Without saying a word, I stood, zipped my pants, threw some money on the floor, and left her sitting there.

**‖ ★ ★ ★ ‖**

It was extremely late. Not accustomed to drinking, my head was spinning. At the door, I fumbled with the keys thereby dropping them onto the ground. I made another attempt to unlock the door. Suddenly, the door opened. I could see Ariel's shadow coming from behind it. I took a minute to take a deep breath to calm what I knew would turn into something very ugly very quickly if she said the wrong thing.

"Where have you been?" Ariel asked, as I strolled pass her.

Reeking of liquor, I said, "A kid was shot today." I threw my keys at the couch and missed.

"You've been drinking," she said, following me.

Ariel had on a pair of slippers that slapped the bottom of her feet as she walked. The sound was so loud and annoying it felt like someone was slapping me upside the side of my head.

"Yeah, I'm sorry, but I had to find a way to get that image out of my head."

"Did it help?" she asked, still walking and still making the noise with her feet.

"What?" I said, flipping around and facing her.

"The alcohol," she said.

Deciding that I couldn't take the noise that was coming from her mouth and her shoes anymore, I lifted each one of her legs and removed the slippers.

"What are you doing?" she asked.

I took the slippers outside and threw them into the garbage can.

"Why did you do that?" she asked, looking both angry and confused.

Without looking at her, I said, "I'll talk to you in the morning."

# CHAPTER
## 32

I was hung-over. I felt like crap. I smelled like shit and I had an overwhelming desire to throw-up. Ariel was walking around with her lips stuck out. I should have cared, but the only thing I wanted was to wash that horrible stench that was coming from my pores off of me. I was undressing when Ariel walked into the bathroom. Completely forgetting about what happened the night before, I removed my clothing and was getting in the shower when she spotted them.

"What is that on your back, Izrael?"

"What are you talking about now, Ariel?"

"What am I talking about now?" she asked, in combat mode. "I'm talking about that shit on your back."

Still not remembering all of the events from the night before, I said, "I don't know what you're talking about."

"Then you better try and see what I'm talking about," she said.

"I'm not in the mood for your shit this morning. I'm sure that whatever it is, it's some shit you did."

"Excuse me, I would have remembered doing that shit!" she said, at the top of her voice.

Cringing, I said, "Stop overreacting. I'm sure it's nothing."

Grabbing the bottle of alcohol from the sink and pouring it over the wounds on my back, she said, "Does that feel like nothing?"

I buckled over in pain. Before I knew it, my hand was going

toward her face. "Bitch!" I yelled before hitting her. "What the fuck is wrong with you?!"

She fell to the floor. "You hit me!"

My chest was heaving. I wanted to hit her ass again.

"You have lost your fucking mind. You don't put your hands on me. You must be crazy." She stood up and walked toward me.

Before I could walk away, she was swinging her arms at me. Each blow coming faster than the other. I grabbed her hands. Now we stood face to face, both of our chests were rising. For a minute, no one spoke. Finally, I broke the silence.

"Don't do that shit again," I said, sternly.

"Don't you ever put your hands on me again," she insisted.

Looking down, I saw her stomach. My back was still of fire, but I tried to regain my composure. "I'm sorry. I didn't think. I just reacted."

Trying to get free, she said, "Let me go."

I let her hands go. She reached back and with all of her strength, she hit me. My head went back. When it came forward, the side of my face was burning. My bottom lip was bleeding. The bells in my head went off. I wanted to hurt her, but I restrained myself.

She stepped up to me so close that I could smell the toothpaste on her breath. "The next time you have the desire to call somebody a bitch, you better pick up the phone and call your mama. Also, don't ever put your fucking hands on me again or I'm going to catch a case. Do you hear me?" she insisted.

Licking the blood off of the side of my mouth, I looked at her. I shouldn't have hit her. Although, I was wrong, I wasn't feeling apologetic. To down-play the seriousness of the situation, I yelled, "Sir, yes sir!"

She rolled her eyes, turned, and left slamming the door behind her.

## ❙❙ ✯ ✯ ✯ ❙❙

"Damn-it," I said in the shower as the soap and water burned the welts on my back. As the water fell over my head, I recalled the events from the night before. *The prostitute.* I thought to myself. I remembered the things that she let me do to her. Thinking about that night, I found myself repulsed and aroused at the same time, but it was therapy. That's all it was.

# CHAPTER
## 33

I went back to the bar. She was there...waiting for me. We ordered some drinks and when I was at a point where I could barely stand, we left and ended up at her apartment again. We weren't in the door good before she was bent over with her ass in the air. The only thing I could think of at that moment was that she had been sitting on that bar stool all night with no panties on. It's a good thing I came prepared. It took all of thirty seconds to put on my second skin.

I was so drunk that my aim was off. I pushed. She screamed. She screamed. I pushed. The more she screamed, the more I pushed. I couldn't climax. The screaming was making my head hurt thereby throwing my rhythm off. "Shut up," I told her.

"But it hurts," she said.

Not caring, I said, "Shut up."

"It hurts," she pleaded.

She tried moving away from me. I grabbed her by the hips and continued to push. She pleaded for me to stop. I was on a mission and she needed to shut the hell up until I completed it...successfully. Since she couldn't do it herself, I decided to help her. I grabbed her by the throat and I squeezed gently at first not trying to hurt her, but to get her to shut up. She began to claw at my hands. I pushed. She clawed. I pushed. She clawed. I pushed. She clawed. Her muscles tightened. My back arched. Her neck snapped. I climaxed. I released her. She went limp.

Her body fell to the floor. I looked at her, removed the condom, and then zipped my pants. I stood over her. I went into the bathroom, flushed the condom, waited to make sure it went down, and washed my hands. When I came out of the washroom, I noticed that she hadn't moved. I stood over her, watched her, but there was nothing; not even a smile, a frown, a breath, or a heartbeat.

*I wonder how much I owe her.* I thought to myself. *An honest days pay for an honest days work.* I reached into my wallet and noticed that I didn't have anything left, but twenty dollars. *Damn.* I took out fifteen of the dollars, and placed it on the floor next to her. *Sorry, but a brotha gotta catch a cab.*

# CHAPTER
# 34

After a ten mile run, I greeted the morning with five hundred sit-ups and five hundred push-ups. When I entered my home, Ariel was crying.

"What's wrong with you...now?" I said, trying to catch my breath.

She ignored me.

I asked her again. "What's wrong?"

She didn't respond.

I thought that I would give it one more try. I walked up to her, stroked her hair, and in the gentlest voice, I said, "Ariel, sweetie, are you okay?"

Pushing my hand away, she said, "You will never understand."

That was code for "it's going to be a long day". I decided to walk away. I wasn't in the mood for it so I left her sitting there. Instead, I went into the kitchen, grabbed a bottle of water, and went into the bathroom to take a shower. When I was done, I was drying off when she walked into the bathroom wearing jogging clothes.

"I'm going running," she said, bouncing up and down in the doorway.

"Stop that Ariel and go sit down before you hurt yourself or the baby."

"Exercise is good during the pregnancy."

"I don't think running is good."

Frustrated, she said, "I'm losing my mind Izrael. I need to get out of this house. I have to do something. These four walls are making me crazy."

"This ain't about you. You are carrying a baby now. You have to take care of the baby."

Pouting, she said, "This isn't fair. We are both having a baby, but I'm the only person getting fat and being forced to wear spandex. I sit in this house waiting for you to take me out and what do you do? Nothing, you won't even have sex with me. You treat me like I'm a leper. "

"Ariel, I come home from the military to be with you…"

"You make loving me…being with me sound like a damn chore," she said, putting her hands on a waist that used to measure a size 28.

I didn't respond. I turned toward the sink. I didn't want her to see the aggravation on my face. The fact that I was clearly ignoring her did not detour her. She continued to complain while I brushed my teeth. I rinsed my mouth. I shook the aftershave can and applied some on my face. I removed my razor from its stand and proceeded to shave. Listening to her complain was the equivalent of someone dragging their nails across a chalkboard. I was imagining her without a tongue when she said something that she knew would piss me off.

"I wish that I wasn't pregnant." Pointing at her stomach, she continued, "I want it out of me."

I dug the razor deep into the side of my face. I was hoping that I was dreaming. When the blood began to stream down the side of my face, I knew that this moment was really happening.

*I love my wife. I love my wife. I love my wife.*

With blood running down the side of my face and dripping onto the sink and floor, I said, "Ariel, come sit right here." I patted on the toilet seat to indicate that's where I wanted her to sit.

"For what?" she asked, suspiciously.

Calmly, I said, "We need to talk." Ariel's words hurt, but I wouldn't let on.

"I've been trying to do that all morning," she said, with her hands on her hips.

"Ariel, please come sit down," I said again.

Reluctantly, she sat down. I leaned over her – blood dripping onto her lap. Looking her straight into her eyes, I said, "I know you didn't mean that. So I'm going to forgive you. I will admit that when you first told me that you were pregnant, I wasn't happy. It was too much, too fast, but it's done now and you now carry my child – my legacy. Now, if my memory serves me correctly, I was the one who said that I didn't want a baby and you were the one insisting that we give your parents a grandbaby. Do you remember that?"

"Um no, when you came home you were the one insisting that we get pregnant. Why would I want to get pregnant and mess up this beautiful figure? Do you know how many years..."

I interrupted. "Are you freaking serious?" I asked, ignoring the pool of blood forming in her lap. "I remember clearly that you were the one who wanted to have a baby. I remember that as if the shit happened just yesterday...what the hell is wrong with you?"

"It ain't me sweetie, it's you," she said.

"It's me what, Ariel?"

"If you believe that I wanted to get pregnant and that it was all my idea then you are crazy as hell."

With a piercing stare, I looked her straight in the eye and said, "I know that I'm not crazy...I know what happened, so here's what we are going to do. You are going to behave yourself. You are going to ease-up off of me and give me some time to adjust to everything. You are going to sit your ass down and act like you are carrying a baby. Okay?" I asked and then answered my own question, "Okay." I stood and walked back over to the sink. "I'll be done in a minute." Without looking at her, she had been dismissed.

She stood, gave a dismissive wave, and left the bathroom, mumbling to herself all the way down the hall.

I stood staring into the mirror. Ariel's words replayed in my mind. I was pissed. The wound on my face began to hurt. My heart began to race. My eyes became red – blood red. I threw cold water on my face to douse the fire burning within. I changed the bandage on my back and treated the cut on my face. I walked into the bedroom. Standing in front of my closet, I removed a pair of jeans and a faded t-shirt. After slipping into my clothing, I bent over to put on my sneakers. A sharp pain shot across my temples. I searched around the room for something to ease the pain, I couldn't find anything. I needed something. *The prostitute.* I thought to myself. When I came out of the bedroom, I found Ariel asleep on the couch. I left and locked the door behind me.

**|| ✶ ✶ ✶ ||**

This shit was becoming better than any therapy or painkiller I had ever taken; find one, do what you have to do, and walk away with no strings attached.

I slapped her again. She moaned.

"What else can I do to you?" I asked.

"Anything you want...it's your money," she said, spitting blood onto the floor.

"Really?" I asked, intrigued and feeling a certain need to be aggressive.

"Really," she replied, bracing herself for what was coming next.

*A freak...I like that.* "Turn over," I instructed as I untied her from the bedposts.

"What you got in mind?" she asked.

"Do like I tell you," I said, forcing her over.

She purred and stuck her ass high into the air. I removed the belt from my pants. I hit her across her thighs. She moaned. I hit her across her back. She moaned again. I hit her across her butt. Her body began to jerk. She screamed, "It feels so good!" I hit her across her back again. She begged me to fuck her and I did as hard as I could. I released. I couldn't tell if she climaxed and I didn't care. When I turned over to close my eyes, she said, "You have to go…my next john will be here any minute."

I stood and put on my pants. "Call me a cab."

"Okay," she said, picking up the phone.

I placed two hundred dollars on the table.

She looked at the money and then said, "It's a hundred extra for the spanking."

I looked into my wallet. "I don't have it."

"Pay me tomorrow," she said, going into the bathroom.

"Tomorrow…yeah, tomorrow…umm?" I said. I realized that I didn't know her name, but decided not to ask her for it. She was a prostitute and I was a john…a soldier who found another way to keep the demons at bay.

**‖ ★ ★ ★ ‖**

In the cab, I rested my head on the car seat. I thought about some of the things me and my boys did – crazy shit; drugs, alcohol, prostitutes, blew our checks gambling and buying expensive toys like cars and other material things – whatever it took to numb our senses. It was hard – dealing with the lies was hard. We did what we had to do.

When the cab pulled up in front of my home, I asked the driver to wait a minute. I couldn't go into the house. After about five minutes, I told him to drive me down Lake Shore Drive to give me some time to think before facing Ariel.

# CHAPTER
## 35

The next morning, I found myself lying in bed trying to put the pieces together. I couldn't separate fact from fiction. What felt real was being at home with Ariel, the wound on my back, and this migraine headache. Everything else felt like a bad dream.

I stood and walked over to the dresser where the medals I received as a soldier were displayed. Looking at them brought back memories – both good and bad. I was reminiscing when I heard someone shouting at someone. I walked down the hall to find that Ariel was talking to herself. Before asking her what was going on, I carefully surveyed the room. There was no one there, but her.

"Ariel, who are you talking to?"

"No one, why do you ask?" she responded, calmly.

"I ask because I could have sworn that I just saw you talking to someone."

Waving her hand, she said, "Oh, I was just praying."

"You weren't on your knees, Ariel."

"You don't have to kneel to pray. Special provisions are made for the disabled."

"Who's disabled, Ariel?"

"My big ass. I am unable to get my butt on the floor and get back up without help."

"Ariel, you are letting this weight thing become a problem. You are pregnant. You are supposed to gain some weight…it's for the baby."

"That's what they say…"

*Here we go.*

"You won't even touch me," she said.

I didn't comment.

"You see…I was right. I figure if I lose maybe ten pounds then you would spend more time with me."

"Ariel, I've never heard of anyone trying to lose weight while they were pregnant. That doesn't make any sense."

"Look at me, Izrael," she said, throwing open her robe and exposing her beautiful round belly. "There ain't nothing sexy about this. You loved me more when I wasn't pregnant."

Reminding her of our previous conversation, I said, "We've had this conversation. I thought that you were going to stop talking this way."

"You also said that you were going to spend more time with me."

Annoyed and frustrated, I said, "Before I returned home, what did you do for entertainment?"

She snorted a response. "I hung out with my friends. I did volunteer work. I went shopping."

"Why don't you do that now?"

"My friends didn't do this to me," she retorted, pointing at her belly.

At the brink of a boiling point, I said, "Since I've been home you haven't done shit, but complain…"

She stopped me. "You haven't been home that long and since you've been here it's been one thing after another."

"You want me to leave?" I asked, hoping that she would say 'yes'.

Still complaining, she walked over to the refrigerator and removed a can of beer and opened it. I ran over and slapped it out of her hand.

"Izrael, what are you thinking?"

"I'm thinking that you've lost your fucking mind. What are you doing drinking beer and when did you start buying alcohol? What is wrong with you?"

"Are you crazy?" she asked, ripping paper towels from the holder thowing them on the floor. "First thing, I can't drink. I'm pregnant." She pointed at her stomach like it wasn't obvious. "Secondly, I wasn't getting it for me. I was getting it for you. I thought that it would calm your ass down like it did last night."

"Last night, what the hell are you talking about?"

"You and Eddie watched the fight here last night." She tried to bend down to pick up the paper towels, but failed. Giving up, she said, "You know what? You pick this up. You made the mess."

Confused, I said, "I was here last night?" I walked over to the kitchen table and sat down. "We didn't fight yesterday?"

"We fight everyday, Izrael. You cut your face yesterday. Don't you remember?"

I reached up to touch my face. The scar was there. *I'm losing my fucking mind.* Rubbing my head, I said, "So I didn't leave the house last night?"

"No, you stayed up all night making noise and keeping me up."

"I was drinking…here?" I asked, scratching my head.

"Yeah, one of your new habits," she confirmed.

I stood and walked over to the phone. I dialed Eddie's number. He answered sounding like he was still asleep. "What's up?"

"Eddie…"

He stopped me, "Man, I'm sorry about the carpet."

I turned to look over my shoulder. There was a stain on the carpet.

He continued, "Man, I thought I could hold my liquor, but…"

I dropped the receiver onto the floor and ran into the bedroom.

"Izrael, come and clean up this mess…Izrael!"

**‖ ✶ ✶ ✶ ‖**

A few hours later, I decided to drive around to clear my head. I needed to get myself together. I went to the bar. The guys, that I had been hanging out with lately, weren't there. I did not want to be alone, but I couldn't go back home. I jumped back into my car, rested my head on the back of the seat, closed my eyes, and fell asleep.

# CHAPTER
## 36

At breakfast the next day, I was distant. My thoughts were on the recent events in my life. Feeling disconnected, I followed the conversation adding things here and there trying not to let on that shit wasn't right. Ariel was talking for about fifteen minutes when I said, "Huh?"

Repeating herself, she said, "Baby, we haven't had sex in a while...what's wrong," Ariel asked, putting the dishes away.

"Until we get the okay from your doctor, it's probably not a good idea to have sex," I said, sitting at the kitchen table praying that the drum beating in my head would stop.

"The doctor said that sex is good during pregnancy. It's supposed to feel better than having regular sex," she said, sitting down into my lap.

"Is that what he said?" I asked, looking at how big her belly was getting.

"Yep...and just think...we can have sex as many times as we want without worrying about getting me pregnant," she said, laughing and placing my hand on her stomach.

"I don't know if I want to do that to him."

"Who said it's a "him"? And don't get me wrong you're big, but I don't think you can hurt the baby."

"You underestimate me...believe me."

"I wish I could testify to that, but if it wasn't for the big belly, I could tell people that I'm a virgin…again." She stood and walked over to the kitchen sink. She grabbed one of the sponges, sprayed some disinfectant on the counter and began to clean.

I looked down at my finger. For the first time, I noticed that I didn't have my wedding band, but I remembered having it the night that I was with the prostitute. *Did I lose it?* I thought to myself. That was strange. I tried thinking of our wedding day, but the memory was vague. I tried my best to conjure up a memory, but nothing came to me. The energy I used to remember one special moment of that day was causing the veins in my head to swell.

*Was it real? Did I really marry her or is this whole moment a figment of my imagination? It has to be real. Who would imagine such unhappiness?*

I was lost in my thoughts when they were interrupted by the scent of bleach coming from the area Ariel was standing in.

"That shit stinks?"

With her mouth turned up, she said. "It's bleach. I use it all of the time to clean the house."

I knew that it was bleach. The scent filled my nose making it difficult to breathe. Although, I've smelled it many times before, but something about it…about this time wasn't right.

"It's a common household cleaner. You know sweetie, if you helped out more with the chores around here the scent wouldn't be a stranger to you."

Through clinched teeth, I said, "Would you like for me to clean up?"

Throwing the sponge onto the counter, she said, "I'm done now, but thanks for asking." She wobbled down the hall. Before reaching the bedroom door, she stopped and yelled, "Are you coming to bed?"

"Not right now. I think I'm going to watch a little television instead."

"Okay, but don't stay up too long."

I walked over to the sofa and then plopped down in front of the television. Over on the end table was a photo of Ariel and I on what looked like our wedding day – the clue was the bouquet of flowers in her hands and the strained look on my face. I closed my eyes again to try to remember that day. I remembered that the ceremony was held at a City Hall. A Justice of the Peace performed the service and a janitor stood as witness. On that day, for the first time in my life, I was scared to death. I loved her – I think. I wanted to spend the rest of my life with her – I think. I don't know what my thoughts were then. All I know is, right now, I'm not sure about anything.

**‖ ✳ ✳ ✳ ‖**

"Harder!" she screamed.

"You want it harder?" I asked her.

"Yes!" she screamed.

"Okay…" I raised her legs over her head. "Is this what you want?"

"Yes!"

I was about to climax. "Get on your knees."

She obeyed.

When it was all over, I was about to pay her when she said, "Don't worry about it."

Confused, I asked, "Are you sure?"

"Just promise me you'll be here tomorrow."

Not questioning the freebie, I said, "Don't worry…I'll be here."

# CHAPTER
## 37

Yesterday was a complete blur. They called me in for work, but I declined. Instead, I decided to call Eddie to organize a basketball game in the park. I felt good. I was working up a sweat maintaining a lead in a game of 21.

"Damn man, I see you got your game back," said Eddie.

Pretending to stumble to try to fake him out, I said, "Man, I haven't felt this good in a long time."

A couple of young ladies sitting on the bench watching the game began to cheer me on.

"Whatever it is you got going on, you need to let me in on your secret," he said, trying to take the ball away.

Smiling, I said, "You know that I'm going to be a daddy."

Snatching the ball, he said, "Damn brotha, when were you going to tell somebody?"

"I'm telling you now," I said, taking the ball back and running down the middle of the court for a lay-up.

The young ladies cheered again.

Retrieving the ball, Eddie said, "Congrats man, I'm happy for you." He threw the ball to me.

Standing at the free-throw line and dribbling, I said, "Thanks man." I missed my first shot, but I smiled in spite of it.

Eddie gave me a strange look. "Are you sure you're okay."

Taking my second shot and missing, I said, "Yeah, why do you ask?"

"Something about you is different," he said, reaching into his pocket and taking out a small white bottle. Shaking the bottle into his hands, he took two pills and threw them into his mouth.

"Everything is fine…just fine." Retrieving, the ball, I ran it down the middle. I felt a sharp pain in my legs. My knees buckled underneath me. "Son of a bitch," I said, grimacing in pain.

Being a competitor, Eddie stole the ball and took a shot. After making the shot, he walked over to help me. "Are you okay?" he asked, extending his hand. "What happened?"

"I don't know. I must have tripped over something," I said, taking his hand.

"Well, you know that shot put me in the lead for the win."

I looked at him.

I don't know what he saw, but beads of sweat began to form on his forehead. He was scared of something…someone.

After careful consideration, I said, "You saw an opportunity to take your man down. I like that. That's how it should be done. I ain't "hating" on you." After standing and regaining my balance, I stuck out my hand to give him "dap."

He hesitated at first, but then returned the gesture. He wrapped his arm underneath my shoulder blades to assist me to my car.

"Can you drive?" he asked, after helping me into the car.

"I'm good man, this ain't nothing. I'll be fine."

Before closing my car door, he said, "If you're feeling better tomorrow, maybe we can get another game going?"

"Maybe," I said, rolling down the car window.

Eddie was walking away when I said, "By the way, that shit that happened on the court today…that only happens once," I said, rolling the window back up. Walking slowly towards his car, he never took his eyes off of me.

# CHAPTER
## 38

That night, I insisted on taking Ariel out for dinner thinking that it could ease some of the tension between us. I thought that it would be nice to take her to an upscale restaurant downtown.

From the moment she got into the car she talked. I waited for that moment when she would get tired – run out of things to say or take a breath, but it never happened. She just went on and on and on. When we entered the restaurant, she was still talking and when we were seated by the maitré d, she was still at it. We ordered. Shortly afterward, the waiter brought our salads and dinner rolls.

"My mama thinks that if it's a girl we should name her after my grandmother and if it's a boy, I should...I mean, we should name him after my father."

Snapping out of an "Ariel-induced" coma, I said, "That's not going to happen."

"Excuse me," she said, looking bewildered.

Clarifying myself, I said it again. "That's not going to happen."

"Izrael..."

Without taking my eyes off of my dinner salad, I said, "If it's boy, we are going to name him after me and if it's a girl, she will be named after you or me."

Frowning, she said, "Izrael that's silly. I would never name a little girl, Izrael."

"Just like I would never name him or her after your grandmother and father," I said, without hesitation.

She started going off. "You don't have the right to tell me what *we* are doing…"

Having had enough of her voice for one night, I mumbled, "Shut up," in an attempt not to draw anymore attention to us.

With a mouth full of food, she said, "What did you say?"

I sipped from my glass of water. "Please be quiet. I'm trying to enjoy my dinner. I'm trying to enjoy an evening out with my wife."

"Humph," she said and for the first time the entire evening, she was quiet.

Over Ariel's shoulder, more drama was going on. A young lady was being dumped by her boyfriend. Suddenly, the man stood and left the restaurant; leaving her there alone.

She was crying when she looked over in my direction. There was something truly beautiful about her. Through the tears and the running eye makeup, I saw them…the most beautiful eyes I'd ever seen. I smiled at her. She blew her nose and then smiled back.

When Ariel excused herself to go to the bathroom, I walked over and introduced myself. We talked for a couple of minutes, exchanged numbers, and then I walked back over to my table. When Ariel returned, I spent the rest of the evening staring at her and she stared back. When Ariel wasn't looking, I made faces in an attempt to make her laugh. She did and that went on the entire evening. On our way out of the restaurant, I turned and waved goodbye to her. She waved back.

When I got home that evening, I looked at the number. I held it in my hand. I admired the beautiful handwriting. I enjoyed the way the paper felt in my hands. It felt real – tempting. I gave it one last look and then threw the number into the garbage.

**|| ★ ★ ★ ||**

After a short nap, I took Ariel for her late night craving for Mickey's Ds. Watching her stuff down a fish filet sandwich it all came back to me. When I first met her, I didn't know she came from a wealthy family. She seemed so common and regular like me. We dated modestly...nothing fantastic. She enjoyed the simple things like making stove-top popcorn and eating Snickers while watching the Three Stooges. It wasn't until one night, when she decided to stay over late, that there was a knock on the door. The gentleman standing in my doorway indicated that he was sent by her father to pick her up. At this point, I was already in love with her and it didn't matter, and shortly after dating, I made the decision to marry her.

Crying, on the day that I left, she said, "Don't leave me Izrael."

"I won't be gone long...I promise," I said, holding her.

"What if something bad happens...I can't lose you," she said, as her chauffeur stood close beside her handing her tissues.

"Don't talk that way. I will be fine."

Stamping her feet and folding her arms, she said, "No...I won't have it. Now you go home and unpack your bags right this instant." My heart began to swell. Fighting back tears, I said, "Don't do this Ariel. You're making this so hard."

"I won't have it," she insisted.

Opening my arms, I said, "Come here and let me hold you."

She fell into my arms. "I'm going to really miss you." She held me tightly.

"I'm going to miss you too."

As I walked away, I remember her waving goodbye, crying, as her chauffeur continued to hand her tissues.

Now, here we are five years later and the woman I've promised the rest of my life to…the mother of my child had a face full of tartar sauce and was a complete stranger to me.

## ‖ ✭ ✭ ✭ ‖

I wasn't born into a world of money. We barely had food to eat because there was so many of us. My parents did the best that they could, but we still struggled. The youngest of ten kids, I had it a little better because I was the baby. My clothes were hand-me-downs, but they were always hand-washed clean. Our home was small. At least it looked that way because there were so many of us living there. It was a three bedroom ranch on the Southside of Chicago. My mom and dad had a room and the rest of us shared the remaining two bedrooms.

When I was young, I remembered that we didn't have to lock our doors and everyone knew and took care of each other. By the time I was a teenager, the neighborhood turned into a war zone. Young men and innocent bystanders were being killed all of the time. My mother refused to lose her children to gunfire so as we became older we were shipped to live with other relatives in the family to keep us safe.

It was one day, when I was visiting my parents, that one of my brothers was killed by a gang member. The gang member thought that he belonged to a rival gang and gunned him down right on the steps of my parent's home. He was putting his keys in the door, when a car pulled up and opened fire. When the bullets hit the door, I thought that someone was knocking and went to open it. My brother's bloody body slumped into the doorway. I fell to my knees and held him as he took his last breath. I looked out into the street.

I saw the car and the boy who pulled the trigger. We exchanged glances. He smiled as they pulled off.

I remember my mother running towards me screaming and crying. I watched as she tried to wake him...pleading for him to come back. He didn't respond. I looked down at my hands. They were covered in blood. Frightened, I ran to wash them. Even though they looked clean, I could still see the blood. In the distance, I could hear the sirens. I didn't go back to where my brother's body lay; I sought refuge behind the closed door of the bathroom.

**|| ✫ ✫ ✫ ||**

After they pronounced my brother dead, I went storming out of the hospital. I gathered three of my boys from the neighborhood and I went on the hunt. That day, I did not find the guy who killed him – which was a good thing because the only thing I brought with me was anger.

That night, I did not sleep. I paced the floor as I listened to the cries of my mother in the next room. Before I knew it, it was daybreak. My mother and father left to make funeral arrangements. I walked into my parent's room, went into the closet where I knew my father kept his gun. I stuck it in the front of my pants and with the cold steel rubbing against my skin, I went looking for the boy who killed my brother. After searching for two hours, I spotted him, in the park, talking to a girl. As I crossed the park, the vision of my brother's lifeless body replayed in my mind.

I walked up to him. Without saying anything, I pulled the gun from my pants, pointed the gun, and pulled the trigger. Nothing happened. For a moment, time stood still. I looked at the gun and noticed that the gun had a safety on it. As I removed the safety, the boy pulled his gun. Before he had time to aim, I pulled the trigger again. I shot him in the ear. He dropped his gun and grabbed his ear. The girl began to scream. I pointed the gun at her face. She stopped screaming and stood frozen. I turned my gun back on the murderer.

Trying to stop the blood, he said, "Damn man!!!! What the fuck did you do that for?"

"Do you remember me?" I asked, scared, but the adrenalin rushing through my body wouldn't allow me to feel it.

"Naw man, who the fuck are you?" he asked, as blood flowed down his arm like water.

"Maybe you remember my brother," I said, with my finger still gripping the trigger.

"Who the hell is your brother?"

I didn't say anything. I just looked at him and as if a light went off in his head, he said, "Now I remember…"

Before he could finish his sentence, the gun went off placing a small hole between his eyes. He stared at me. I stared back. His eyes rolled to the back of his head. He dropped his hands to his side. Next, his body fell backward. I dropped my hand to my side. I looked to find that the young lady was still standing there. I looked at her. We didn't say anything. I turned and walked away.

A few days later, we buried my brother. As they lowered my brother's body into the ground, I looked across the yard to see that they were burying the body of my brother's murderer.

I walked toward them. My grieving mother called for me in the background to come back, but I didn't listen. I walked up to the murderer's mother.

She stopped crying and looked up. "Can I help you?"

"No."

"Did you know my son?" she asked.

"The question is…did you know your son?"

"Excuse me?" she asked.

"You need to teach your kids that 'you reap what you sow'."

"Huh? Who are you?"

I didn't answer. I walked away.

The last time I went home, I went to move my parents out of that neighborhood and I haven't been back since.

**‖ ✯ ✯ ✯ ‖**

Ariel and I spent the rest of the evening, not arguing, but talking about our past and laughing about the happy times. It was 0300 hours when we both began to yawn. In my arms, she drifted off to sleep and for the first time in a long time, I wanted her there.

# CHAPTER
## 39

The next morning, I awakened to find myself alone. The smell of rain filled the room. I looked over at the window to find that it was raining out. My plans to play basketball had been changed so I decided that today would be a perfect day to sleep in. The sound of the rain tapping against the window was soothing. I laid back against the bed and drifted back to sleep. An hour later, I woke up to find that the rain had stopped. I took a deep breath. There was no smell of breakfast – no smell of coffee brewing. I wondered where Ariel was. Before sitting up, I stretched to remove the kinks from last night's slumber. In the process, my hand hit something knocking it onto the floor.

I sat up and allowed my feet to dangle off of the side of the bed. Wiping sleep from my eyes, I noticed a bottle on the floor. When I stepped down to retrieve it, it rolled under the bed. I stooped down on all fours to look under the bed. There was a box under the bed. Forgetting all about the bottle, I reached for the box. I sat down on the floor near the bed and examined the box. It was wrapped in gold wrapping paper with a matching ribbon. I don't know why, but I hesitated to open it. Slowly, I removed the lid. Enclosed inside, were a stack of letters tied neatly with a bow. I removed the ribbon carefully. There were over a hundred letters addressed from me to her and from her to me. I opened one. It said:

*Dear Izrael,*

*Where are you now? It's been three months and I miss you so much. Today is my first day of classes. I couldn't concentrate because I spent the whole day praying for you. I love the photo you sent of yourself in boot camp. You look so sexy in your uniform. Did I tell you that daddy brought me a new car? It's beautiful. It's a BMW coupe. It's jet black and it has leather seats. I love the way the seats embrace my ass. It reminds me of you. ☺ Well, I have to go now because I have to go to the library. I'm thinking about you everyday and every-night. I wish that you were here.*

*Love Ariel*

The next letter was my response to her.

*Dear Ariel,*

*I'm so happy that you are okay. Tell those seats that when I get home, I'm kicking their asses. ☺ I miss you too. I will contact you later. I love you more than life.*

*Love Izrael*

Holding the letters, I tried to remember when I was such a chump. I continued to look through the letters. Underneath them all, was a stack of photos. On top there were photos of Ariel and her father, Ariel and her mother, and Ariel and a few of her friends. Next there was a photo of Ariel. She was wearing a long white gown standing in front of a church. She was standing next to a young man wearing a tuxedo. I looked closely at the image in the photo. It was me, but how could that be. How could I've forgotten having a big beautiful wedding? How could I have exchanged those memories with a ceremony at City Hall? I became overwhelmed with confusion. The room began to spin. Suddenly, the room went black.

# CHAPTER
## 40

Benny Thompson. *Benny Thompson.* A voice said over the intercom in my room. I awakened to find my mother standing over me.

"Daddy, he's awake," she said, shouting toward the hall. "Baby, oh baby, we were so worried about you." She rubbed the top of my head.

"Mama?" I said, disoriented. I heard a toilet flush and then the door to the bathroom opened.

"Hey son," my dad said, walking toward the bed.

"Dad?" I mumbled. "Where am I? Where's Ariel?"

"That crazy woman. I've told you that before. That child is nuts…running around here with that baby…"

My father cut her off. "She's down the hall son. Don't worry about her now…worry about yourself. How are you doing?"

Realizing that I was in the hospital, I said, "My head hurts, daddy. Why am I here?"

"You blacked out. The doctor said that you'll be okay. It's a good thing I stopped by the house…no telling what could have gone wrong."

"Where was my wife?"

They looked at each other. "Who?" they said in unison.

"Her name is Ariel," I reminded them.

Again, they looked at each other.

"Whatever," my mother said. "I'm just glad that your father found you." She started crying. "My poor baby."

My dad walked over to the other side of the bed to comfort her. "There, there, mama," he said, rubbing her shoulders.

Removing a handkerchief from her purse, she said, "I would be so glad when he gets better."

"How long am I in here for?"

"They said, three days," my father said, as he walked my mother over to a chair sitting in the corner of the room. He walked back over to me.

"Why am I going to be in here so long?"

"They want to try you on some new medication before releasing you."

Confused, I asked, "For the headaches?"

Looking like he had answered this question a hundred times before, he said, "Yeah right, son...for the headaches."

"Shit," I paused when I remembered that my mother was in the room. "Sorry mama...anyway, I don't need to sit in here for three days...for no painkillers."

I tried to sit up, but my father forced me back onto the bed. "Rest son, it's only three days."

"But I have to get home to take care of Ariel," I said.

My mother and father exchanged a glance.

"Look son, we will be back in a couple of days to pick you up."

"Ariel will pick me up."

My mother and father looked at each other again.

"Goodnight son," my father said, walking toward the door.

My mother walked over to me. "Goodnight baby, get you some rest." She kissed me on the forehead and walked out of the room.

Shortly, thereafter, Ariel walked into the room. "Hey sweetie."

"Hey Ariel, where were you?" I asked.

"I was right down the hall waiting for your parents to leave."

"They said that I have to stay here for three days."

"That's okay. I will be right here with you."

"Thank you baby." I was going to ask her about the wedding photos, but decided against it. I didn't want to think about anything at that moment other than getting out of there.

# CHAPTER
## 41

Three days later, after being released, I drove Ariel home and proceeded to go to the "low-end" for relief.

"Damn, that's exactly what I needed," I said, zipping my pants. "How much do I owe you?"

"Let's see...we did some anal, some oral, then there was the strangling," she said, rubbing her throat. She paused and then said, "I'll call it even if you agree to have breakfast with me."

"Huh, what did you say?"

She asked again, "Will you have breakfast with me?"

"Are you serious?" I said, trying to keep from laughing in her face.

She smiled. "What's wrong with that?"

"Everything," I said.

"We all eat."

"I eat at home...with my wife."

She looked at me with contempt in her eyes.

"Anyway, here's three hundred. I'm gonna get out here before your next john shows up."

"Since you've been coming here, I've let go of my other johns because I like the time we spend together."

"How long have I been coming here?" I asked, confused.

"You've been coming over here for the past three months."

Confident, I said, "Bitch, I know that I haven't been fucking the same ho' for three months. That's bullshit."

With her hands on her hips, she said, "What? Excuse me?"

"You are excused…real excused," I said.

"For your information "john", we've had a standing appointment every Tuesday and Friday for the past three months. I've had to let my other johns go because of all of the kinky shit we do. I can't fuck nobody else after we're done."

"Gurl, you're crazy. I haven't been coming to see you for the past three of nothing. You have me confused with someone else."

With her hands on her hips, she said, "You're crazy…"

*She called me crazy.* Shaking my head, I thought, *This bitch doesn't know crazy.*

She continued, "You made me laugh and made me feel better about myself. I thought that we had something special."

"Any man could have done that. I don't know what you've been smoking or maybe you need to spend less time on your knees and come up for some air," I said.

"I know what I'm talking about. Remember at the restaurant, I was with my pimp…I was crying…you were with your wife…I gave you my number…I didn't imagine the connection we shared between us."

Remembering that moment, I said, "That wasn't you."

"That *was* me," she confirmed.

"That's bullshit, I would have remembered if that was you."

"Then how would I know about that night?"

There was silence.

She broke the silence, "I know what I am talking about."

"I hear that your *kind* do a lot of drugs…"

"What the fuck? I know what I'm talking about," she reiterated.

Confused about that memory, I said, "I don't know what you are talking about. Sex is the only thing that we shared and the only connection we've ever made was me connecting to that ass. You're fucking your other johns? Did you feel a connection with them?"

"There's something different about you…I saw it that night…the first time we met."

"What?" I asked, confused. *This woman was trying to mess with my head.* I thought to myself.

"You're a gentleman. I mean, you could treat me like shit, but you don't. You see…johns will do anything to you as long as they pay you. I've been burned, cut, robbed, pistol-whipped, raped…some of everything."

"Raped?" I asked, not believing her.

"Yeah, raped," she confirmed. Squinting her eyes, she said, "What? Prostitutes don't get raped?"

"I just never thought about it…I guess you could."

"Yeah, we do. Sometimes johns take it too far…then they don't want to pay us."

"So is it still rape if they still pay you?"

"Yes, it is."

Confused and not really caring, I said, "I don't want to sound cruel, but you don't have to do this."

"Don't judge me. The money's good and when you think about it, we are all hoes if you really look at it. We don't do shit unless we are getting something in return. I just hate that men see me as nothing until they need to get their "thang" sucked. Anyway, if it wasn't for me then what would you do?"

"Find another hoe…there's no shortage and look, if you want to get respected, you need to get a respectable occupation."

"What's a respectable occupation…school teacher, banker, secretary?" she asked.

"It ain't hanging around bars waiting to suck a man's…"
Realizing that the conversation was taking a bad turn, I said, "I'm just saying, we all have a choice."

Clarifying, she said, "It was a restaurant…and I'm no different than some girl working at a bank that meets a man and ends up in the sack and then the next morning to thank her for giving him "some" he gives her carfare or buys her breakfast. Shit, I could easily be some man's wife – lay on my back all day and night – giving him what he needs and in return, he gives me something nice…like a wedding ring. Men are so funny."

"Why do you say that?"

"You say that the woman you marry must be held to a higher standard than women like me, but two seconds into your honeymoon, you're trying to get the freak to show her face. The only difference between me and her, I'm real with mine. I'm free to do what I please to whomever I please, but just know that I can make pancakes, take care of a home, and still take care of my man…if I wanted to."

"Interesting."

"Yeah…interesting," she said.

"Well, thanks for the lesson. I need to get home."

"Will I see you tomorrow?"

"We'll see," I said.

I was walking to the door when she jumped in front of me blocking my path. "If I didn't do this…do you think that you could want to be with me?"

Walking around her, I said, "Do what? Fuck strangers for money? A minute ago, you were acting like Norma Rae…"

"Who?" she asked, with a dumbfounded look of contempt on her face.

"Norma Rae was a woman who..." Realizing that a history lesson would be wasted on her, I said, "Never-mind...I couldn't imagine that we could...not to say that there's anything wrong with you or what you do."

"Really," she asked, looking like she wanted to say something else, but decided against it.

"Really," I confirmed.

There was an awkward silence.

"Okay," she said, conceding, "Well, I'll see you."

"Yeah," I said, not looking back. I could tell that she was staring at me. I jumped into my car. Once in the car, I glanced over my shoulder to find her waving. Frowning, I pulled off.

# CHAPTER
## 42

"What do you think honey? Aren't these the cutest little shoes you've ever seen?"

In a trance, I nodded my head. We had been shopping for things for the baby all day. Ariel was getting close to her due date and wanted to get the nursery ready.

"I'm so excited. Aren't you sweetie?" she said, admiring the miniature pair of gym shoes.

"Yes, I'm excited." Distracted, I was thinking about the prostitute...thinking about all of the things that I wanted to do to her. Feeling the tension rising in my back and developing a hard-on, I said, "Look, how long are we going to be out?"

"Just a little longer, I want to go look at the diapers and *all* of the other baby things," she said.

Adjusting myself, I said, "We've been here too long already. Plus, you need to get off of your feet."

Agreeing, she said, "Well okay. We can go home, but you know that the baby will need some more things."

"The baby only needs us. All of this other stuff, *you* want. Now, can we go home?"

"Okay, okay, you big baby. We can go home," she said, wobbling toward me.

Not joking, I said, "There is a God."

# CHAPTER
# 43

fter a long day of bonding, I needed something therapeutic. I needed to relax. My head was in so many places. I needed to find a balance. It was a few hours later, after making sure that Ariel was content, that I found myself patronizing the local talent. As the light crept through the blinds in the living room, I stared down at the top of her head as she worked to earn her money.

"My name is Wanda," she said, wiping her mouth.

"Huh," I said, as all of the blood rushed to my head.

"My name is Wanda," she said again, now standing to put on her underwear.

Wiping the sweat from my forehead and trying to catch my breath, I said, "Okay."

"Okay?" she asked.

Shaking away the euphoria, I said, "Yeah okay…your name is Wanda."

"What's your name?" she asked.

"Look Wanda, don't take this personally, but I'm not trying to be your friend. What we have is strictly business. You provide a service and I pay you for it. Once we start exchanging names, things will become complicated."

Angry, she said, "So all I am is just a piece of ass to you."

Trying to be sensitive to her feelings, I said, "You make me feel good. You good people…"

Hands on her hips, she said, "I make you feel good…"

Frustrated, I said, "Yeah, why do you think I keep coming back. Why are you tripping? I pay you." I tried to remind her of our supposed arrangement.

"I thought that you were different," she said, pouting.

"I'm a john…we have sex…why would you think that I was different?"

She stormed out of the room. I placed the money on the table and left. When I arrived at home, Ariel was already asleep. I showered, climbed into bed, and dropped off into what seemed like a coma. Suddenly, there was a crash. I jumped up and ran into the living room where I found a brick lying on the floor surrounded by shattered glass. On the sidewalk, standing in front of the house, was the prostitute. We stared at each other. I opened my door. She ran and jumped into her car. I ran behind her and grabbed her car door. We struggled. I pulled the door open and snatched her out of her car.

"What is wrong with you?" I asked, shaking her.

Trying to break free, she said, "You come and fuck me and then drive home to your wife like nothing happened. If the bitch did what she was supposed to do you wouldn't need me, but you use me and then toss me to the side like a used paper towel."

Shaking her, I said, "Bitch, have you lost your mind? You are a hoe…it's your job to be used. You have the nerve to follow me home. All we did was fuck…you stalk all of your johns?"

"I just thought that you were different," she said as her eyes filled with tears.

Pushing her into the car, I said, "Bitch, do I look like your ticket out? You are nuts. If I gave you the impression that you were anything else other than a 'means to an end' then I'm sorry." I closed her car door. "Take your ass home and don't come back over here. You don't know me." I gritted my teeth and lowered my voice. My rage was growing by the second. I knew that she needed to be dealt with, but I refused to do it in front of my home.

Crying, she pulled off. Heading back toward the door, there was no sign of Ariel. I went back into the bedroom to find her sleeping peacefully. I went into the kitchen to grab a broom. Sweeping up the shattered glass, I tried to understand what was happening. The more I thought about what happened, the angrier I became. I was pissed. After picking up the glass, I woke up Ariel and explained to her that someone had attempted to break-in. She accepted my excuse, got dressed, and I took her to her mother's house. I needed to secure the home.

I was at a hardware store purchasing materials to board up the windows when I picked up a hammer. Looking at it closely, I thought about the incident again...thought about losing Ariel. I couldn't let that happen. I had to protect her and my unborn child. I knew what I had to do. I purchased the materials and left the store speeding until I found myself sitting outside of the prostitute's apartment. Removing the hammer from the bag, I looked at it again. My body became feverish. I began to sweat. *Soldier, get your shit together. There's a war going on.*

*Yes sir!* I said to myself. *Yes sir!* I left my car, placing the hammer behind me. Initially, my breathing was heavy, but it leveled-off the closer I came to her door. I knocked on the door.

She answered. "I'm so sorry. I don't know what came over me. I don't know what I was thinking coming over there. I will pay for the glass. I'm so sorry..." She continued to talk as she fell to her knees. She unzipped my pants and began to suck as she continued to apologize between breaths.

*Soldier, you know what you have to do.* I raised the hammer. I swung it. I heard something crack. She stopped sucking and grabbed the side of her head. "What did you do? Why did you do that?"

I didn't say anything. I just looked at the violator. I knew the rules of engagement – when, where, and how much force should be used. She looked at me and then I remembered her...in the restaurant with her beautiful sad eyes.

"I'm sorry," she mumbled. I hit her again. She stopped moving. I stood over her watching the blood flow down the side of her face. Her body fell backward. I waited to see if she would move...nothing. I zipped my pants and began to leave. As I wiped my fingerprints from the doorknob, I looked back at her lifeless body.

"Take care...Wanda," I said, leaving her lying there.

**‖ ✶ ✶ ✶ ‖**

When I arrived at home, the house had cooled due to the air coming through the window. I walked in. The house was dark. I looked around to make sure that no one had entered when I left.

I was alone. I walked into the bathroom with the hammer in my hand. I looked at it. Turning the water on, I washed it and my hands. I noticed that there was blood on my pants and shoes. I removed them, placed them in the trash, and then took them outside. I walked back in and looked at the window again. I thought about Wanda. Nothing came to me. *I wondered what her last thoughts were as life escaped her body? God only knows.* I will never forget the look on her face – the look of bewilderment as the Angel of Death called. It was almost amusing watching her try to figure out what had just happened to her. I'm sure that she knew that it would come one day – death. I guess if anyone had to show her, I was glad that it was me who did it.

I was too tired to board up the room so I decided to deal with it in the morning. Instead, I lied across the couch in the room with the broken window and went to sleep.

# CHAPTER
## 44

I was shaking from the cold air coming through the window. I reached for a blanket, but couldn't find one. I opened my eyes. The light coming from the broken window was blinding. I shielded my eyes. The smell of coffee brewing was in the air. I jumped up, looked into the kitchen, and said, "How did you get here?"

Walking in the room with a Danish in one hand and a cup of coffee in the other, she said, "I was feeling claustrophobic so I asked mother to have Jackson drive me home."

I looked at the window. The hole was still there. *How the hell did she get in here without me hearing her?* I thought to myself.

"I can't believe someone tried to break in here...it's those damn young folks with nothing better to do than to tear up the houses of law abiding citizens," Ariel said, sitting next to me on the couch. She placed the coffee and the Danish on the table and leaned over to kiss me.

I stood up and in my underwear, I went outside to retrieve the materials to fix the window. When I returned, Ariel was eating the Danish and rubbing her stomach. She watched TV while I put up the wood to cover the gaping hole in the window.

"I am so glad that you were home," she said.

"Me too, baby," I said, mumbling through a mouth full of nails.

"I can't believe I slept through the whole thing. Boy, this baby is wearing me out."

"Uh huh," I mumbled.

"It's hard enough carrying myself. Now, I have to carry somebody else. It's a lot of work," she said, placing her feet upon the coffee table.

I was listening to her when I began to examine the hammer closely. I stared at it. There was no blood. I remembered Wanda's lifeless body. I didn't feel anything. No emotion came to me. *I've been trained to kill...trained not to feel.*

Ariel was still talking. After securing the window, I walked over to her, fell by her side and began to rub her belly. My hand jumped.

"Oops, did you feel that?" she asked, smiling.

The baby jumped. "Yes, I felt that." We didn't say anything else. We sat quietly as we felt the little life moving inside of her.

# CHAPTER
## 45

The seasons were changing and it was getting colder outside. I hadn't seen Eddie in a few weeks. I decided that it was time to get together and hang out. I pulled up in front of Eddie's home. It was quiet. I rang the doorbell. He exited from the side of the house. I walked around to greet him. He was cooking out back. I grabbed a seat in one of the lawn chairs and waited for the food to cook.

"How's Ariel?" Eddie asked, sipping a glass of cola.

"She's fine," I said, zipping up my jacket and enjoying the rays coming from the afternoon sun.

He handed me a glass of soda and then out of nowhere, he began to breakdown. He said, "Man you are so lucky...a beautiful wife...a baby...your baby...on the way..." he paused to wipe tears from his eyes. "That bitch...I would have done anything for her." Eddie placed his hands over his face and began to sob uncontrollably.

"Man, you still crying over this shit? You are young. This ain't the end..." I said, trying to console him.

Wiping his face with his apron, he said, "I loved her."

"I know man, but you have to move on...unless you want her back."

"How can I go back? How do you play a "blue-eyed" baby off? My family would freakin' flip...right after my mama has a damn heart attack. Are you nuts? I couldn't take her back if I wanted to...it's

192

about the principle of the matter. It ain't the point that she cheated…I understand that, but shit, if you gon' be shady be discreet with yo' shit. A baby? Damn." He reached into his pocket and removed a small bottle from it. He shook two pills from it, placed them into his mouth, and washed them down with some cola.

Listening, I thought about the prostitute and then I thought about Ariel.

He continued, "I could have forgiven the infidelity…five years is a long time to be without. Man, when I found out, it took everything to keep from catching and hurting her and that piece of shit that she was fucking. That motherfucker doesn't know how lucky she was."

"Man, let that shit go. Every minute you give her is a minute you can't get back. She ain't worth it."

Eddie turned to look at me. "Maybe you're right."

"I know I'm right," I said

Laughing, he said, "If Ariel had cheated on you, I would be talking to you through bars."

"Maybe…maybe not," I said, sipping from my glass.

Laughing and rejoining me at the table, he said, "Maybe my ass. Ariel's ass would be dead and your face would be all over 'the news at nine.'"

"I'm just saying man…you sitting here whining and she's somewhere living and loving. Don't get me wrong we all do shit that ain't right…may have been right or felt right at that moment, but it wasn't right. Ain't none of us perfect, but life is too damn short. I was there when you two said your 'I dos'. You were so happy. I was there when you did your "time" and not a day went by that you didn't think about her and your future together and here you are, still talking about the same shit. She didn't just cheat. She left."

"Damn that's some "deep" shit," he said, wiping the remaining tears from his eyes.

"Our hands ain't clean either. Ain't none of us right."

"What are you talking about?" Eddie said, with a confused look on his face.

*Let he who is without sin cast the first stone.* Staring off into the distance, I said, "How can we say anything? We are licensed murders...trained to kill. Yeah, they say that we're supposed to kill the enemy, but ain't none of them ever did shit to me, to you, or to our families. They say that it's to protect the country...we didn't kill them here on our soil. We went to their "house"...knocked on their doors and killed them. I still have images of dead children...blown to pieces...and for what? Nothing. Not a fucking thing."

"Man, what are you talking about? What is wrong with you?" he asked.

Suddenly, I drifted off. I was rambling. Then I saw myself holding the body of an infant struggling to breathe. "Hold on lil' one...help is on the way." My eyes became wide, I started to shake, and began to sweat.

"Izrael," Eddie said, shaking my arm. "Izrael."

"Help! Help!" I screamed.

"Izrael! Man, snap out of it," he said, still shaking me.

I placed the baby on the ground. I grabbed the soldier by the collar. "Help him or he's going to die."

Gasping and pulling at my hands, Eddie said, "Man, let me go."

"We have to save him," I pleaded.

"Who? What the hell are you talking about? Let me go." We began to struggle with each other as he tried to break free. He reached for the glass of soda that was sitting on the table and then threw it in my face.

Snapping out of my trance, I said, "Where am I?"

Fixing his clothes, he said, "A place where you were about to get your ass kicked. What's wrong with you?"

Helping him fix his clothes, I said, "I'm sorry man. I don't know what came over me."

"A case of "crazy" came over you…that's what. I ain't never seen anything like it. Your eyes were bugging out of your head and you were talking about some baby."

Taking one of the ice cubes from the glass and rubbing it on my face, I said, "I was?"

"Yeah, man, I'm telling you it was crazy. I tried calling your name, but you were somewhere else. You need to have that shit checked out. How long have you been doing that?"

Bewildered, I said, "I gotta get out of here. I'll talk to you later."

"Well, you need to have that shit checked out for real. You scared the shit out of me."

"I'm sorry man," I said, looking over my shoulder. I ran to my car. I had to get out of there.

**❚❚ ⋆ ⋆ ⋆ ❚❚**

I was anxious. I couldn't sit still. After I left Eddie's place, I decided to take a drive. It was around three in the afternoon. I drove pass the school where I once "subbed". School was letting out. I sat in my car as I watched the students flow out of the building. I was about to pull off when one of the female students from one of my classes spotted me sitting in my car.

"Hi…ummmm?" she said, snapping her fingers trying to remember my name. "Mr. Sub, right? Yes, it's Mr. Sub…Fine ass Mr. Sub."

I watched as she leaned into my car window bringing attention to her cleavage. Nervously, I adjusted my collar.

"Yeah, I remember you…tough and sexy," she confirmed.

I didn't say anything. I should have pulled off, but curiosity kept me parked.

"I haven't seen you around the school. What have you been up to?" she asked, blowing bubbles with her bubble gum.

"Don't you have some dolls or something else to play with other than grown men?"

"I want to play with you," she purred.

*Really.* I thought to myself.

"Where are you headed, Mr. Sub?" she asked, reaching into her purse to retrieve something. She took something from her purse and slowly applied it to her lips. I watched as she attempted to seduce me as she puckered and licked her lips. "How much money does a substitute teacher make?" she asked.

"Excuse me?" I asked, frowning.

"Well, you look good and I look good..."

I interrupted, "Whatever you're thinking...stop it. I'm a grown man and you're a child. I'm not one of these little boys."

Agreeing with me, she said, "I know." She reached down and grabbed my "package".

I grabbed her by the hand placing a tight grip around her wrist to emphasize that she was out of order for touching me like that. "Don't do that."

Offended, she said, "I thought that's why you were here...checking out the possibilities. Unless you have a kid that goes to this school."

"I don't, I'm just sitting here minding my own business."

"You can do better than that. Why are you really sitting out here?" she asked and then said, "There's another guy who used to come by here...pick up little girls...take them for a ride in his limo...Do you know who I'm talking about?"

"No, I don't know any pedophiles."

"Huh?" she asked.

I shook my head. "What am I supposed to do with a little girl? Not to mention that I'm a married man," I said, trying to turn her off.

"She leaned in closer, looking me directly into my eyes, and licking her lips, she continued, "These tits don't belong to a little girl and I won't tell your wife if you don't. Anyway, for your information, I'm eighteen and about to graduate."

While she talked, I wondered what her mother would think of her little girl if she could see her right now. "Look, it was nice seeing you…" I said, looking away and placing the car in drive not taking my foot off of the brake.

She stood and then said, "I have a few friends who really like to party. I can invite them to ride with us. What do you think?"

"I think you should play with folks your own age. That's what I'm thinking. Now get away from my car before somebody sees you."

Frowning, she said, "You're a "sub". I know that you're not worried about losing your job."

*She had a point. Sassy lil' bitch.* I thought to myself.

"So what's it gonna be? I have to get home to do my homework," she said, popping her gum.

Annoyed, I looked at her. Seeing her standing there looking like a grown woman with her big breasts, big hips, and matching big butt, I wondered if her breath still smelled like breast milk. She had no idea who she was messing with. Before I could open my mouth, she leaned into the car and began to rub my thighs. Slowly she brought her fingers to the spot between my legs. She rubbed gently. I began to get hard. I grabbed her hand. "Look, I gotta go."

She didn't like being rejected. "Well, fuck you then. Probably couldn't even handle it," she said, smacking herself on the ass.

Changing my mind and accepting the challenge, I said, "You know what? Get in the car."

Smiling, she said, "That's what I'm talking about. You want me to call my girls?"

"Who can't handle who…look at you calling in the "reserves.""

"Huh?" she asked looking confused, again.

"Forget it." *Fine, young, and stupid.*

"Oooo, I like it when they take charge. You gone spank me too?" she asked, jumping into the passenger side of the car.

*I'm going to do more than spank you. You can believe that.*

# CHAPTER
## 46

*Now how did that get there?* I thought to myself as I wiped blood off of my shirt. Looking in my rearview mirror, I thought about the events that had taken place earlier. *So sad.* She screamed as I took her virginity. *What a waste.* She was so young. She tried to act experienced – grown. She screamed for her mama until she took her last breath. I drifted off. *I wonder what Ariel cooked for dinner.* I wiped the blood on an old napkin resting on my seat. I looked at it. It had a big castle on it. *I wish that Ariel wouldn't eat that shit while she's carrying my baby, but I knew better than to stand in the way of a pregnant woman and her cravings.* I retrieved the phone from my coat pocket.

"Hey, did you want me to pick up anything?" I asked.

Smacking in my ear, she said, "The baby wants oysters and butter pecan ice cream."

I heaved, but nothing came up. "Ariel, that sounds gross as hell."

"Hey, I just do as I am told," she paused and then said, "Mama came by earlier, she wants us to come by for dinner."

"I can't do that right now."

"Izrael, don't start."

"Ariel, I don't want to be bothered."

"Here we go…," she said.

"What Ariel? 'Here we go', what?"

"Izrael, look, I'm hungry. I'm not going to talk about this."

"Me neither," I said. We both fell silent.

Breaking the silence, she said, "Izrael, you're upsetting me and the baby."

Calming down, I said, "Look, I'll pick up the stuff you want...I mean I'll pick up the stuff the baby wants."

"Thank you baby, I'll be waiting."

**|| ✶ ✶ ✶ ||**

During dinner, Ariel and I decided to watch television. I was scanning through the channels when Ariel insisted that I stop.

"I want to see what's on the news," she said, eating the oysters right out of the can.

Watching her made me sick to my stomach. "Sure," I said, leaving the room.

Standing in the kitchen, I could hear the weatherman's forecast of 60 degree weather and sunny skies for tomorrow.

"You think that after breakfast tomorrow you could take me for a walk?"

"Yes," I mumbled, getting a refill on dinner.

"My ass is spreading all over the place," she said.

"Sure, whatever," I said, looking into the refrigerator for something to drink.

Next there was breaking news. Ariel turned up the volume.

*The body of a young African-American female between the ages of fifteen and twenty was found brutally murdered in the park near Oak Street Beach...*

*Bam!* I hit my head on the refrigerator door. "Damnit!" I shouted in pain.

"Are you okay, sweetie?" Ariel yelled from the living room.

I walked into the living room, grabbed the remote, and changed the channel.

"Hey!" Ariel yelled. "Why did you do that?"

"I don't think that it's a good idea that you watch stuff like that while you're pregnant."

"Why?" she said, as she struggled to retrieve the remote.

Coming up with something I was sure that she would believe, I said, "The baby can hear everything...you have to be careful about what he hears."

"He, huh?"

"He," I confirmed.

Giving up on getting the remote, she said, "I think that it would be better if it was a girl. They're cute with their little bows, dresses, and patent leather shoes," she said, rubbing her belly.

"Sounds expensive," I said, glad to change the subject.

"Boys can be expensive too," she said.

"Boys are happy with anything. That's how we are."

"No child of mine is walking around looking like 'anything'."

"No child of yours?"

"I mean ours," she said.

"I thought so," I clarified.

"Well since you want to take part ownership for something, why don't you come take half of these stretch marks and swollen ankles?" she said, trying to find her feet, but was unsuccessful.

I just looked at her.

I joined her back onto the couch. "Let me rub your feet." She couldn't lift her legs because of her protruding belly. I slid onto the floor, removed her slippers, and began to rub her feet. She rested her head onto the back of the couch. As I rubbed her calves, she began to purr. She rubbed the top of my head.

"Sweetie, Big Mama could use a little bit."

Raising my eyebrow, I said, "I don't feel like it tonight." I stood to join her on the couch.

"What do you mean, 'you don't feel like it'?" She leaned over to kiss me.

Returning her kiss, I said, "I thought we talked about this."

"We did, but…" She stuck out her bottom lip.

For some odd reason, I started feeling exceptionally charitable so I said, "Sure."

She was so excited like a child on Christmas morning. She placed her hand between my legs. "Ooooo," she moaned.

We kissed. She stopped and tried to lower her head to my crotch, but her belly got in the way. Then she tried to get on the floor, but she was having a hard time doing that too. I asked her to bend over so that I could enter her from behind, but just as I tried to the baby kicked.

She yelled. "Ouch! Lil' Bugger…I guess he doesn't want us to do anything."

I fixed her clothes and said, "Yes, I guess he doesn't." Zipping up my pants, I said, "Come on, let me take you to bed."

"He's messing with my sex life," she said, wobbling down the hall.

After tucking her in, I went to take a cold shower. As the water ran down my spine, I looked down to find that the "Big Easy" wasn't going away. I touched him. He responded. I stroked him. He responded more. I closed my eyes. Out of the blue, I could see her…young and pleading for her life. I pulled harder as I imagined her allowing me to take her virginity. She screamed, I moaned, and I released as she took her last breath. I climaxed, hard. I awakened from my trance to find that the "Big Easy" was living up to his name. I drained the life out of him. *Little girls playing grown up games*, I thought to myself. I watched as the water washed away the memories of her.

# CHAPTER
## 47

A fter sleeping peacefully beside Ariel, I awoke to the alarm clock that was set to radio. I reached over to turn it off, but couldn't find it through the sleep in my eyes. I laid there rubbing my eyes when the newsflash discussing the discovered body of a young woman was being broadcasted. I listened quietly as they described her. As I listened to the details, I realized that I felt nothing. I was numb. It was actually kind of funny listening to their description of the assailant.

*Young male, tall, brown-skinned, about 6 feet tall, and weighing around 200 pounds.*

*That could be anybody.* I chuckled to myself.

Groggily, Ariel asked, "Baby, could you turn that off."

"Sure," I said, sitting up. After turning it off, I rose to leave the room. "I'm going to make some coffee."

Ariel mumbled something and then turned over and went back to sleep.

I strolled down the hall. The telephone rang. I ran to catch it before it woke up Ariel. "Hello," I said.

No one said anything. "Hello," I said again.

"Oh hey man, sorry about that. What cha' doing?" Eddie asked.

"I'm about to make some coffee. What's up?"

"I think we should go down to the hospital today and visit our boy."

"Sure Eddie, who's driving? Me or you?"

"Man, I'll pick you up," he said.

"Good, let me get my coffee. I'll be ready when you get here." I placed the phone on the receiver. As I was walking to the kitchen, I heard what sounded like the toilet flush. "Ariel," I called out. No one answered. I walked down the hall, looked into the bedroom to find Ariel soundly asleep. An eerie feeling came over me. I walked slowly to the washroom. I noticed that the door was slightly opened. "Is anyone in there?" I asked, but no one answered. I went back into the kitchen to retrieve a knife from one of the drawers. I went back to the washroom. "Is anyone there?" I asked again, but there was still no answer. I pushed the door open. The image in front of me frightened me so bad that I found myself floored. My legs fell from under me. There was blood everywhere. A woman in garb screamed as she kneeled over her dying baby. She reached out to me. "Help me!"

Catching my balance, I screamed back, "Mam, you have to get out of here!"

"My baby...my baby!"

"Mam, you have to clear out of here." I stumbled toward her.

"Help me! Help my baby!" she pleaded.

"Mam, troops will be coming through here any minute. You have to leave." I reached out to her, but suddenly there was nothing there. She was a ghost, a figment of my imagination. "Mam...mam," I called out, hoping that I wasn't seeing things, but she was gone. The baby was gone. There was no blood. I sat, confused, on the bathroom floor covered in sweat.

## ▌▌ ✶ ✶ ✶ ▌▌

I was shaken and confused. In the car with Eddie, I sat quietly trying to sort things out. Eddie was rambling on and on about his "ex" that he didn't notice that I wasn't listening.

"Hey man, what is up with you?" he finally asked.

Feeling plagued by everything that's been going on, I went off, "Man get the fuck off my jock."

"What?" he asked, confused.

"I said, get the fuck off my jock. Damn, it's like being in the car with Dr. Phil."

Throwing his hands in the air, he said, "Hey, I'm sorry." He quickly placed his hands back on the steering wheel.

Sick of his shit and all of the shit that's been going on, I said, "You're sorry alright...that's why that skank cheated on you. Man, I've always found that interesting. How can the lowest piece of ass we both know, fuck around on somebody? You walk around sweating that ass when the truth is, she's sucked on more shit than a Hoover vacuum cleaner. It's what she does."

"Damn man, I thought that you wanted me to forgive her and get back with her."

"Is that what you thought? I don't remember saying that shit or remember anything else for that matter, but if anything, what I really want is for you to stop running around acting like a bitch over that hoe. It's hard to respect a motherfucker that I've seen go into enemy territory, ready to lose his life, and all he does is cry over some female. Pathetic."

"Man, I'm sorry..."

Banging my hands on the dashboard, I said, "Will you please stop saying that you are sorry. Do you know who apologizes more than you? Fucking politicians...and you know why, don't you?" Without waiting for his answer, I said, "Because they are full of shit. The question you should ask yourself is, are you full of shit or is she full of shit? If it ain't you then shut the hell up and let that bitch do the apologizing." I huffed and then looked out of the window.

Eddie was shocked at first, but then looked like he was taking my words to heart. We didn't say anything else until we arrived at the hospital. When we exited the car, I said, "Man look, I've been under a lot of stress lately. I don't know what came over me."

"It's cool man. Some of the shit that you said made a lot of sense."

"I could have said it better, but as long as we are cool...I'm sorry," I said, patting his shoulder.

"Are you full of shit?" he asked, referring to what I said earlier.

I smiled and said, "I gotcha, brotha."

We went upstairs to Greg's room. When we got there, Greg was sleeping. We stayed for a couple of hours and then left.

# CHAPTER
## 48

The next day, Ariel convened a two o'clock meeting with me and fifty baby magazines in the nursery.

"So what do you think of this color?" asked Ariel, waving paint swatches in my face. "I'm thinking we should keep the base color white, but then sprinkle the room with shades of yellow, light blue, light green, and just a little bit of pink. That way, if it's a girl or boy, our bases will be covered."

I decided that I would let Ariel handle all of this. I didn't have to do anything, but say 'yes'. Her parents hired someone to design the room.

She continued, "Now, I'm thinking that we could get a bassinet for now, but until the baby is old enough, he or she should sleep with us."

"Sure," I said, without enthusiasm.

"The baby shower…"

I stopped her. She had my attention. "Baby shower? Is that when you invite a bunch of women over and you guys male-bash?"

"No silly, we sit around and "ooo" and "ahh" all night. We don't male-bash…at least not on purpose., but you know there has to be at least one scorned sistha in the group."

"Only one?"

Slapping me on the shoulder, she said, "Be nice."

"All I ask is that you give a brotha a heads-up a week in advance so that I can make myself scarce."

"You're not going to be there?"

"I would rather re-enlist first. I would rather kill..."

She waved her hand. "I get the point."

*If only you did.* "Are we done here?" I said, feeling anxious.

"You're dismissed."

# CHAPTER
## 49

"Hey man, what are you doing? I'm feeling a little claustrophobic," I said.

"Nothing, why?" Eddie said, answering my question with a question.

"Look, I need to get out of here…I need to relieve some tension."

"I thought that's what Ariel's for," he chuckled.

I didn't respond.

"I can see that you're not in the mood for jokes."

"Not when it comes to my wife."

"Sorry man."

"Anyway, back to what I was saying…I need to get out of here. I'm feeling claustrophobic. I need to clear my head."

"Do you want to talk?" he asked.

"Okay…maybe I'm not saying it right. I said that I need to get the fuck up out of here," I said, adding emphasis.

"Okay man, damn. What do you want to do?"

"I just need some air."

"Well, you know that we promised Greg that we would try to see him everyday. He would be happy to see us again."

"Yeah…our boy. That's a good idea. Let's go to the hospital."

"Well, could you come pick me up? My car ain't actin' right."

"Sure, I'll be there in thirty."

"Cool," he responded.

I hung up the phone. Getting dressed, I noticed that the wound on my back was still oozing. As I changed the dressing, I thought of our friend in the hospital. Thought about the man he was and the man he had become. I couldn't understand why watching the withering body of a friend…of a man who once stood strong…stood for his country against an enemy that was not his own, would give me peace…a chance to run from my own pain…my own demons.

After getting dressed, I gently kissed Ariel on the forehead and quietly left the house. On the way to Eddie's house, I fought back images of the woman and her dying child. It seemed so real. My heart began to race and my hands began to sweat so badly that I could barely hold onto the steering wheel. I struggled to breathe. My vision became blurry. I had to pull over. I turned off the engine. I closed my eyes and rested my head on the steering wheel. I drifted off. Suddenly, there was a tapping on the vehicle's window.

"Sir, are you okay?" the officer asked, sincerely.

Heart beating fast again, I answered, "Sure, officer. Why do you ask?"

"Some people saw you in the vehicle and called it in. They said that it looked like you were having a seizure. Are you sure that you are okay?"

"I'm fine," I said, wondering what would cause people to think that I was having a seizure.

The officer paused, looked inside of my vehicle and then said, "Could I have your license and registration?"

Confused and anxious, I asked, "Why officer?"

"Sir, I'm not going to ask you again," he insisted.

"Okay, but I just wanted to know what brought this on."

The officer didn't say anything. He waited while I retrieved the items that he requested. When I leaned over to remove the papers from the glove compartment, he placed his hand on the handle of his gun. I stopped. "Officer, I'm just getting my papers."

"Then get them," he said, his hand still on his gun.

I retrieved and handed him the papers. "Here you go, officer."

"Wait here," he said, as he began to walk toward his car.

I watched through my rear-view mirror as he typed the information into his car's computer. I waited like I was awaiting the electric chair. I thought about the hookers, the man at the mall, and the young student. Moments later, he walked back to my car, holding something other than my papers in his hand.

"Get out of the vehicle," he instructed.

"May I ask why?"

"Because I told you to. Now, we can either do this my way or your way. Please note that my way is less painful."

"Okay officer, but I don't understand what's going on," I said, as I exited my vehicle.

"Sir, have you been drinking?"

"No sir, why do you ask?"

"Sir, as a precaution, I am going to have to ask you to take a Breathalyzer Test to insure that your behavior isn't the result of inebriation. Now here, breathe into this."

I began to breathe into the strange apparatus. The officer examined it closely. He then looked at me. "Sir, I advise you to go home."

Relieved, I said, "Sure officer, I will do that and thank you."

He handed me my papers. "Sorry for the inconvenience. You take care."

"Oh I will," I said, jumping into my car. I restarted my vehicle and slowly pulled away from the curb. The officer pulled up behind me. He followed me for about ten blocks and then he turned to go into a different direction. My heartbeat began to recede. I steadied myself and tried to focus on my destination. When I arrived at Eddie's place,

I saw him in what seemed like a heated argument with his "ex". I rolled down my car's window to hear what was being said.

"I love you Eddie. Don't do this," she pleaded.

"Are you serious? You better get the hell away from here," he said, pointing toward the street.

"Please let's talk," she pleaded. "I know that I fucked up, but I do love you."

Folding his arms, Eddie said, "What we had is over and done with. I have a new woman and she's a hell of a lot better than you. I wish you and your blue-eyed baby all the best."

Falling to her knees, she said, "I would do anything...just tell me what you want me to do."

"I want you to get your ass off of my property before my woman sees you," he demanded.

Crying, she ran to her car and pulled off. When I saw her drive off, I pulled into the driveway.

I said, "Hey man, what was that all about?"

"Who knows and who cares." He walked toward his door. "Let me get my keys and lock up. I'll be right out."

I went to sit in my car. While waiting I decided to turn on the radio.

*...A witness in the investigation of the murder of the young woman found near Oak Street Beach has come forward. She insisted that she did not see the assailant, but she did give a detailed description of the vehicle she saw driving away from the crime scene...*

Eddie locked the door to his home and walked over to the car. When he entered, he put on his seat belt and was about to say something when he turned up the volume on the radio.

*...the vehicle has been described as a black Lexus SUV. The witness was unable to give any further information.*

"Hey man, you have a black Lexus SUV," he acknowledged.

"Yeah me and a whole lot of other folks," I said, pulling out of the driveway.

"That's right," he said, pointing at a vehicle that had just passed the light. "There's one right there."

"See, I told you so." Changing the subject, I said, "So you don't want to talk about what I pulled up on."

"Naw man, I'm telling you it wasn't shit…just like her. She wants us to try again."

"What happened to the baby's daddy?" I asked.

"I don't know and I don't care. Right now, I'm enjoying my freedom."

"But I heard you tell her that you had a woman."

"I do and she's right here and I mean 'right' here," he emphasized while looking at his right hand.

I laughed. "Man, you are sick."

"Hey, *it* never gives me any lip, doesn't complain when I leave the toilet seat up, doesn't cheat, and is always ready to give me what I need without complaining of a headache."

I laughed again. "Man, your ass is crazy."

"Am I lying or am I telling the truth?"

Agreeing with him, I said, "Naw man, you ain't never lied."

We talked and laughed all the way to the hospital. The laughter stopped once we pulled into the parking lot. We sat in silence for what seemed like a lifetime.

"Here we go," I said, turning off the ignition.

"Yep, here we go."

**‖ ★ ★ ★ ‖**

"Excuse me sir, you will have to put on this mask and protective clothing," said the nurse who stopped us before we entered Greg's room.

"Why," I inquired.

"Your friend's disease is progressing. To protect you and your friend, we ask that you put this on."

*Damn.* I thought to myself. I looked over at Eddie to find him wiping tears from his eyes.

I shook my head. "Look, you have to cut that shit out. You can't upset him."

Wiping his face, he said, "Okay, I'm good. Let's go."

I grabbed his arm. "Don't go in there crying like no bitch."

Snatching his arm away from me, he said, "I said that I'm good. Now let's go."

We walked into the room. The room was so clean that the smell of disinfectant made me dizzy.

Greg was asleep. We walked closer to the bed to find that Greg had tubes in his nose, hands, and chest. His face was sunken in. He had lost a considerable amount of weight since the last time we saw him. He had no more hair and as we got closer, we noticed that there were sores on his face and scalp. I heard someone gag. I turned to find Eddie holding his month and running out of the room. *I told his ass...*My thoughts were interrupted.

"Wha, Wha," Greg mumbled. "What's up, man? What are you doing sneaking up on a brotha like that?" He tried to laugh, but ended up coughing instead.

"How are you doing man?" I asked, forgetting the obvious.

"I'm dying man and you?" he said, trying to sit up.

"I'm sorry man. That was a dumbass question," I said, apologetically.

"It is what it is...you know what I'm saying?"

*No I don't.* I thought to myself. There was a moment of silence. I began to rub the back of my neck. He could sense that I was uncomfortable.

"Could I get you anything?" I asked.

"Do you have some time that you can spare? A brotha could really use some more time." He tried to laugh again, but ended up coughing.

"I'm glad that you are still finding a reason to smile."

"Man, my life is over. I know it, you know it, and those mother-fuckers who keep sticking me with those needles know it. I don't have nothing left. My family barely comes to see me anymore...probably picking out the suit they are going to bury my ass in as we speak. The last time my mother came to see me, she started crying, reached out to hold me and my father snatched her back to keep her from touching me...ignorant ass. Doesn't he know that you can't get this shit by touching somebody?" He coughed again. "You know what? Fuck them all. That's what." He paused and then said, "Where's Eddie?"

"Umm, he went to go get some chips from out of the vending machine," I said lying.

"Damn, I wish I had known." He pointed to his IV and continued, "Chips would taste so good right now." He rubbed his stomach and continued, "They would probably only give me the shits anyway. They have me on a very strict diet."

"I understand."

Just then Eddie walked into the room. "Hey man," he said, trying to hold on to the remaining contents of his stomach.

"Hey man, where's the chips?" Greg asked.

"What chips?" Eddie asked, confused.

I gave him a hard look. "You know what chips."

Picking up the hint, he said, "Damn, those chips. Man, I ate those chips so fast...talking about good...I damn near bit my hand trying to get them into my mouth." He tried laughing at his own joke, but couldn't.

I frowned at him to indicate that he was taking the lie too far.

Eddie walked up to Greg to give him the brotha's handshake, but realized that he had gloves on. There was an uncomfortable silence. Greg broke the silence. "Hey, let's play some cards? I could use the money to help pay some of these hospital bills." We didn't laugh. He did.

We played cards for hours, laughed at some of his dry humor, and shared stories of the war until he drifted off to sleep still holding his cards in his hands. I reached to take his cards. Looking at his hand, I said, "Man, he had a Full House."

"Lucky ass," Eddie said, throwing down his hand.

"I don't think that the word 'lucky' applies here."

We put the cards away and turned off the lights as we exited his room. We were in the hall when suddenly we heard a long beep. There were alarms going off at the nurse's station. They all went running into Greg's room. We ran back into the room. One of the nurses escorted us out.

"Sir, we are going to have to ask you to leave," she said.

"Sure, let's go Eddie." I pulled him out of the doorway.

We found two chairs in the hall. I sat quietly as Eddie paced back and forth in the hallway. Suddenly, a nurse came out.

"He has been stabilized for now. There is nothing else we can do right now, but wait. We ask that you let him rest. We will watch him closely and if anything changes, we will call you."

"Thanks nurse," I said, rising to my feet.

"Yeah, thanks," Eddie said.

On the elevator, there was nothing, but silence. We didn't speak on the way to the car or on the way home. I couldn't imagine what Eddie was thinking right now. I just wanted to go home to my wife.

# CHAPTER
## 50

"Izrael, something's wrong," Ariel said, standing at the door, holding her stomach, and crying.

"What's wrong?" I asked, frantically.

"I don't know. Ahhhhhhh!!!!" she screamed, buckling over in pain.

"Come and sit down. Let me call the paramedics?" I took her gently by the arm and led her to the couch.

"No!!!" she screamed between breaths.

"What did you do, Ariel?"

"What do you mean 'what did I do'? I didn't do anything. Help me!"

"Okay Ariel, we have to get you to the hospital. Now come on. Let me help you."

She fell to her knees. "Ahhhhhhhhh!!!!!" she screamed. "I'm wet."

"Wet? Wet where? What are you talking about?"

"There's something wet between my legs." She reached down. When she brought her hand back up it was covered in blood.

"Let's go right now." I picked her up and rushed her to the car. I strapped her into the vehicle. I started the car, turned on the hazard lights, and rushed her to the hospital. On the ride there, Ariel held my hand tightly. She moaned and cried all the way there. Seeing her in that much pain brought tears to my eyes. I wanted to save her.

The tears began to roll down my cheek. *Suck it up soldier. There's no time to cry.*

"Ahhhhhh!!!" she screamed, clenching my hand so hard that I thought that she was going to break it.

"Ahhhhhh!!!!" I screamed back.

"Ahhhhhh!!!" she screamed, again.

"Ariel, please hold on. We are almost there."

Once there, I jumped out of the vehicle and ran over to the passenger's side of the car. Opening the door, Ariel's body almost fell out. "Ariel, speak to me," I said, lifting her body. Looking over my shoulder, I screamed, "Somebody please help me!"

A nurse who was taking a cigarette break heard me screaming and ran over. Putting the cigarette out, she asked, "Sir, what happened?" She tried to take Ariel's pulse while we walked over to the hospital's door. Her limp body hung heavily in my arms. She was hemorrhaging. Her pulse was weak.

"I don't know. I came home and she was bent over…screaming in pain."

Once inside, the nurse called for additional help. An orderly came over with a stretcher. When I placed her body onto the bed, I looked down to find that I was covered in blood.

"What is her name?" they asked.

"Ariel," I said, almost unsure.

They called her name. I called her name. There was nothing. I watched as they rolled her down the hall and out of sight.

As I sat there waiting, I could only think of the worst. Shortly, a short gentleman in a doctor's uniform approached me.

"Sir, are you here with the patient they just brought in."

"Her name is Ariel. Yes, Yes," I said, interrupting him. "How is she? Where is she?"

"Sir, she has lost a lot of blood. Are you her husband?"

"Yes, of course, I am."

"Sir, your wife lost a lot of blood. We are going to need your permission to give her a blood transfusion."

"I...I...I can't make that decision for her."

"If you don't she could die."

Pacing back and forth and rubbing the back of my head, I said, "Is there any other way?"

"No and you need to make the decision fast," he paused and then said, "I understand your concerns, but the blood has been tested. She will be fine."

Reluctantly, I said, "Okay, just bring my baby back to me."

"Yes, we will. I will send someone out here to talk to you. There are some documents that require your signature."

"Whatever you need...doctor, just please get back in there and save my wife...and my baby," I said, frantically.

The doctor walked away. As I sat there, thinking about a life without Ariel made my head hurt. I rested my head against the wall while they worked to save my wife and child.

## ▌ ✫ ✫ ✫ ▌

"Sir," the doctor said, standing over me. He placed his hand on my shoulder.

"Yes...where's my wife?" I asked, jumping up out of the chair I was sitting in.

"She's fine," he said.

"And the baby?" I asked.

"Sir, I need you to sit down," he said, placing his hand back on my shoulder.

Pushing his hand from my shoulder, I said, "No, tell me about my baby."

"She delivered prematurely. We are doing the best we can. He's fighting for his life."

"He? Did you say 'he'?"

"Yes, you have a little boy."

I fell into the chair. I covered my eyes and began to sob uncontrollably.

"Sir, I spoke with her doctor. He informed me that everything was fine and that he expected your wife to carry to the end of her term...Was there an accident or anything?"

"No." I paused and then said, "What are you saying, doctor?"

He looked at me. "It's nothing."

There was an uncomfortable silence.

"Sir, can I get you anything?" he asked.

Wiping my eyes, I asked, "Can I see him?"

"It's going to be a little while before you can see him, but you can see your wife."

"Yes...where is she?"

"I'll take you to her. She's weak."

"I understand."

Walking into her room, I saw her lying there. She looked like an angel resting peacefully. I brushed her hair back from her face. She mumbled, "Izrael."

"I love you," I said, kissing her on the forehead. I sat in the chair sitting next to her bed. I grabbed her hand and kissed each finger gently. I was so happy that she was safe.

In a weakened state, she closed her eyes. Seeing her lying there, I couldn't help, but remember all of the blood. Suddenly, the image of the woman on my bathroom floor came to me. I remembered her cries as she pleaded for someone to save her baby. I shook the images from my head.

*I will save you, Ariel. I will save you.* I thought to myself. I didn't sleep that night. I stayed awake and watched over the mother of my child.

# CHAPTER
# 51

"Good Morning beautiful," she said, tapping me on the hand. I smiled and said, 'You're the one who's beautiful." I turned the television off to give all of my attention to Ariel.

Realizing where she was, she said, "Where's my baby?" She jumped up from the bed.

I rubbed her shoulders and said, "It's okay Ariel…he's okay. They are taking good care of him."

Relieved, she said, "Him? So it's a little boy."

"Yes."

"Have you seen him?"

"No, not yet," I said.

She began to panic. "I want to see my baby. I want to see him right now."

"Relax Ariel, let me go talk to the nurse." I stood to leave the room. "I'll be right back."

I went into the hall to find one of the nurses that were on duty. I approached one. "Excuse me, Where's my son?" I asked.

"What is your son's name?" she asked, without looking at me.

"We haven't given him one yet," I said.

"Well, what is your name?" she said, looking through a stack of files on the desk.

"My name is Izrael."

"The Angel of Death," said the nurse who finally looked up.

"Excuse me?" I asked.

"Your name means, the Angel of Death. It is said that Izrael is the angel who separates the soul from the body before death."

"How do you know that?" I asked.

"It's a hobby of mine. I study the meaning of people's names."

Intrigued, I asked, "That's interesting. The Angel of Death, huh?" I leaned on the counter that separated us.

"Yes," she said, staring at me and looking into my eyes. Suddenly, she became pale as if she had seen a ghost.

Noticing her sudden agitation, I asked, "Is there something wrong?"

"No...no," she stuttered, breaking her stare and looking away. I smiled.

With a look on her face that indicated that she wished that she was somewhere else, she said, "Yes, but back to my original question...what is your name? I mean, what is your last name."

"He would be listed under my wife's name...Williams."

Confused, she looked at her clipboard, she said, "Oh, here he is. I can't bring him to you because he's under special care. I can take you to him if you like."

"Yes, I would love to see my baby."

"Okay, right this way," she said, looking over her shoulder in an attempt to keep an eye on me.

We walked down the hall to a room that had about five newborns in it. The nurse led me to a small glass case. Inside was a tiny little body. The body was so small I could hold him in the palm of my hand. There were tubes coming out of him. It hurt to see him this way, but I reminded myself that it could have been worst.

Staring at him, I asked, "Can I hold him?"

"Not yet, sir, but soon," she responded.

"How long will he be in that case?"

"Not long," she said. "Look, I'm going to leave you here. I have rounds to make." She turned to leave, but turned toward me and said, "He's a fighter. He's going to be fine."

I said, "Thank you."

"You are welcome," she said, before leaving the room.

I stared at him – falling deeply in love the more I watched him. Seeing him in that case made me think of the way they showcased diamonds and other rare and fragile jewels. *That's what he was…a rare and fragile jewel.* He was a fighter like his father. I wanted to hold him; tell him that I would do anything in the world for him, but the glass box prevented me from doing so. I decided to speak to him through the glass hoping that he could hear me.

I smiled and said, "Hey, little one. This is your daddy talking to you. Wow, did you hear that. I said the word "daddy". I didn't think that those words would ever pass my lips, but here you are." I paused. The feeling of shame swept over me. I continued, "I've done some bad things. I've hurt some people…badly. I didn't mean to, but it happened. I've never admitted this to anyone, but you…I've killed some people. I know that it's wrong, but you have to understand that I didn't mean to. I've done a lot of bad shit." I stopped and covered my mouth. "Oops, I'm sorry for saying that word, but just know that I'm going to change. I'm going to dedicate every minute of my life to being the best father I can be. I love you little one." I kissed two of my fingers and placed them to the glass. "I will see you soon."

I walked back to Ariel's room. She was resting. I decided to go to the hospital's Chapel to pray. At the altar, I prayed for my wife and my son and I begged for God's forgiveness for all of the sins I had committed. I promised Him that I would never shed another person's blood for any reason and if He would allow me the chance, I would dedicate each breath that I take to making things right.

# CHAPTER
## 52

Every night until Ariel's release from the hospital, I slept in my son's nursery looking forward to him coming home. Every waking moment was spent thinking of him and my life with him as his father. I imagined buying him his first baseball glove and bat. I imagined us tossing a football in the backyard. I thought about what I would say to him when he asked me, "Daddy, where do babies come from?"

When she was finally released, we spent every minute visiting our son at the hospital. Unable to hold him, we just stood there and watched him. Ariel hated not being able to bring him home. She thought that his being born premature was her fault because she thought that she was a terrible mother. I tried convincing her that she wasn't, but I couldn't.

Initially, we both went together, but after awhile getting Ariel to go see her own son was like pulling teeth. I couldn't understand why a mother would become so withdrawn and have no desire to see her own son. She wasn't herself anymore. She was crying all of the time. She wasn't eating. She was complaining about her body and the weight she gained during the pregnancy. She wasn't well and when I insisted that she tell her doctor about the things she was experiencing, she would yell and scream that I was wrong and blame it all on me.

One day, after I spent all morning trying to get her out of bed and trying to convince her that our son needed her, she snapped. She ran into our bedroom closet and threw everything out onto the floor. She was ranting and raving like a crazy person. I had to restrain her.

"Get off of me! Do you hear me? Let me go!" she shouted at the top of her lungs.

Holding her tightly, I said, "Ariel, stop this before you hurt yourself."

"Get off of me you son-of-a-bitch! You did this to me!"

I let her go so that I could see her face. "What?"

"You heard me, you bastard. Look at me. I'm fat and disgusting because of you. That's why you won't touch me and then you fuck my body up so that no one else will touch me."

Scowling, I said, "Are you serious?"

Scowling back, she said, "Yeah, I'm serious." She pulled away her clothing to expose her body. "Look at this shit," she demanded. She pointed at her stomach, breasts, and thighs. "I look like a freakin' alien and it's your fault."

I was about to walk away before I hurt her feelings when she ran up behind me swinging and clawing at me. I turned and grabbed her hands. "Let me go!" I held her. She cried while I held her.

*I love my wife. I love my wife. I love my wife.* I thought to myself.

After exhausting herself, she fell asleep in my arms.

**‖ ✶ ✶ ✶ ‖**

The next morning, I awakened and Ariel was nowhere to be found. Groggily, I looked for her. I stopped at the baby's nursery. Her back was turned to me. She was in the rocking chair, humming.

"Ariel," I said, but she didn't respond. "Ariel," I said again, but still no response. I slowly approached the chair she was sitting in. "Ari…Ariel, what are you doing?" I asked, taken-aback. I rubbed my eyes to remove all traces of sleep to make sure that I wasn't hallucinating.

"I have to practice. The baby will be home soon," she said, grabbing and pulling at her breast, with a wide-eyed look on her face.

Looking around the room for any indication that this was a dream, I said, "Ariel, stop that."

"But why?" she asked.

"Because that shit ain't normal," I said, pointing at her as breast-milk dripped all over the front of her shirt.

"Well, I just thought that I should get ready."

Kneeling at her feet, I took her hand into mine. "Ariel, are you okay?"

"I'm fine, why do you ask?"

"'Cause you've been acting really strange lately."

"Strange?" she asked.

"Yes, you don't think sitting here, by yourself, humming, and milking yourself like a cow isn't strange?"

"You're overreacting," she said, putting her dripping breasts away.

Realizing that I was dealing with something "special", I said, "Ariel, let's get dressed and go see the baby. You need to get out of this house...we both do."

Out of nowhere, she began to cry. "I'm a terrible mother."

Confused, I asked, "What are you talking about...now?"

"It's my fault."

Trying to draw on the patience of a saint, I said, "Ariel, you just had a baby. I'm sure that parents blame themselves all of the time when their babies don't come into the world the way that they expected, unless..." I paused remembering the time she insisted on going jogging during her pregnancy.

"Unless what?" she said. Now she wasn't crying, but taking a defensive stance.

I looked at her.

"It's you…you're the reason why my baby's in the hospital."

"What?" I asked, tired of her blaming me for this shit.

"It's all of that shit they gave you in the military. You brought the shit home. Those drugs probably fucked up your sperm. You left here one way and came back a mess."

As she screamed, I ran my hand over my head, carefully searching for the appropriate words to say. The voices inside of my head began to speak to me. "Slap the shit out of that bitch," one voice said while the other voice said, "Grab her and hold her…tell her that you love her."

"Izrael, do you hear me talking to you? This shit is your fault," she said, with her hands on her hips.

The voices inside of my head, speaking to me, were becoming louder. "Slap the shit out of that bitch," one voice said again. "Grab her and hold her…tell her that you love her," the other voice said, still disagreeing. Suddenly, I imagined how different things would be if she had no tongue. How quiet my world would suddenly become.

I continued to look at her waiting for her mouth to stop moving. I stood trying to block her out. I remembered how I felt when I almost lost her. The voices began to scream. I didn't want to hurt her. Suddenly, in an attempt to shut them up, I began to chant out loud, "I love my wife. I love my wife." Realizing that I was ignoring her, she finally became quiet and then stomped out of the room. All of the noises stopped.

**|| ✶ ✶ ✶ ||**

I visited my son everyday. Most of the time, Ariel stayed home. She wasn't eating or sleeping. This was putting more strain on our relationship. I was spending all day at the hospital and all night taking care of Ariel. My headaches were getting worst. I wanted to get away, but I couldn't. I couldn't understand what was going on. Nothing was making sense. I was having strange dreams – horrible dreams. I was forgetting things. My head was always hurting and I was having difficulty taking care of myself. Now, I had to deal with this shit.

One morning, I awakened to the old Ariel. She had put all of the clothing that had been lying on the floor for days, back into the closet and made breakfast. She walked into the room humming a song as she brought me breakfast in bed. "Sweetie, hurry up and get ready so that we can go see the baby," she said.

I looked at her like she was a stranger. So happy that she was doing okay, I ate quickly, got dressed, changed the dressing on my wound, and we were on our way.

In the car, everything was fine until I noticed that she was unusually quiet. I didn't want to ask her what was wrong, because I knew that I would regret it, but I did it anyway. "Ariel, are you okay?" She didn't say anything. I asked again, "Ariel, are you okay?" She still didn't say anything. When we came to a light, I looked over at her. She was clenching her chest and was struggling to breathe. I pulled the vehicle out of traffic. I threw the car into park and ran over to her side of the car. I opened the door. I removed the seat belt. "Ariel, what's wrong?" She grabbed at her throat. "Put your head between your legs. Try to slow down your breathing," I instructed. She did as I asked. After several minutes of this, her breathing regulated itself. She looked up. Her eyes were filled with tears. "I can't do this."

"You can't do what?" I asked.

"I can't do this."

"This what?" I asked.

She sighed heavily. "Can we just go to the hospital?"

"No Ariel, let's talk."

"No Izrael, I don't want to do this now. I just want to go to the hospital."

I looked into her eyes searching for something – anything that would give me a clue as to what was going on. Suddenly, I felt a chill. As I looked, I saw something so familiar. I've seen that look before.

**|| ★ ★ ★ ||**

We were standing in front of the case that held our son's body when Ariel asked, "So what are we going to name him?"

"I haven't thought about it. Wait a minute, I will be right back."

"Izrael, where are you going?" she asked, nervously.

A strange feeling came over me, but I ignored it. "I'll be right back," I insisted.

I walked the halls, back and forth, looking for the nurse who knew the meaning of names. I found her checking the IV of a patient in a room. "Nurse, could you please help me."

She looked up and with that same look of fear on her face that she had the first time we met, she said, "Sure...Just give me a minute."

"Okay," I said, waiting patiently in the hall for her.

"Yes, how can I help you?" she asked, joining me in the hall.

"I'm trying to name my son. I want something powerful. He is such a little angel," I said, sounding like a proud father. "I want something Biblical."

"Well, there's the name Michael," she said, fearful that she had given the wrong answer.

"And Michael stands for?"

"Is this is your first child?" she asked.

"Yes, he is my first."

"Well, it is said that Michael means, 'One who is like God'."

"I like that. Then my son's name will be Michael. He can be an angel like his daddy."

"Yeah, like his daddy," she mumbled.

"I can't wait to tell my wife." We were standing there for a second when the monitors behind the nurse's desk began to sound off. She ran toward the desk. I strutted down the hall back to the room. At the door, I could see that the glass case was empty. I walked slowly into the room. I walked toward the case. Looking around the room, I could hear someone humming a lullaby in the corner of the room. I feared the worst. I dropped my head and hesitated to look in the direction of the song. When I finally got the nerve, I glanced out of the corner of my eye. "Oh my gawd Ariel, what have you done?"

She was rocking his lifeless body back and forth. "He didn't want to be in that case anymore so I took him out," she said, trying to breastfeed him.

Falling to my knees, I cried, "Ariel, no!!!!"

In a gentle voice, she said, "Izrael, why won't he eat?"

Responding to the alarms, nurses and doctors ran into the room. "Ariel, no!!!!" I covered my face. "How...how could you?"

Taking the baby from her arms the doctors and nurses began to try to resuscitate him.

"Ariel, why?" I said, sobbing into my hands.

With the look of an angel, she said, "He didn't want to be in that box. He wanted to be with me."

Everything around me became hot. "He wanted to be with you?" I asked, wanting to kill her.

"Yes," she replied.

I was so overwhelmed with anger and grief. I stormed out of the room. I ran out of the hospital searching for my car, but my thoughts were so clouded that I couldn't remember where I parked it. I went running into the street almost being hit by a car. I kept running until I found myself alone in a park. I sat on a bench and cried until my chest hurt. Hours had passed before I realized that it was dark outside. After going through all of the stages of grief in a matter of minutes, I found myself left with the only emotion that has been a refuge for the man that I've become – anger. A fire began to burn deep inside of me. I looked at the sky and began to speak with the person who has failed me once again. The first time was when my brother was killed. The second time was when I went to the war…and now this.

"Why? Why him?" I asked. "I thought that we had a deal. You took my son from me. Why? He didn't do anything. He didn't deserve to die. Why would you take him when there is so much scum on this earth that deserved it more than he? You could have taken me, but instead you take an innocent child – my only child." Suddenly, my conversation was interrupted by a young lady jogging down the road. I looked at her, but then I turned my thoughts back to the sky. "You took my son. You took my baby." Suddenly a fire raged inside of me. I was pissed. I wanted to take from Him like He took from me. I wanted to get even. "It's on. Do you understand? The next time you hear from me it will be when I arrive at Heaven's door for judgment. Peace."

I turned my attention back to the woman jogging on the trail. I ran behind her. She didn't hear me coming because she was listening to her IPod. Before I knew it, I was upon her, grabbing her from behind. I wrapped my arms tightly around her throat. She struggled. I squeezed harder. Images of my son's body flashed before my eyes. The images of dead women, men, and children flashed in front of my eyes. I squeezed harder. She struggled. I thought about the prostitutes, the young man, and the teenager. They deserved to die. They weren't innocent, but she was. A wave of satisfaction swept over me. I squeezed harder. Suddenly, there was no movement. She was dead, as dead as my only son. I let her go and watched as her life-less body fell from my arms. I stood and walked away with a feeling of peace. We were even.

# CHAPTER
# 53

I didn't go to my son's funeral. I couldn't come to terms with him leaving me so quickly. It hurt knowing that I would never have the chance to hold him, to kiss him, or to tell him how much I loved him.

The following months were hard on Ariel and me. We barely spoke to one another. I even started sleeping on the couch. Most of the time, she was heavily medicated. I had to take care of her every need because she slept most of the time. When she was awake, I was force-feeding her and bathing her.

One winter morning, I was sitting in front of the fireplace in the living room while she slept. As I watched the flames dance among the firewood, I thought about all of the things that happened over the past year. There were so many gaps. As I tried to put the pieces together, the image of Ariel holding my son appeared in my mind. I became sad. I hated myself and I hated Ariel. I really hated Ariel.

The house was quiet. The only sound came from the drum playing in my head and chest. I paced the floor looking around for a distraction, but my thoughts consumed me. *You don't hate Ariel. I* reminded myself. *You are just angry. She didn't know what she was doing. She wouldn't intentionally hurt the baby. Would she?* I tried shaking the thoughts from my mind. *She loved him. Didn't she?* I continued to pace back and forth. Then I remembered her behavior and the things she did and said. *"I wish that I wasn't pregnant"*, *she said.* Something inside of me snapped. I walked into the kitchen. Sitting on the counter were a set of carving knives. I removed one and became seduced by the light bouncing off of its blade. Never thinking twice about what I needed to do, I walked into the bedroom where Ariel lay.

She was sleeping peacefully. I stood over her, lurking. I imagined taking the blade across her throat, but thought that would be inhumane because she may not die right away. I imagined plunging it into her chest, but she would awaken and I didn't want that memory. As I stood there contemplating ways to give my little one justice, Ariel began to mumble, "Michael...Michael."

My heart grew heavy. I walked out of the room.

**|| ✯ ✯ ✯ ||**

The next morning, she decided to break the silence that has held on to us since the death of Michael.

Having spent so much time in bed and letting herself go, she began to look like her mother more than my wife.

"We can't go on like this," she said.

I didn't say anything.

"Izrael, did you hear me?"

"I heard you."

Standing in front of me, she wrung her hands desperately searching for the right thing to say. "I think we should try again."

*That wasn't it.* "Try what?"

"Izrael, we should try to have another baby."

"Are you fucking serious?" I said, trying to do what should have been done a long time ago.

She broke down into tears. "You will never understand."

"Understand what?"

"You make it seem like it's my fault."

"Are you serious?" I asked, trying to suppress the rage burning deep inside of me.

"You think that I killed him. I know you do. You think that I'm unfit to have a child."

"Don't tell me what I'm thinking Ariel."

"I loved my baby as much as you did. I could never hurt him...I just wanted to hold him."

Becoming angry, I said, "You took him off of his life support. What mother would do that shit? You fucking took him off of his life support. I can't believe you did that and you know what you got for doing that shit?" I answered my own question. "A fucking 'get out of jail free' card...that's what you got." Knowing that I had no right to say that, I continued anyway, "So while I morn the loss of my son, I'm forced to take care of the motherfucker who took his life. You took my son away from me. He was fine one minute, I leave you in the room with him, I come back and he's dead."

"Izrael..."

I cut her off, "They claimed that you were depressed, gave you some pills, and made you my burden. I hate you and my son hates you too."

She looked at me then she ran into the bedroom and slammed the door behind her. I followed her to the room. I wasn't done with her. I wanted to wring her neck. I placed my hand on the handle. It was locked. I started banging on the door. "Open this fucking door. Do you hear me?" There was no answer. "Open this fucking door." There was still no answer. I was so angry that I turned and slammed my fist into the wall.

When she didn't respond, I walked back to the living room. I turned off all of the lights and sat in the dark quietly trying to calm down. I was pissed. My thoughts were all over the place. My head began to hurt. I was hearing things. I shook my head trying to get rid of the voices. I needed to do something to stop the pain...to stop the noises. I stood to walk toward the bedroom when I heard screams coming from the bathroom. The door was still locked. I walked back down the hall, ran as fast as I could, and kicked the door in. When I entered Ariel could not be found. I called out to her, but she didn't answer. Suddenly, I could hear whimpering coming from the bathroom. I ran in there to find Ariel lying in the bathtub – blood oozing from her wrists. "Ariel," I called out to her. "What have you done?"

"I don't deserve to live," she mumbled.

I ran into the bedroom and grabbed the phone and dialed 911. I ran back into the bathroom.

All of my earlier thoughts were a memory. "Ariel, I forgive you," I whispered into her ear. She didn't answer me. I watched as the tub filled with blood. I tried to help her. I wrapped both wrists with a tourniquet, but the blood soaked through. By the time the paramedics arrived, Ariel was gone too.

# CHAPTER
## 54

"Amazing Grace, how sweet the sound…" the choir repeated over and over as they lowered Ariel's body into the ground. I looked around at all of the faces of her family and friends. It was clear by their expressions that they were mourning, but I couldn't hear them. My family didn't come, they refused to see her.

Noticing how particularly beautiful it was out, I saw it. The one thing I've avoided since his death – my son's grave placed next to the grave of his mother. As I resisted the urge to cry, the words 'you reap what you sow' came to mind. Finding the humor and irony of this whole situation, I began to laugh – at first quietly, but then loudly like a mad man. Everyone around me stopped to look at me. I laughed louder and harder. I looked into the sky and said, "Good one." I shouted, "Do *You* hear me? I get it."

**‖ ★ ★ ★ ‖**

Within a year, I had buried both my wife and son. I had lost everything that I fought my entire life to have. Now I'm alone in the dark with nothing, but the memories of my sins.

The phone rang and rang. At first, I didn't want to answer it, but it seemed like the person on the other end wasn't going to stop calling until they got through.

"Hello," I said, without emotion.

In a squeaky voice, I heard, "Izrael? Izrael honey, how are you?"

"I'm doing as best as I could under these circumstances, grand-mamma."

"Well baby, I know these are bad times for you, but you have to lean on your family son. You just can't shut the people who love you out. You gotta let us in. Yo' mama told me that you haven't called or visited since…" she hesitated and then continued, "Look son, the Bible says in **Psalm 55:22** – *Cast thy burden upon the LORD, and He shall sustain thee: He shall never suffer the righteous to be moved.* You have to lean on Him now. You need to ask Him for His love and understanding."

"What I need to ask Him is why would he take my son and my wife? Why would he do that, grandmamma?"

"When things like that happen, you need to ask yourself what you've done in your life that would cause Him to punish you that way."

"Excuse me?"

"You heard me son. God is a merciful God. He wouldn't take both your wife and son unless he felt that you didn't deserve them anymore or he felt that He needed to protect them from something. You need to ask yourself, what have you done that would warrant Him to put this type of raft upon you."

As she spoke, I thought about all of the people I've killed. I became uncomfortable. "Grandmamma, I gotta go."

She continued. "Just don't forget that we's here for you," she said, before hanging up.

Her words left me feeling empty. I knew that she was right. I did some horrible things. It was hard to believe that God would take the lives of the innocent to punish the guilty. What if he was trying to protect them instead? Maybe, grandmamma was right, but the fact that she was right only made me angrier. I loved my family. I wouldn't have done anything to hurt them. He didn't need to protect them from me. He needed to protect me from myself.

# CHAPTER
## 55

One day, I just couldn't take it anymore. I missed Ariel. I missed my son. I was feeling so messed up inside. My world was crashing down around me. I was tired. I covered every window in my home, with the black sheets that Ariel and I used to make love on, to keep the sun out. I took the phone off of the hook. There were knocks at my door, but I didn't answer. I refused to eat or drink anything. I sat in the recliner in my living room and waited for my fate, I wanted it – I welcomed it.

The first couple of days, it was okay, but then the silence took over. I'm not sure if this makes sense, but the silence was so loud that it was becoming deafening. I began to "trip". I started to hear noises. I began to hallucinate. After about a week, I really began to freak-out.

The "tick-tock" coming from the clock on the wall reminded me of the clocks strapped to the chests of children on a Kamikaze mission. I could see them waiting for their time to run out while their dreams, futures, and contributions were suddenly blown away.

The walls began to close in on me. "What was that? Did you hear that?" I asked myself. "It was nothing. Yeah…Yeah…it was nothing," I said looking around the room. I began to laugh at myself. The laughter bounced off of the walls making it like sound like I wasn't alone. The room began to spin. I grabbed my head trying to make it stop. When I removed my hands, I realized that I wasn't in my living room anymore. Suddenly, out of nowhere, I heard the sound of gunfire. Next, there were bombs going off. I had to find cover. I ran and ducked behind the sofa. There was gunfire all around me. I began to look around for my guns. I patted my chest and legs in search of them, but they weren't there. I remembered that I had left them on the truck. I had to get to them, but there were shots coming from everywhere. I had to think quickly. I dropped close to the floor and crawled to my truck. I reached under my seat to find a loaded pistol. I crawled back to cover. I let off a few rounds. They shot back. I shot again and again until there were no bullets left. I knew that there was nothing left to do, but to rush the enemy. I took a deep breath and ran out. I tripped on something. As my body became a victim of gravity, I tried breaking my fall only to have my hands give way to the floor. My head broke the fall. There was a bump against the cherry hardwood floors. Next, everything went black.

## ❚❚ ✯ ✯ ✯ ❚❚

Dazed, I asked, "Where am I?" I tried to sit up. "Am I dead? Awww!" I yelled, grabbing the side of my head, "Son-of-a-bitch." I looked at my hand to find that it was covered with blood. *Damnit, a reprieve.* Looking up at the ceiling, I said, "Why couldn't *You* just finish me off?"

# CHAPTER
## 56

"Our father, which art in heaven," I prayed.
*Soldier it's time to go.*
"Hallowed be thy name," I continued.
*Let's go soldier.*
"Thy kingdom come."
*Now soldier!*
"Wha...What...What's going on? Where am I?" I awakened panting heavily. My clothes were soaking wet. Looking around the room, I recognized the setting. I was at home.

"My head," I grimaced in pain. I wiped the sweat from my head and then I went into the bathroom to splash cold water on my face. I was looking in the mirror when a reflection of the tub appeared. I stared at it. I fell to my knees. I placed my hand inside of the tub. She was gone – *because of me, she was gone.* I fell to the floor along side of the tub. "What have I done? What have I done?" I shook my head. I was confused. *What am I doing?* Looking up at the ceiling, I asked, "What is going on? Why are you doing this to me?" I was so angry. I wanted to curse Him. I needed to blame someone. I didn't understand any of this. Why would He sit back and watch as people die senselessly? Why would He take my wife and son when I am the one undeserving of life? I couldn't understand.

Looking down into the tub – at the place where Ariel took her last breath, I became enraged. "Ariel!" I screamed. "Ariel!"

Remembering that I was alone, I whispered, "I'm sorry, Ariel." I climbed inside of the tub to place myself closer to her memory. Not understanding where my life was headed, I made her and my son a promise. I had to make it up to them. I had to change. I thought about what I was going to do to keep that promise as I crawled into the fetal position and fell back to sleep.

The next morning, I was awakened by the sprinkle of cold water on my face.

"Hey! What the hell?" I asked, flailing my arms to avoid the cold water.

"Your mama called me and told me to check up on you. Since you were already in the tub I figured I would just turn the water on," Eddie said.

"Damn man, turn that shit off. How did you get in here?" I asked, frustrated and disoriented.

"You left the door open. Now get up and get dressed."

"For what?" I asked, trying to get out of the tub, accidentally falling backward and hitting my head again. Grabbing the back of my head, I screamed, "Shit!"

Eddie didn't attempt to help me. He walked out of the bathroom shaking his head.

Confused by his reaction, I said, "Why are you here?"

"Look, you can't change what happened. You have to get your shit together. I'm here because I promised your mama that I would help you do that."

"Man, I don't need your help. I need to go see my doctor," I said, removing the water soaked clothing.

"That's a start. Give him a call and I will make sure that you get there."

Now standing in front of Eddie completely naked, I said, "I will. Could you leave the room and give me some privacy."

"I'll be in the living room waiting for you."

I retrieved a pair of sweats from the bedroom closet. "Hey man, I appreciate your help, but I got this." I shouted through the bedroom door.

"I promised your mother…" he said.

I interrupted. "I said that I have this." I opened the door and joined him the hallway. "I promise that I will go to the doctor. I'll call you when I get back."

Eddie was about to say something when I grabbed my keys and left him standing there.

# CHAPTER
## 57

Nothing has been right. I made a sacrifice and in return, my life has been nothing short of a disaster. Nothing was making sense. In my quest to separate fact from fiction, I've made a lot of mistakes – I think. I wasn't sure about anything anymore. The killing in the war, the killing of strangers, the death of my wife – none of it felt real. Then there was the anger. It was the only thing that I could feel. It was the only thing that made sense – the only thing that felt real.

Whether real or imagined, every memory gave way to a feeling of retribution – a need to get back at someone – at life. It was the only consistent thing in my life except for the pain. I knew that I needed to see my doctor, but deep down inside he couldn't help me – no human could.

"It's been a long time Izrael. How have you been?"

"I haven't," I said, cold and emotionless.

"Well, since I haven't seen you I assumed that all was well."

"Well, it hasn't."

"What's been going on?"

"First, could you look at this thing on my back again? I don't know what it is, but it won't heal."

"Okay, let's take a look at it."

I removed my shirt and he removed the dressing. Putting on some plastic gloves, he said, "How long have you had this?"

"I don't know...I can't remember when it happened. I can't remember a lot of shit for that matter?"

"I'm going to have to clean it. It looks infected."

"Okay," I said.

The doctor walked over to the medicine cabinet removed some cotton balls and antiseptic. He poured the antiseptic over the wound. I gritted my teeth to hold back the scream fighting to get out.

Examining the wound, he said, "That's odd."

"What?" I asked.

"So this isn't a tattoo gone bad?"

"No, why do you say that?"

"If I didn't know any better, I would swear that it's an upside-down cross."

"Really?" I stood and walked over to the mirror. "That's strange...it does look like that."

"Let me put something on it." He began to put a dressing on it. "And you don't remember when this happened?"

Trying to remember, I said, "I think this happened about a year ago."

"And it hasn't healed? Why didn't you come and see me?"

Confused, I said, "I did. You gave me some medicine, but it didn't work."

Looking at my chart, he said, "There are no notes about this in your chart. Are you sure?"

"Yes, I'm sure," I said, becoming agitated.

"Calm down, I'm going to take care of it. What else has been going on?"

"A lot has been going on. So much that I wouldn't know where to start."

"Why not start at the beginning?"

"This could take awhile. Don't you have other clients to see?"

"I do, but they are not here yet. Let's focus on you right now. Now tell me...what's been going on?"

"I can't tell you."

"I'm your doctor. If you can't talk to me, then who?"

"Everything I say will be held in the strictest confidence?"

"Nothing you say will leave this room," he confirmed.

I hesitated, but then I said feeling like I had nothing to lose, "I've killed someone. Well, not just one person, but several people."

"I know that you were in the war. It was your job," he said.

"No, that's not what I'm talking about." I paused, took a deep breath, and then continued. "Since I've been back home I've killed a couple of people."

Clearing his throat the doctor said, "Since you've been home?" He stood walked over to the door and told the nurse, "Cancel all of my other appointments."

I heard the nurse say, "Sure doctor."

After sitting back down, the doctor said, "Now where were we? Since you've been home? What do you mean?"

"Well, you see doctor. When I came home I thought that I was okay, but then I started having nightmares. Then the nightmares came to me during the day. There were moments when I would blackout and find myself back on the battlefield. Initially, small things would trigger it, but then they became as frequent as taking a breath. So I came to see you."

"What about the medications I prescribed for you?"

"I didn't fill the prescriptions because I didn't think that I needed them. I took the painkillers you prescribed, but they made me sick so I stopped taking them. Then there were the prostitutes…"

He interrupted, "The who?"

Like someone had opened a flood gate, the words were just coming out. "Well there was more than one. The first one was an accident. I snapped her neck trying to shut her up. She wouldn't be quiet. The second prostitute…she was a little clingy…The nutcase showed up at my house…said her name was Wanda…I hit her in the head with a hammer. Yep, Wanda's dead too."

The doctor walked over to the water cooler, filled a cup full of water, and gulped it down nervously.

I continued, "Her death gave me peace for some odd reason. For a moment the demons stopped, but that feeling didn't last long. Then there was a teenager..."

At this point the doctor's hands were shaking. "Teenager? What teenager?"

"This little girl at school. Not anybody in particular. Just somebody who decided that she wanted to be next."

A light bulb went off in the doctor's head. "Are you talking about the little girl that's all over the news?"

"I don't know. I don't get to see much TV. Then there was this other lady. I killed her just because I had a debt to settle."

"Because of what? A debt to settle with who?"

I pointed at the ceiling, "With Him." Scowling, I said, "I didn't want to, but you gotta do what you gotta do."

The doctor looked at me.

Snapping my fingers, I said, "Damn, I almost forgot about ol' boy. That idiot stole my wife's purse."

"How did he die?" the doctor asked.

"Let's just say that it wasn't pretty."

The room became quiet. We stared at each other. The doctor broke the silence.

"You have to turn yourself in."

Shaking my head, I said, "I can't do that."

"Why not?" he asked, confused and afraid for his own life.

I began to laugh. "Look, I'm not going to do no such thing."

"But you have to," insisted the doctor.

"Or what?"

The room became quiet again. We stared at each other like two men dueling, waiting to see who would pull their gun first.

I broke the silence. "Well, you know what doctor. Thanks for this moment to share. I actually feel better. We need to do this often." I stood to leave. At the door, I turned and said, "I don't have to worry about you telling anyone about this right?"

"Well…"

"Well what?" I asked.

"Well, you do understand that I cannot keep the information you disclosed in confidence."

I closed the door and stepped back into the office. "But you said that you would keep everything said between us a secret?"

"I did until you confessed to murder. I have an obligation to report this to the appropriate authorities."

I raised my eyebrow and smiled, "The only obligation you have is to me and to keeping your mouth shut. Believe me…talking to the authorities is something that you don't want to do. Plus, none of it was real. You see, it was all just a dream. Since I've been back, I've been having a lot of crazy dreams. So, I'm not worried about it and neither should you." Standing directly over the doctor, grabbing his stethoscope and pulling it tightly, I said, "Like right now…I'm not choking you. You're not gasping for air; struggling to breathe. I'm actually at home, eating some cereal, and watching TV. None of this is real, right?"

The doctor nodded his head "yes".

Letting go, I said, "Good, then I'll see you in two weeks."

**❙❙ ✳ ✳ ✳ ❙❙**

That evening, I went back into the bathroom. I sat on the toilet and stared at the tub. I threw my hands into my face. I closed my eyes. I could see her, so clear, it was as if she was standing right in front of me. I thought about how much we fought. I reflected back to a moment when we were happy.

I remembered one evening when she decided to seduce me with

food. She had the crazy idea to pour chocolate syrup all over herself so that I could lick it off.

"Come on, daddy," she said, carrying a can of whipped cream and a jar of maraschino cherries.

I thought that it was so funny watching her trying to dance as the syrup dripped to the floor. It was really funny when she found herself stuck and unable to move.

"Izrael, help me," she pleaded.

As I reached out to help her, the scene changed to the night that her body lay in the tub with blood pouring from her wrists.

I could hear her crying out. "Izrael, help me," she pleaded. "Help me."

I uncovered my face and ran from the bathroom. I found myself kneeling at the foot of my bed. I threw my face into the mattress. When I looked up, I could see where her body left an indent on her side of the bed. "Ariel," I called out. "Ariel." On the floor, I threw my body into the fetal position. "I did all of this for you...to protect you and then you leave me. Why?" Lying in that position gave me a view of the floor underneath the bed. There was a bottle on the floor. I reached for it. I noticed that it was empty. I examined it closely. It belonged to me. The prescription was for Haldol. I stared at it for a long time trying to remember when I had this prescription filled. I stood and walked over to the computer that sat on the desk in the room. I blew away the dust that had accumulated on the keyboard and screen.

I failed at my initial attempt to log in because I couldn't remember the password. I pondered for a while trying to think of what it could be. I tried everything. I was about to give up when I entered the date of my return home from the war. The computer responded. I logged into the internet and did a search on the prescription. I found a website that said that the prescription was for people who were schizophrenic, bipolar, or psychotic. I didn't remember getting these pills or even taking them, but what I couldn't understand was why the bottle was empty.

# CHAPTER
## 58

The next morning, with my head resting on the keyboard, I awakened to the sun's rays creeping through my bedroom window. I stood and walked over to the bed. I laid down on the side of the bed where Ariel once slept. There was a trace scent of her perfume still on her pillow. I smothered my face into it and inhaled. I was enjoying this moment when the phone rang.

"How you holding up, man?" he asked.

"I'm good. I think," I said.

"You're in a better mood."

"Going to the doctor was good for me. I was able to get a lot of stuff off of my chest."

"You up for some b-ball?" he asked.

Looking around the empty room, I said, "Sure, let's meet at the court?"

"Good, sounds like a plan. Are you sure that you're up to this?" he asked.

"Just don't show up without your A-game," I said.

"See you on the court."

Eddie was about to hang up the phone when I called out, "Eddie, I have a question."

"What's up man?"

"Have you ever seen me take any medications?"

"No, but I remember times when you needed some medication."

"Man, I'm serious."

"I am too."

"Look, just forget I ask. I'll see you in a little bit."

"Cool," he said, before hanging up.

■■ ☆ ☆ ☆ ■■

I was dribbling the ball and Eddie was trying to take it from me. I dribbled the ball between my legs, did a behind the back move, and then took the ball to the hole. Flying through the air, I made contact with the rim, almost shattering the glass.

"Yeah boy, that's what I'm talking about. Did you see that shit? The shit was so fly that Michael Jordan's taking notes."

Some young ladies who were watching the game began to stand and cheer.

*Let's get physical*
*Get down, get hard, get mean*
*Let's get physical*
*And beat that other team!*

One of the young ladies began to move her body as if she was in a rap video. I watched her for a minute, but then looked away. Eddie, on the other hand, began to drool. Using his distraction as an opportunity, I snatched the ball and then took it to the "hole."

Embarrassed, he said, "Alright man, calm down."

"You wasn't ready for that."

"I was ready. I just wouldn't think that a man who's mourning his wife and son would be at the top of his game."

"Weren't you the one who said that I had to move on?"

"Yeah…I just expected something different."

"Look, don't use my wife and son to distract me. I'm having a good time. Don't do this because you're losing."

"That's low man. I would never do that. I'm just saying that you've done a complete turn around."

"Someone once told me that you're either living or dying. I choose to live. Ariel would want it that way."

Patting me on the shoulder, he said, "I'm glad man."

Snatching the ball out of his hand, I said, "Good, now let me commence to finishing this ass-whooping."

**ll** ✶ ✶ ✶ **ll**

After the game, the young lady that was doing the seductive dance approached me. I was taking a sip of water, when she said, "Hi."

I looked at her.

"I was wondering if you would like to hook up sometime," she said.

In a serious tone, I said, "Little girl go home."

Insulted, but determined, she said, "I'm not little."

"I'm old enough to be your father."

"That's good because my daddy spoils me. Do you want to be my daddy too?"

"No, I want you to take your young ass home."

Sticking out her hand, she said, "Well, if you change your mind…"

I looked down to see what she was handing me and I thought about the day my sergeant committed suicide. I automatically looked for his car… for him, but there was nothing.

"Get away from me. Believe me, you don't want none of this."

"Let me be the judge of that…call me," she said, skipping away – ponytails bouncing up and down.

Eddie walked over to me. "Man, I would have tapped the hell out of that ass."

"Yeah and you would have took your pedophile ass to jail too. Believe me, that little girl did the smartest thing she could have ever done… and that was walk away."

# CHAPTER
## 59

"Slow down," I whispered to some woman I picked up at a bar in an attempt to relieve some tension.

"It feels so good," she said, jumping up and down.

"I said, slow down. I need this to last," I said, watching her take all ten inches of me.

"Oh-but-it-feels-so-good. Awww!"

"I said, slow down. You're going to make me..." Before I could finish my sentence her body began to shake and then she went limp. Pissed and frustrated, I threw her onto the floor. "Get your ass up and get the hell out of here."

"I'm sorry. I didn't mean to, but it felt so good."

"Whatever."

Dropping to her knees, she said, "Let me make it up to you."

"I said, get out."

"I'm sorry. I'll leave, but can we see each other tomorrow?"

"Have you ever heard of a one night stand?"

"Yes," she said.

"Have you heard of a hit and run?"

"Yes," she said again.

"You've just experienced both. Now get the fuck out."

"You bastard," she said, grabbing her clothes and screaming as she left the house.

I shook my head. She didn't realize how close she came to...my mind went back to the pressing issue between my legs. Sighing, I said, "Now I need to find somebody who can take care of this," I said, stroking myself. Suddenly, someone knocked on the door. I stood, put *it* away, and then answered the door.

"Look, I'm sorry. I really want us to have a good night. Let me take care of you. I promise I will."

Frustrated, I said, "I need somebody who can listen…take orders."

"I won't be able to sleep tonight unless I'm able to satisfy you."

Giving in because I wasn't in the mood to look for anyone else, I said, "Just come on in."

"Okay," she said, closing the door behind her.

I turned off all of the lights and walked over to the couch.

"You want to do it in the dark this time?" she asked, still standing by the door.

"Get over here," I instructed.

There was a bang. "Ouch! I hurt my knee," she said.

Before she could say another word I had her bent over and touching all fours. I tore her panties from under her skirt. She screamed. I don't know which hole I fell in, but it felt good. Real good.

"Ariel," I begged.

"Huh?" she said.

"Ariel," I begged some more.

"Huh?" she said again.

"ARIEL!" I screamed. My body began to jerk and then I collapsed right on top of her. I rammed her face into the couch.

When I was able to catch my breath, I stood to fix my clothes.

She stood to fix her clothing. "You don't mind if I use your bathroom, do you?"

"It's down the hall to the left," I said, pointing in its direction.

"Thank you." She left the room.

I sat on the couch to catch my breath. Before I knew it, I dozed off. When I awakened it was three hours later. Everything was quiet. I stood and looked out of the window to find that the woman's car was still there. I couldn't call out to her because I neglected to get her name. I went to the bathroom. No one was there. I continued down the hall. When I arrived at my bedroom door, my eyes grew wide. My breathing became so labored that I began to hyperventilate.

"What the fuck do you think you're doing?" I asked.

"Wha...wha?" she said, groggily.

Dragging her off of the bed by her hair, I said, "Bitch are you nuts?"

Fighting to get free, she said, "I didn't think that it was a problem. I was tired."

"Does this look like the damn Holiday Inn? What the hell is going on with you women? I go to the war and come home and every woman I have sex with think we got something going on." Dragging her ass to the front door, I turned and slapped her. "You were laying your head on the side of the bed that belongs to my wife."

Grabbing her face, she said, "You're married?"

"Until I die, bitch. Now get the fuck out."

"You shouldn't have hit me. You had no right," she said, screaming as she walked to her car.

I didn't say anything. I just slammed the door behind her. Hours later, there was another knock at the door. When I approached, I could see the red and blue lights flashing through the window. I unlocked and opened the door.

"How can I help you officer?"

"Well, lookie here. Don't I know you?" he asked.

He looked kind of familiar. "How can I help you this evening?"

"We got a complaint. One of your neighbors called and complained about a disturbance."

"Everything's fine officer. There's no disturbance here."

"Interesting, well you don't mind if I look around to make sure that everything is okay?"

"Sure officer, go right ahead," I said.

First, he took a tour around the outside of the home. Then, he came in. He walked around. I waited at the door while he walked around inside. When he came to the door, he looked me up and down.

"Your wife keeps a beautiful home."

"My wife is dead," I confirmed.

"I'm sorry to hear that."

"Thanks."

Once on the steps, he said, "Look, just keep it down okay."

"Sure," I said, agreeing so that he would get out of my house.

When he pulled off, I closed the door and went quietly to sleep.

# CHAPTER
# 60

The next day, I decided to visit my parents. I knew that I couldn't avoid them too much longer. At times, I regretted visiting them because I knew that my visit would guarantee a lecture. The thought of having to listen to it made me want to kill myself. It was strange how my mother had a way of making me feel like a child every time I was around her.

"Hey baby, how are you doing?" she said, standing over a hot stove making lunch for my father.

"I'm fine mama and how are you?" I kissed her on the cheek.

"I'm better now that you're here," she said, kissing me back.

"Thanks mama."

She looked me up and down. "Have you been eating? You're as thin as a toothpick."

"Yes mama, I've been eating."

"No, you're not. Look at those boney arms." She lifted my arm and shook it in the air. "Tsk, tsk, tsk. It's a shame. Just wasting away. Go sit out there with your daddy while I make you something to eat."

"Yes, mam." I did what I was told. I walked outside to the sunroom to find my father napping on the porch. He looked so peaceful. I didn't want to bother him.

As if he felt my presence, he jumped up and then said, "Hey, young pup."

I smiled. "Hey daddy, how did you know that I was standing here?"

"You ain't the only one who has done a tour."

I smiled. "Sometimes, I forget."

"Sit down junior before I have to subdue you." He stood and pretended to put me in a headlock, but gave up when his back began to hurt. "Ouch!"

"I thought so ol' man." I began to help him sit down.

"Boy, you better be glad. I'm telling you…back in the day, I would have given you a run for your money."

We both laughed.

Rubbing his back, he said. "Whew, that took a lot out of me."

"Me too," I said, pretending to rub my back too.

We laughed again.

"Daddy, how you doing?" I asked.

"I'm fine. Why do you ask?" he said, trying to adjust the chair.

I reached out to help him. "I was just wondering."

Slapping my hand to indicate that he didn't need any help, he said, "Wondering about what?"

"Just things," I said, rubbing the place where he hit me.

"Izrael, what's going on?"

My father always knew when something was wrong. I paused and then said, "I've been going through some things."

"Like what?"

"I can't really explain it." I wanted to tell him about the things that have happened over the years and tell him about the wound that wouldn't heal, but I knew that he wouldn't understand and it would only worry him.

Looking at me, he tried to explain what I couldn't. "It's hard to wash the horrors away. It's hard to ignore the continue screaming and cries." Briefly, he looked like he was being tormented by something. He shook his head, took a deep breath and then continued, "Even now…after all of these years, I still see bodies lying in the streets...babies blown to pieces," he paused, wiped tears from his eyes, and then continued, "You never get over that shit. No one prepares you for that crap, but you're stuck with the bad memories and the bad feelings that come from it for the rest of your damn life."

"That's for sure," I said, in agreement.

Recalling a moment from his past, he said, "Let me tell you a story, son. You know I remember, as a young boy, a friend of mine was so desperate to get in a gang. I never understood his need to belong to something that would make you kill your own people...steal from your own people...sell drugs to your own people, but he did...no matter what the price." He looked at me as if I could tell him why, but decided not to revisit my ugly past, he continued, "Well, after a night of partying at one of the neighborhood house parties, we all gathered in the street to laugh and talk. Suddenly an argument broke out. A crowd of people formed a circle around the two individuals that were arguing. I was curious. I wanted to know what was going on so I made a path through the crowd and found myself in the front row. One of the individuals arguing was my boy – my friend. He and this person were arguing about which one of them was the toughest. Suddenly, the argument took an ugly turn. The other person pulled out a gun, placed one bullet in the barrel and spun it. My heart began to race. I grabbed my friend's arm and pleaded for him to walk away, but he didn't. He had something to prove. I watched nervously as each person took a turn placing the gun to their head and pulling the trigger. This happened five times before finally, it was my boy's turn. He pulled the trigger. The gun went off. My boy stood there, for what seemed like a lifetime with his eyes bulging out of his head and his mouth hanging open. Suddenly, a stream of blood rolled down the side of his head. He looked at me. I looked at him. Next, his body fell to the ground. The crowd dispersed. I stood over his lifeless body as the blood continued to stream from the hole in his head. I stood there asking myself why? What did he prove? Why would he sacrifice his life for something so meaningless? I couldn't understand it. Suddenly, like everyone else, I ran away, but I never stopped thinking about him or that night.   One day, as a soldier, we were doing a sweep to count the casualties and the ones still alive. I found a body lying on the ground. I remembered my friend and I asked myself those same questions. To this day, I still can't figure this shit out."

There was a long pause. I thought that he was done with his story, but then he started again. "You know what I realized? I realized that the only thing that separated me from those boys lying on the ground is that I am still alive to tell the story. Other than that, we all put our lives on the line for shit we would never understand or even make sense. You understand what I'm trying to say?"

"Yes daddy, I understand," I said.

"I say all of that to say this…we will never be able to figure any of this shit out. We just have to figure out a way to deal with it…a way to get through it."

"How do you deal with it daddy?" I asked, trying to find the answers to a lot of unanswered questions.

"I devote a lot of time to helping others like us – to help them get back on their feet. For every life that I've taken for my country is a life that I dedicate my life to save."

"Is that all?"

"No son, I pray. I pray a lot."

"Daddy, sometimes I feel like I'm going crazy. At times, it's hard to figure out what's real and what's not."

"You are going to feel that way for a while. Those motherfuckers think they understand the war…they have no clue. A lot of young men…some of the smartest people in the world are fucked up!" he said, with a lot of emotion.

My mother yelled out. "Daddy, watch your mouth!"

"Sorry about that mama!" he yelled over his shoulder. He grabbed my hand and held it tightly. "I love you son."

"I love you too, dad."

Nothing else was said that afternoon. I knew what I had to do.

# CHAPTER
## <u>61</u>

I thought deeply about the things my father said and he was right. I've done some bad shit and now it was time to change my life. At about 2300 hours, after visiting with my father, I ended up on the steps of my family's church. I did so many bad things in my life that I thought that once I stepped over the threshold, the ground would open up and suck me in, but that did not happen. Once inside, I walked through the building until I found the preacher sitting in his study.

I walked through the door without knocking. "I want to give my life to God," I said.

Accustomed to having lost souls wander in, in the middle of the night, he said, "Really? And why do you want to do that, son?" He closed the book that he was reading.

"I've done some bad things, Reverend." Standing there I realized that the preacher didn't recognize me. I had to admit that I hadn't sat in one of the church's pews since I was a child.

"Before you give your life to God, it is recommended that you confess all of your sins and repent before Him."

I laughed. "God and I have an understanding."

"Do you want to tell me about it?"

"You don't want to know, Reverend. Plus, if I told you, I would be forced to kill you," I said, taking a seat in one of the chairs.

The preacher laughed, but stopped when he realized that I wasn't laughing with him. He cleared his throat before saying, "Well huh…have you ever been baptized, son?"

"No sir, that's why I'm here. I've done a lot of bad things in my life. I know that I cannot completely fix things by saying I'm sorry. I have to find a way to give back…to do right. I believe that I should start here."

"In **Acts 2:38** – *Peter said to them, "Repent, and each of you be baptized in the name of Jesus Christ for the forgiveness of your sins; and you will receive the gift of the Holy Spirit."*

"That's all well and good, but I didn't come here tonight for a Bible lesson."

"Son, don't forget where you are."

"Sorry about that."

"All is forgiven."

"Okay, so when do we start?" I asked, eager to change the things in my life.

"It's not that simple. There is a process. First, you must repent. Second, we require that you take some classes to prepare you to be saved. The classes will also give you more insight of His word and what will be expected of you. Plus, it's the middle of the night. What's the rush?"

"Look," I said, seriously. "I don't have a lot of time. You see, I need this. It's a matter of life or death…mine or someone else's."

Twitching nervously, the preacher said, "Well, I've never had someone request an emergency baptism before."

I didn't say anything.

"The pool isn't ready. I can "bless" you – pray over you right here and then later, we can get you baptized," he suggested.

I leaned closer to him. "Maybe you didn't understand me. I said that I want to be baptized. So, you need to figure out a way to get that pool filled."

There was an uncomfortable silence. Fifteen minutes later the pool was ready. The preacher offered me a robe, but I refused it. I didn't want anything between me and my salvation. I removed all of my clothing. The preacher looked away.

"Let's do this," I insisted.

The preacher walked into the water first. I watched as it rose to his waist. I followed closely behind him. The water felt cold against my skin. He quoted a scripture as I entered the water.

"**Acts 2:38** *says, Then Peter said unto them, Repent, and be baptized every one of you in the name of Jesus Christ for the remission of sins, and ye shall receive the gift of the Holy Ghost.*"

I closed my eyes and received the word.

The preacher began to pray. As he prayed, I whispered my sins in an attempt to cleanse my soul – to seek peace before the cleansing.

"And forgive us our trespasses," he prayed.

*The bloodshed of innocent women and children.*

"As we forgive those who trespass against us," he continued to pray.

*The prostitutes, the guy in the bathroom, the teenager, and the jogger.*

The preacher stopped praying. "Excuse me?"

"Stop talking and do your job," I instructed.

He frowned. "Where was I? Oh yes, and lead us not into temptation, but deliver us from evil." He looked me up and down.

*Yes, deliver us.*

"Amen," he said.

"Amen," I repeated.

Suddenly, he placed one hand in the arch of my back and placed the other hand on my chest. He threw my body back into the water and held me there for what seemed like forever. I didn't fight him. I floated in the water. I could see him through the current.

I remember thinking that I could lay there and end it all – completely give my life to God, but as I waited for the cleansing to take place I realized as justified as taking my life would be for the lives I've taken, I didn't want to die – at least not now.

I couldn't hold my breath any longer. I grabbed for his hand. He let me up. When I stood, he had a disappointed look on his face – as if someone had diverted his plans. I wiped the water from my face. I looked at him. He looked back.

I smiled. "I guess that God have other plans for me."

"I guess so."

We looked at each other.

"How do you feel son?" he asked.

"Like a new man…like a new man."

# CHAPTER
## 62

The next day, I awoke feeling like a new person. Before my shower, I removed the dressing on my wound. I smiled. The wound had healed. I was so excited. I looked closely at the wound. Upon close inspection, I could see it – the cross was no longer upside down. I laughed; glad that it had finally healed, I showered, dressed, and left.

I jumped into my vehicle and drove until I found myself parked in front of a VA hospital on the west side. I waited outside for a minute to think about what I was doing. I wanted to make right all of my wrongs. I wanted to give back, but was I making the right decision. Did I really want to volunteer my time reliving the atrocities of war? While I contemplated the idea, I could hear the words, *"Soldier, it's time."* I stepped out of the vehicle and walked toward the building.

After spending what seemed like hours in the Office of Human Resources, I was given the honor to volunteer. I was assigned a badge, given the responsibilities of my position, told to stay away from the twelfth floor, and that my first responsibility was to visit with each bedridden veteran on the first floor.

The first day was hard. Looking at all of the dismembered bodies of the once young and healthy made me angry. I became upset. I ran down the hall to the men's washroom to calm down.

"Why?" I asked myself repeatedly. "They didn't deserve this…none of us." I banged my hand so hard on the sink that it almost came completely out of the wall. A janitor walked in.

"Are you okay man?"

Turning on the water and splashing some on my face, I said, "I'm fine." He left and I stood staring in the mirror. A voice spoke to me, *You have to suck it up soldier. While you are in here there is a war going on out there…now get your shit together and get out there.* I screamed, "Yes sir," and then dried my face. I saluted the image in the mirror and then left the bathroom.

My first visit was with a young man who lost both of his legs via complications of some infected bullet wounds. When I walked into his room, he didn't acknowledge my presence. He never diverted his attention away from the television which was on a cartoon channel.

Every once in awhile, he would laugh, but he never looked at me. At first, I wanted to introduce myself, but decided against it. Instead, I sat in the chair next to his bed. This went on for about a week until one day, right in the middle of *Tom & Jerry*, he turned off the television and said, "Hello."

I was so taken-aback, that I didn't know what to say.

"Don't worry. That happens a lot around here," he said, nonchalantly.

"I'm sorry. My name is Izrael," I said, extending my hand.

He extended his. That's when I noticed that he was missing two of his fingers.

Again, I didn't know what to say.

"I told you," he said.

"I'm sorry, man."

"Stop apologizing, you didn't do anything. Unless, that was you shooting from behind that parked vehicle."

"Naw man, that wasn't me."

"I didn't think so. Now, don't tell me. They sent you in here to cheer up the cripple."

"Naw man, I just came in here to see if you needed anything."

"I need some legs and some fingers if you got any," he said.

I didn't say anything.

Looking around and trying to change the subject, I said, "I noticed that I've been the only one here to see you."

"My mother usually comes through here on the weekends."

"And your father?" I asked.

"I don't get to see him much. He hates me."

"Why do you say that?"

"I went to the war instead of going to college. I had a full basketball scholarship. Long story short, I don't see any lay-ups in my future."

"I'm sorry to hear that, man."

"Again, don't be sorry. Anyway, what can a brotha do to get a change of scenery around here?"

I laughed. If I wasn't standing there talking to him, I would swear that he was a ghost. I thought that having blonde hair and pale skin from the lack of exposure to the sun would exclude anyone that had those characteristics from being a brotha. I guess you don't have to be black anymore. Maybe the rules changed while I was doing my tour.

"You never told me your name," I said.

"Names complicate things. You probably won't be around long."

I thought about that and then said, "Don't say that."

"Yeah right," he said, sadly.

Wanting to change the subject, I said, "Let me go ask the nurse if I can move you."

"Man, you don't have to ask her shit. It ain't like you are trying to break me out of here and believe me, you can't hurt me. That's already been taken care of."

I stepped into the hall. I stood against the wall out of his sight.

Seeing that young man lying in that bed, left me overwhelmed with emotion. Suddenly, the walls felt like they were closing in on me. I was pissed. I wanted to put my hand through the wall...I wanted to hurt someone. I wanted to make someone pay for his pain. I couldn't understand why I was feeling this way for a complete stranger, but I had heard his story before read from the lips of other wide-eyed and disillusioned young men. I closed my eyes to see them singing and marching toward the unknown. I could hear their cries for help. My chest began to hurt. I grabbed my head hoping that the noises would stop. Suddenly, as if someone intervened, the noises stopped and my chest stop hurting. A weird calm came over me. I found myself looking up as if I wanted to hear Him take responsibility for the sudden sense of peace, but there was nothing. I let it go for the moment.

After getting permission to move the patient, I received a wheelchair and some advice from one of the nurses.

"Look, a lot of these people want you to feel sorry for them. Don't do it. Treat them like you would treat any other cripple on the street – talk about them behind their backs and then park in their handicap spaces." She hit me in the back and laughed so hard that she almost choked on her tongue.

"You think that shit was funny?" I asked.

"Yeah, you know how they are...whine, whine, and whine. I need this and I need that...what they need is to shut up and be glad that they didn't come home in a body bag." She laughed again. "That's all they ever do. They're not like the rest of us."

My eyes grew cold. I leaned closer to her. "Really? I'm not like you. You see, I am one of them. Although, I'm not lying in one of those beds, I suffer from a condition that causes me to randomly snap the necks of ignorant motherfuckers." I leaned in closer, so close, I could count the hairs on her chin. "Are you an ignorant motherfucker?" I didn't allow her to answer. "Yes, you are, but you're going to change right. It's not hard. Just imagine repeating that dumb shit, you just said, through a hole in your neck." Her body began to shake. This pleased me. "Now, if you tell anyone, I would swear up and down that you are delusional. Now here's what you are going to do to make up for the dumb shit you just said. Later, my friend over there would like a porterhouse steak, cooked hard...he's seen enough blood in his life. He would also like a baked potato, steamed vegetables, and a glass of wine."

Nervously, she said, "But I can't do that. That's against the hospital's rules."

"I'm sure that being an asshole is also against the hospital's rules. Now, you can and you will. Also, my man could use a blowjob. You can make that happen after I leave. I will expect to hear all about it when I come to visit him tomorrow." I stepped away from her. "Now, let's get on top of that meal." She attempted to say something. I placed my fingers onto her lips. "Shhhhh. Now be a good girl and get on that." I walked away. She stood watching me until I disappeared out of sight. At his bedside, I lowered the railing and lifted his body from what seemed to be turning into his casket. I wrapped a blanket around what was left of his legs and pushed him down the hall. We went into the visiting room where there were other visitors and their families. I pushed his chair close to a window. He smiled. He seemed to enjoy having the sun's rays on his face.

"Would you like to go outside?"

Excitedly, he asked, "Can you do that?"

"I don't think that we would have a problem," I assured him.

"Sure."

I rolled him down the hall pass the nurses' station. I smiled at the nurse. She looked away. I rolled the patient to the elevator that took us to the lobby.

"I can't believe that we are actually doing this."

I smiled.

I rolled him to an area where there were benches. He looked at the sky, smiled, and said, "My name is Benny. People call me, Lil' T."

"Why do they call you, Lil' T?"

"My last name is Thompson. I'm a junior."

"That's strange, me too," I said. I extended my hand. "It's nice to meet you Benny...I mean Lil' T."

We didn't say anything else for the rest of the afternoon. I began to notice that he was too quiet. I looked over at him to find that he had fallen asleep. I rolled his chair back to his room. When I attempted to lift his body back into bed, he woke up.

"Hey, what's going on?" he said.

"You fell asleep. I will never accuse you of being the perfect host."

"Funny," he said, pulling his blankets over himself. Suddenly, the door opened. The nurse walked in pushing a cart carrying two trays. When she removed the tops that sat on top of the plates, Benny's face lit up.

"Oh wow, it isn't my birthday."

"I know. This kind nurse just felt like being nice. Didn't she?"

She nodded her head, "Yes" and proceeded to leave the room.

"Oh nurse, don't forget desert," I said, reminding her.

She huffed and then left the room.

"We're getting desert too?" he asked.

"Not 'we', just you. You deserve it."

"So you did all of this? Thanks man. I really appreciate it." He licked his lips. "I don't know where to start."

"Just enjoy it, man."

We were about to dig in, when he stopped us to say grace. I listened until he was finished. "Amen."

"Amen," I echoed.

We ate. We laughed. After dinner, he fell asleep and then I left. As I waited to get on the elevator, I looked down the hall towards Benny's room. I saw the nurse enter his room. I smiled, entered the elevator and then went home.

# CHAPTER
## 63

The next day, Benny was smiling from ear-to-ear.

"What's up man? What happened to you?"

He motioned for me to come close. "Man, the nurse came in here after you left and...let's just say that she hooked me up. Damn, felt good as hell. It's been a l-o-n-g time since I've had that done."

Laughing, I said, "Really?"

"For a minute, I thought that I had died and gone to Heaven – almost made me get up and walk." He started laughing. "I'm telling you man. She did it like her life depended on it."

"You don't say," I said, coyly.

"I do say. Man, she even asked me if I wanted seconds. I don't know where it came from, but I'm glad it came. I only have one complaint. I wish it was that chocolate honey that shares that desk with her. Man, I've had a lot of fantasies about that one, but don't get me wrong...with my eyes closed she could have been ShanayNay off of the Martin Lawrence show...fo' sho'...I don't even care. That shit felt good," he said, extending his hand to give me "dap."

Listening to him made me laugh. I was just glad that he was happy. That afternoon, I gave him a shave and a hair-cut. We laughed and played cards all night. Later, his mother arrived. She spoke and introduced herself. I excused myself to allow them some privacy. When I walked in the hall, I noticed a portly gentleman sitting outside of Benny's door. I walked passed him, but decided to go back. I stood in front of him. He looked up.

"Can I help you?" he asked.

"Are you Benny's father?"

"Who wants to know?" he asked.

"His friend." Saying that made me feel awkward.

"Well friend, I don't think it's any of your business who I am."

"Really?" I took the seat next to him. "Well if you are Benny's father, I think that it's real fucked up that you sit out here instead of going in to visit him."

He was about to say something, but I interrupted him. "Hear me out. Do you like knowing that he lies in that bed alone wishing for your love and approval? Do you think that it is okay for that young man to lie in that bed day-in and day-out thinking that you've abandoned him? He's already loss so much, does he have to lose you too?" I stood and began to walk away.

He walked up behind me.

With a face that had been ravished by the years, he looked at me. "He's lucky to have you."

"He'll be luckier to have you," I said, as I continued to walk away.

# CHAPTER
## 64

"Hey man, where have you been? I've been calling you almost everyday for the past couple of weeks. It's a good thing that you answered the phone. I was about to fill-out a missing person's report," Eddie said.

"Ease-up man, it's all good. Matter of fact, things couldn't be better." I knew that my parents had appointed Eddie as my "keeper" so I didn't get upset when he was all up in my business.

"What's going on? You dating?" he asked.

Frustrated, I said, "Do you have a piece of paper and a pen handy?"

"For what?"

"I need you to write something down."

"Okay, I have one right here. Go ahead."

"Start writing the following...No woman could ever...ever take Ariel's place. Did you get that?"

"Dude, why did you ask me to write that down?"

"Because I want to make sure that I never have to say it again and if you have the desire to ask me, just refer to your notes."

"Damn man, why you gotta be like that?"

"Because I know how easy it is for some brothas to move on and maybe this makes me a punk, but I will never stop loving Ariel, no matter what."

"Awww, that's sweet as hell. Almost made me cry," he joked.

Dismissing his comment, I said, "Whatever...why did you call?"

"I wanted to see if you wanted to get out on the court today?"

"I can't man."

"Okay, I know what you told me, but there is no way you can tell me that there isn't another woman in your life. A woman is the only thing, short of death, that would keep you away from the court."

"Do you have that piece of paper handy?"

"I'm just saying," he paused and then said, "You got a job?"

"No...well, sort of."

"What's 'sort of'?"

"I'm doing some volunteer work over at the VA hospital."

"Really?"

"Yeah, why?"

"Because you don't seem like the charitable type," he pointed out.

"I don't seem like a lot of things. It's all about evolution."

"E-v-o...who?"

"Some advice man, instead of spending so much time playing babysitter, you might want to pick up a dictionary. It will make our conversations go a lot smoother."

"You are on a roll today," he retorted.

"If you say so. Anyway, I have to get out of here. I'll be late. I'm glad you called. I feel kinda special."

"Whatever...anyway, call yo' mama so that this brotha can get some sleep."

"I gotcha. I will call you later."

"Sure," he said, before hanging up.

Glancing over at the clock on the kitchen wall, I noticed that it was getting late. "Well Ariel, here I go again." I said, talking to myself. Suddenly, a sense of loneliness swept over me. I walked over to the picture frame that held our wedding photo. I ran my finger over it. "I know that you would never intentionally hurt our son. I should have told you that while you were alive. Maybe, you wouldn't have killed yourself." I kissed the photo. "It was a mistake. Just know that if I thought that you were behind the death of my son, I would have killed you myself. I love you, honey." I put the photo down, grabbed my keys, and headed for the hospital.

# CHAPTER
## 65

"How are you doing, Benny?" When I walked into Benny's room, he wasn't lying in bed, but already sitting in a wheel-chair waiting for me.

"Better than ever man…so what are we doing today?"

"Whatever you want to do man," I said.

"I was wondering if we could go down to the visitors' lounge and maybe play some checkers."

"That sounds like a plan. Have you eaten already?"

"Yeah man, I had steak and potatoes for breakfast too. I feel like a king."

I smiled. "Well, I'm glad." Grabbing the bars on the back of his chair to push him down the hall, he stopped me.

"I got it man," he said, taking control of the chair.

This made me smile.

When we entered the hall, I noticed that the nurse was smiling.

"What's up with ol' girl?" I asked him.

"Man, she's been coming in my room taking good care of me. I had to break her off a little bit this morning. She can't seem to get enough."

I began to laugh so hard that my chest began to hurt. "What are the odds?" I said, without realizing that I had said it aloud.

"The odds of what?"

"Nothing man, just get ready to get your ass whooped, okay?"

"Yeah, right."

# CHAPTER
## 66

Today Benny didn't look good. I could tell that something wasn't right. He kept drifting in and out of sleep. We were playing cards. He was winning, but couldn't enjoy the game because he was so lethargic. I rolled him back to his room, lifted his body onto his bed, and placed his blankets over him. I didn't want to leave him. I wanted to be there when he woke up. I needed to know that he was okay.

I was feeling a little tired myself. I put two chairs together that were sitting on the opposite sides of the room. I removed the pillow and blanket from the empty bed and made a place to rest. I turned the television to the cartoon channel and decided to watch. I was drifting off when I saw a gurney carrying a sheet covered body being pushed down the hall. On any other occasion this wouldn't have bothered me, because I've seen a lot of dead bodies while I served, but something made me get up from my chair.

I followed the orderly and gurney down the hall. He stopped at the elevator at the end of the hall, pushed the button, and when the door opened he entered. I stepped into the elevator with him. He didn't acknowledge my presence. When the elevator stopped at the designated floor, he exited. I followed and again he didn't acknowledge my presence. As I walked, I noticed that the lighting in the hall began to dim. What was once a brightly lit hall was now becoming darker and darker. He rolled the body into a room and then lined it up against the wall with the others. I was standing in the doorway  taking in the image when the orderly walked pass me without speaking.

I walked in. There were four bodies in the room – two on each side of the room. One by one, I looked at them, pulling back the sheets to reveal their wounds – their stories. The first body had multiple holes in its chest. The second body was covered in open sores. The third body had no arms or legs – just a torso remained. I approached the last body. I stood over it – afraid. For the first time in five years, I felt fear. A chill ran through me. I hesitated. Then with hands that were now shaking uncontrollably, I pulled the sheet back.

He looked so peaceful – young. It was hard to see why he lay among the dead because there were no visible wounds or scars – at least that's what I thought. I was looking at his face, his chest, and then my eyes found themselves focused on what at first seemed like a birthmark right below his navel. I reached out to touch it. Suddenly, blood began to ooze from it. I stepped back. I looked down to find that there was blood on my shirt. The spot became bigger. I touched the spot where the blood was. Something wasn't right. I lifted my shirt to find a hole in my abdomen. Next, the corpse lifted his head. "Help me," he pleaded. "Help me." He reached out to me. I began to panic. I began to convulse with fear. I opened my mouth to scream, but nothing came out. I ran out of the room. Stumbling down the hall, I looked back to find that nothing was there. I began to push the button to the elevator. I continued to look over my shoulder frantically while I waited for the elevator. Suddenly, the door of the elevator opened. I looked inside. The corpse was standing in front of me. "Ahhhhh!!!!!" I screamed.

"Please help me," he begged. "Help me."

"Ahhh!!!!" I screamed, kicking the covers off of my legs.

Benny grabbed the remote to turn the television down. "Damn man, what the hell is wrong with you?"

"Where am I?" I asked, hysterically.

"You are in the hospital, man…visiting me," he said, confused.

"Man, I just had the scariest dream. Benny…the shit was so real."

"What man? What are you talking about?"

As I was about to replay the events of my dream to Benny an orderly walked pass the room with a covered body on a stretcher.

"I gotta go," I said, running out of the room without saying good-bye.

**❚❚ ✯ ✯ ✯ ❚❚**

The next day, we played cards for hours. When he became exhausted, I rolled him back to his room. After tucking him into bed, we had dinner and watched television until he fell asleep. We did this for several weeks until one day I walked into his room to find his mother standing over him in tears. His father stood next to her – rubbing her shoulders to console her. I looked up to find that the television wasn't on. I looked in the direction of the bed. Benny wasn't moving. I walked over to his bed. I looked at his face. It was so peaceful. He even had a smile on his face. I touched his hand. It was cold. I stared at him. I felt weary like I suddenly had the weight of the world on my shoulders. My eyes filled with tears.

Without looking at his parents, I asked the obvious. "Is he dead?"

"Yes," they both said simultaneously.

I sighed. I turned to leave the room when his father stopped me. He grabbed my hand. He placed a photo in my hand. My vision was so blurred, I couldn't see the image. I walked into the hallway to find the nurse that had befriended him crying. I walked down the hall to the elevator. Once I was on, I wiped the tears from my eyes. I looked at the photo. It was Benny in a high school basketball uniform holding a basketball and smiling like it was the happiest day of his life.

# CHAPTER
# 67

"He's dead, Eddie," I said.

"Man, I'm so sick of this shit."

"What man? What are you talking about?"

"Another young man cut down in the prime of his life and for what?" Not waiting for my answer, he said, "For nothing. That's what. I can't take it man. I'm telling you I can't take it."

"What are you going to do? You can't change shit."

"I could write the President…"

I interrupted, "And say what? I could hear you now. 'Hello, Mr. President. You gotta a minute? Ummm, this war shit doesn't sit well with me and I think that you should put an end to it right now. Also, could you give every brotha in the world a Cadillac? We would really appreciate it." I started laughing. "Get the fuck out of here. He don't care about you. He don't care about me. He don't give a shit about none of us. I thought that you knew that."

"Man, I'm just saying. Makes me so mad…just makes me want to do something."

"Do what? All you can do is the same thing that everyone else is doing and that's praying for a safe return of the young men and women already over there, and that this shit would be over soon."

He didn't say anything.

"Eddie, did you hear me?"

"I heard you man. Look I have to go. I'll talk to you later?"

"Yeah man, later."

It bothered me to think that Eddie was right, but he was. As I was sitting there thinking of the things he said, someone knocked on the door.

"Who is it?" I asked, looking through the peephole. It was a man in a police's uniform. I opened the door. I recognized him.

"Hello officer, how can I help you?"

"Well, Mr. Izrael, it's funny that you ask. We were at the crime scene where a jogger was killed."

I pretended not to know what he was talking about. "Okay?"

"And we have an eyewitness that said that she saw you there."

"I'm confused. What are we talking about?" I asked.

Last year, a young lady was murdered on a trail while jogging. The incident happened at the hospital you were visiting at that night."

"And you know this how?"

"Because we have a video tape of you leaving the building right before the murder," he confirmed.

"I was there, but I didn't kill anyone."

"I didn't say that you killed anyone," said the officer as he took out a note pad and a pen. "I just thought that maybe you could shed some light on some things."

"I just assumed that was why you were here...sorry about that."

"Interesting." He wrote something down in his pad and then continued, "No, I just thought that maybe you saw something."

"No, I didn't."

"Who were you visiting at the hospital that night?"

"My son had just died..."

"I'm sorry to hear that."

I continued, "I needed to get away from the hospital so I ran to the park."

"And you didn't see anything?"

"No, I'm sorry, my mind was on my son."

"Can your wife corroborate your story?"

"No, she's dead too."

"Damn, that's right...that's messed-up. Sorry to hear that. So both of them are dead?"

"Yes."

"Tragic."

"Yes."

There was a moment of awkward silence.

"Closing his pad, he said, "Well, I'm sorry to have bothered you."

Opening the door, I said, "Not a problem. I'm sorry that I couldn't help you more."

"It's not a problem. We're going to catch this guy. It's just a matter of time."

"Well, I wish you luck in finding him."

He smiled and said, "Thank you."

**‖ ✮ ✮ ✮ ‖**

I drifted off to sleep in front of the television. A few hours later, I was awakened by someone calling my name. "Izrael," the voice said, gently. I looked around the room. Again, I heard, "Izrael."

"Who is it," I asked.

"Izrael," the voice continued to call.

"Where are you?" I asked again, looking around the room.

"Right here, Izrael," the voice said.

"Where?" I asked again.

"Right in front of you."

I looked around the room. Then I looked down at the television screen. The screen was black. Suddenly, as if I touched the remote, a movie came on. Curious, I watched. Initially, I didn't recognize anyone in the movie, but then the scene changed. There was a woman on her knees pleading for her life. She's hit in the head with something. Blood squirted from her head and like something out of the Twilight Zone the blood came through the television and ended up all over me. She screamed, "My name is Wanda...Wanda!"

*Wanda is dead.*

Freaking out, I stumbled backward. *This ain't real. This ain't real.* As I stood to back away from the television, the screen changed again. I was walking away when I heard the voice of someone else. I recognized that voice. I came back over to the sofa and sat down.

"Did you remember?" he asked.

"I told you that I would never forget."

"Have you done what you've promised?"

"I will," I confirmed.

"Thank you," said the corpse of a soldier with whom I promised I would call his family and tell them that he loved them. I walked over to the phone. Before picking up the receiver, I looked down at my hands. The blood was gone. I picked up the phone. There was someone already on the other line. "Hello," the person said.

Putting the phone to my ear, I said, "Hello."

I recognized the voice. "While we are conducting this investigation, don't leave town," he said.

**‖ ★ ★ ★ ‖**

"Eddie, man, I have been really freaking out lately."

"And hello to you too," Eddie said, groggily.

"I'm telling you man...some really weird shit has been going on."

"What's going on man?"

Recognizing that something was wrong with him, I asked, "What's going on with you man?"

"It's these headaches...not to mention the shit that's going on between me and my "ex."

"You get headaches too and I thought that it was over between you two."

"The answer to your first question is "yes" and the answer to the second is, "me too"...She really wants to get back together."

"Tell me something new. She's been singing that song since she got caught."

"Well...I've been thinking about it and..."

Disappointed, I said, "Don't even say it, man."

"I'm just saying...I'm not getting any younger. I know she ain't shit, but I've been spending some time with her and the kid..."

"When were you going to tell me? I thought that we were boys."

"We are, but I have to admit that I like the idea of being a father," he said.

"What happened to the baby's daddy?"

"I don't know and I don't care. He doesn't have to be from one of my seeds to be mine. Plus, I don't have shit else. I want a family. I want to love and take care of someone. I want someone to need me and I need them. This ain't really all about her. She's low for what she did, but she did it and I don't blame her...completely. Anyway, six years is a long time to do without when you were accustomed to getting it three times a day."

"Damn man, you were putting it down like that?"

We started laughing.

"That's why I thought that I should tell you that we are thinking about moving out of state. With all of the shit going on...everytime I turn around they are finding a body...it's not safe to raise a child here."

Thinking about what he said, I said, "You know what man...do what you gotta do. So when are you leaving?"

"I'm packing now."

"Damn...well, I understand. Just don't leave without saying good-bye."

"Will do."

**❚❚ ✦ ✦ ✦ ❚❚**

A few days later, I decided to stop by and visit Eddie and extend some help for his big move, but when I arrived he was already gone. The house was completely boarded up and the yard looked like no one had cut the grass for months. I looked through one of the cracks in the boards and found that there was nothing. The house looked like no one had ever lived there.

# CHAPTER
# 68

I didn't sleep that night. My head hurt. I placed my hands to my temples to stop the throbbing pain, but it wouldn't stop. I closed my eyes and tried to relax, but the images didn't go away and the pain didn't stop. I went into the bathroom to retrieve the bottle of painkillers, but it was empty. I became angry – frustrated. I turned to kick something out of anger. Without thinking, I kicked the closest thing to me – the toilet. I kicked it so hard that the toilet seat came off and went flying into the wall. I automatically braced myself for what should have been excruciating pain, but there was nothing.

I was confused. I looked down to see if there was a wound or anything on my foot, but there was nothing. Intrigued by this, I ran through the house kicking everything in sight, but there was nothing, but a trail of holes in the walls, kicked shoes, and debris throughout. I found this to be fascinating so I went into the kitchen grabbed a knife and placed it to my thigh and with one quick thrust I lunged it into my leg. Nothing. *What the fuck?"* There was no blood – nothing, but a hole in my leg from where I removed the blade. *Holy shit!*

**❚❚ ✭ ✭ ✭ ❚❚**

"Mr. Williams…What were you thinking?" the doctor, asked looking at the wound.

"Williams is my wife's name and clearly I wasn't thinking or I wouldn't be sitting here with a gaping hole in my leg."

"You could have killed yourself. You just missed the main artery…you could have bled out."

"I could have, but I don't know if you've noticed it…I haven't lost a drop of blood."

"You need to thank God for that."

"I'll thank Him later, but in the meantime, I need someone to explain this shit."

"I can't explain it. I should be looking at a dead man."

"Maybe you are."

"Have you been doing drugs?"

"No."

"Have you been drinking?"

"No."

"Then I don't understand it. You see, a victim heavily under the influence can cause the body to react slowly to trauma or pain."

"Really?"

"Unless there's a blood disorder which we would have to test for."

"Wrap it up doctor, I'm good. Let's not fix what doesn't seem to be broken."

"But sir, you have to let me stitch it up."

"Don't worry about it doctor. Hand me a couple of those bandages. If it gets worst, I'll come see you."

"But I don't think that you understand."

Laughing, I said, "I do understand. I finally understand. Ain't none of this shit real. The reason why my leg didn't bleed is because it didn't happen. You're not even here."

With a caring look on his face, he said, "I think that you should come back and see me so that we can place you under observation."

Walking toward the door, I said, "Observe my ass leaving."

# CHAPTER
## 69

I needed to get out. I decided that although the bar brought back bad memories for me, it was a familiar place and I felt like home there. On the expressway, there was nothing between my thoughts and me. As the rush of cool air entered and bounced off my car windows, I thought about my life and where it was headed. A sudden sensation of foreshadowing came over my thoughts as I envisioned bouts of loneliness, death, and despair. I shook it off and removed the thoughts from my mind.

When I entered, I grabbed a seat at the end of the bar. I was enjoying a game on the plasma television, when he walked in. At first it was hard to recognize him through the dim lights, and cigarette smoke. I watched as he fought his way to the bar. He ordered a beer, sat down, and proceeded to stuff his face with the nuts that were in a bowl. He was watching the game when I decided to say "hello."

Squinting his eyes, he said, "Is this a "cowinkadink" or what? Damn man, how are you?"

His informality made me a little uncomfortable. "Hello officer," I responded, dryly.

Moving his drink, himself, and the bowl of nuts closer to me, he asked, "Who are you here with?"

"I'm alone," I responded.

"Me too," he affirmed.

"Really, I would have never thought," I said, sarcastically.

"Yeah, can you believe it? Anyway, what brings you here?"

"I was trying to get away for a moment."

Sipping his beer, he said, "Man, you can't do that shit in a bar. You can't even be alone on the toilet with cell-phones and everything else that's out there. Because of technology, we are all accessible. Try taking a shit…"

I didn't like where this conversation was going so I decided to find another place to sit. "Look, it was nice seeing you man."

"Hey, where are you going?" He grabbed his drink. "I'll just follow you."

*Damn. Annoying fucker.* "Sure," I said over my shoulder.

"Thanks man, I don't want to look like a loser sitting all by myself."

*Too late.* Finding a booth, I sat down. At first, he sat next to me. After giving him the "Dude, don't be gay" look, he moved to the other side. I watched as he tried to squeeze his big ass belly behind the table. We were talking about the game when he decided to change the subject.

"Remember the case involving the jogger?" he asked, stuffing his face.

Looking over my glass, I said, "Yeah sure."

Pretending to be nonchalant, he said, "Well, you know we found the body of a prostitute and this young girl…"

I stopped him. "You're telling me, why?" I asked.

"It would seem that during the investigation a description of a male, about your complexion, your height, your build…"

"Before you go any further…"

"I know what you are about to say, Izrael…that's your name right?"

"How did you remember my name?"

"It's all in the details, my friend. Plus, I'm a detective. It's my job to remember things. Anyway, like I was about to say..."

"All of us look alike," I said, interrupting him.

He laughed. "I wasn't going to say that at all, but now that you brought that up..."

"Careful officer, you wouldn't want to be considered a racist," I said, being facetious.

"My face is darker than your's brotha'...but, like I was saying...Just for the sake of it...where were you?"

"Look, I don't have an alibi because I don't need one, but if I needed one, I couldn't give it to you because she's dead."

"You're talking about your wife, right? Yeah, that was a shame – especially since you had just lost your son."

"Keeping tabs, officer?"

"It's my job to know about you and everyone else for that matter." He stood and threw some money onto the table. "So, what are you doing now?"

"What do you mean?"

"I mean..." he said, filling his mouth with some more nuts, "What cha' gon' do now? Wife gon' – son gon'. You are all alone in that big-ass house."

*He was tempting me, trying to bait me so that he would have a reason to drag my ass out of here in handcuffs. He didn't know who he was messing with.* Leaning on the table, I said, "Who do you go home to? A wife and kids who loves you dearly? Do you go home to a wife who is faithful? A wife who wants you? Needs you? Do you have kids who respect and honor you? A son who wants to be just like you when he grows up? Huh, Officer All-Up-In-My Business?"

"Huh? Are you being smart?" he asked.

"Naw, I wouldn't do that with someone as intelligent as you," I said, obviously being sarcastic.

Not catching on, he said, "I didn't think so." He turned to leave.

"Well, thanks for the company. I enjoyed it. By the way, stay close."

*Whatever asshole.* "Am I a suspect, officer?"

"Everyone's a suspect until we find out who did it. Now, you have a good evening," he said, leaving.

*So everyone's a suspect...Don't leave town he said...That motherfucker wasn't going to give me any peace.*

I threw some money onto the table and followed him outside of the bar. I saw him get into his car. I located mine, ran to it, jumped inside and decided to follow him. We took a lot of side streets until we ended up on the Dan Ryan Expressway heading south. I followed him for two miles before we exited. We took 95th west until we began to turn off into the Beverly area. I followed closely. We drove around for about fifteen minutes before we began to slow down. I created a distance between us. I watched as he pulled into the driveway of one of the homes. I pretended to drive pass to throw off any suspicion. I pulled around the corner and then drove back around and parked in front of the house.

His house stood out among the other homes on the block. It was white and trimmed in bright yellow – clearly a woman's touch. Every room was dark except for the nightlight which was definitely coming from a child's room. The basement held promise – completely black; its windows sat above the sidewalk completely out of view. The neighborhood was completely quite except for the loud voices coming from my head.

I glanced at my watch. *0000 – midnight.* In the car, I didn't think about what I was doing. I just knew that it needed to be done. *This officer was going to take away my freedom.* I wanted to take his before he took mine.

I waited another hour and then I got out of my car. I circled the house until I found myself in the back. I approached the back door. I jiggled the handle. The door was locked. I crept around to the other side of the house to find some windows leading to the basement. I pulled my shirt sleeve over my hand and began to gently tap against the window pane. It cracked slightly. I didn't want the broken glass to awaken the occupants of the home so I was extra careful. I looked around to see what I could use to remove the glass without making any noise. I was lucky. *Mr. Policeman likes to recycle.* I took a few of the newspapers and used them to continue to break the glass. Once every piece was removed, I entered.

It was dark. I began to feel around the room carefully. Once I found the stairs, I climbed. The steps creaked almost giving my position away. There was a door leading to the rest of the house. I turned the knob. It opened. I looked around and found myself in the kitchen. I stopped by the refrigerator. I looked inside. There were a couple of pieces of leftover chicken in there. I took one. I followed the hall that led me to the bedrooms. I was eating the chicken and thinking what a wonderful cook his wife was.

The first bedroom contained the body of his daughter. She looked so cute snuggled in her *Dora the Explorer* bed sheets. The next room I entered contained the body of a little boy snuggled in his *Harry Potter* bed sheets. I was licking my fingers when I stumbled upon the master bedroom. I stood in the doorway. They were both sleeping soundly. I could tell which side of the bed was his because I could see his big ass stomach from the door. I walked in. I didn't go to his wife's side of the bed. I wasn't interested in her. I wanted him. As I stood over him, I thought about ways I could take him out. Listening to him snore, the thought of strangling him came to mind, but that would be too merciful for someone as annoying as him. Carefully evaluating my options, I realized that I still had the chicken bones in my hand. Then it hit me. What would be more fitting? I stuffed the bones into his mouth. When he tried to snore the bones lodged into his throat. I stood back into the darkness of the room and watched as he struggled to remove the obstruction. The noise made his wife stir.

She mumbled, "Turn down the television. I'm trying to sleep." Then she fell back to sleep.

Suddenly, he fell out of the bed onto his knees with his hands clutched around his throat. He fell backwards onto the floor. I stepped out of the darkness. I stood over him. He grabbed at my leg, clawing, until finally he stopped. I stooped down over him and said, "When you get to Heaven, Big Guy, tell them Izrael sent you."

I left the same way I came.

# CHAPTER
# 70

I felt really weird the next day as if something was off kilter. I knew that I had promised myself that I wouldn't take those medicines anymore because they made me sick, but something wasn't right. I needed something, so I took two pills with a glass of orange juice and then got dressed to leave for the hospital.

When I reported at the front desk to receive my assignment, I noticed the nurses that were usually scheduled, weren't there. The women that were sitting there looked so familiar to me. I couldn't put my finger on it, but I could swear that I had seen them somewhere before.

One of the new nurses told me that my assignment today was to read to a soldier who was a quadriplegic on the eleventh floor. There was nothing strange in her request so I didn't think about it twice. When I entered the elevator, I began to feel sick to my stomach. Elevators never had that affect on me before so I assumed it was the medicine. When the elevator reached the floor that the patient was on, I stepped off. Initially, I wanted to stop by the men's bathroom, but something weird happened. A guy dressed in an orderly's uniform bumped into me.

"Hey man, I'm sorry. Are you okay?" he asked.

Checking myself out, I said, "It would seem that everything is fine." I looked up and shook my head. In disbelief, my mouth fell open. I thought I was seeing things.

"Don't I know you?" I asked.

"I don't think so," the man said, fixing his clothes.

"Naw man, I'm sure that I know you from somewhere," I insisted.

"If you say so, but I can't honestly say that I know you."

My mouth dropped open. "What the fuck? I do know you. Greg?" I asked.

"That's my name. How did you know that?"

"The question is, what the hell is going on? What are you doing here and what happened to your legs? I thought that you had AIDS."

"Damn dude...AIDS...where the hell you get that shit from?"

I dropped to my knees and began to pull Greg's pant leg up to expose what I thought for sure would be prosthetics, but they weren't.

"Hey man, get the hell off me before someone sees you doing that shit. I don't swing that way," he said, pulling his pant leg down.

"What the hell is going on? Am I dreaming?"

"Man, you are tripping. My advice, while you are here, you might want to get treated for that," he said, pointing toward my head.

I stumbled away from him. "This is not right. You were dying the last time I saw you."

"Man, I hope you never get a job writing greeting cards because you are depressing as hell," he said, before walking away. "You have a good day and don't forget to get that looked at."

Something's not right. I needed to talk to Eddie. I tried his number several times, but there was no answer because the number had been disconnected so I decided to call my mother. She picked up on the second ring.

Frantically, I said, "Mama, have you heard from Eddie? I'm trying to get in touch with him."

"Now, why are you doing this?" she asked.

"What mama? What are you talking about?"

"Why are you bringing him up?"

"Mama, what are you talking about?"

"You know that Eddie's dead."

"Oh no! When did he die? What are you talking about?"

My mother's phone clicked. "Look baby, I gotta go..."

"No...No," I said.

"Benny, what's wrong? What's going on?"

"Why are you calling me, Benny?"

"Because that's your name, honey," she insisted.

"No mama! No!"

She was still talking when it came to me, the women at the front desk. I remembered them – the teenager and the jogger. I hung up the phone and ran to the elevator. I must have pushed the wrong button because I ended up on the twelfth floor. As I exited the elevator, I noticed that there were people wandering around and talking to themselves. One of the patients approached me.

"You are under arrest," he said, pointing a make-believe gun at me. My eyes widen. "You...You...the officer?"

"Bang, bang," he said.

I tried to run. I wasn't moving. "What? What?" I looked down. "Where are my legs? Where the fuck are my legs? WHY AM I IN THIS FUCKING WHEELCHAIR?!!!!!!"

"Calm down, Mr. Thompson." The nurse approached me and began to push my wheelchair down the hall. "Now come on, it's almost time for ice cream. Don't you like ice cream, Benny?"

"My name ain't Benny. Stop calling me that. My name is Izrael. My name is Izrael!" I began to swing at the nurse thereby falling completely out of the wheelchair. "Man down!" I screamed. "Man down!"

The nurse called for help.

Looking at the nurse, I said, "Wanda?! It can't be....But I killed you. Remember? What the hell is going on?" I asked. My head began to hurt.

"It's Nurse Wanda to you and yes, you kill me alright...everyday... taking away all of my hopes and dreams. Now, be a good boy and let's get back into your wheelchair."

I tried dragging my torso down the hall. I was trying to get away when two men approached me. At first, I could only see their feet. When I looked up, I began to scream again. "Get your hands off of me you son-of-a-bitch! Wait a minute...I know you. You took my wife's purse."

One orderly spoke to the other, "He's having another episode."

The other one shook his head and said, "They just keep getting worst."

They began to carry me back to my chair. They tried to restrain me, but I fought to keep my hands free.

I screamed, "I killed you! I killed you! I killed all of you!"

Suddenly, a woman walked pass singing to what looked like a baby in her arms. Like an angel she appeared out of nowhere. She was singing the child a lullaby in a sweet and gentle voice.

"Ariel! But you are dead. What is happening to me?" I screamed hysterically wishing – praying that she could shed some light on what I was going through.

She turned toward me. "Yes?"

"Ariel," I pleaded.

"Izrael?" she said.

"Yes...Izrael...You know me. You know me. Ariel, why are these people calling me Benny? What the hell is going on? Tell them that I don't belong here...Ariel...Ariel."

"Yes?" She walked closer to me. "Yes," she said again.

"Ariel," I said as I reached out to her.

She said, "Poor Izrael."

"Ariel, help me."

"You want to see my baby?" she asked, smiling like a proud mother.

I didn't say anything, I couldn't.

In the gentlest voice she said, "Here he goes. Isn't he the most precious thing you've ever seen?"

Shaking, I reached out to hold the baby.

"His name is Michael," she said smiling. "Do you think he's hungry?" She attempted to remove her breasts from her gown. The orderlies rushed to stop her.

Slowly my eyes looked down at the blanket. Carefully, I unwrapped the contents to expose what was inside. Looking into the blanket, I saw that there was nothing wrapped in the blanket. I threw it onto the floor. "Ahhhhhhh!!!!! I'm not crazy! I'm not crazy! Do you hear me? I'm not CRAZY!!!!" I screamed.

Suddenly, I awakened. There was sweat pouring off of me. "Wha...Wha...What is going on?" I asked.

In a room no bigger than a closet, I realized that I was not alone.

*"Yea though I walk threw the valley of the shadow of death, I will fear no evil,"* the man read from **Psalm 23.**

"Who are you? Where am I?"

He continued, "For thou art with me; thy rod and thy staff they comfort me."

I surveyed the room frantically. The room contained a small one-person bed, topped with a mattress and pillow. Next to the bed was a stainless steel sink. The tan walls were completely bare. Adjacent to the bed was a wall with barred windows that allowed a small amount of light into the room. There was a small hanger mounting on the far wall where clothes and towels were hanging. I continued to survey the room. I saw a toilet, also made of stainless steel sitting in the corner. The floor was concrete and cold to the touch. At the top of the cell there was an air vent, and a bright fluorescent light that blinked on and off. The gentleman who sat across from me continued to read from the book in his hand.

I ran to the door, but it had been replaced with bars. The prison bars on the front side of the cell were two inches thick. I shook them in an attempt to get out. "Where am I? Why am I here?" I screamed.

"Prisoner 070566, keep it down. Don't let me tell you again," a voice down the hall said.

"What the hell is going on?" I asked again.

A voice in the cell next to me said, "Psst, Izrael...it's me Eddie. Calm down man...you're only going to make things bad for yourself."

Happy to hear a voice I was familiar with, I said, "Eddie is that you? Eddie, where are we?"

"We're in Hell brotha...We're in Hell."

THE END

# EPILOGUE

The courts found that he was not competent to stand trial for the murders of the three women and two men. A few years later, Izrael was given a reduced sentence, transferred to a mental health facility to serve out the remainder of his term. In the hospital, he was forced to take his medication – forced to deal with his demons – forced to distinguish fact from fiction. With good behavior, because of his condition, he was eventually given parole. A man, who was diagnosed with PTSD (Post Traumatic Stress Disorder), was released upon a society not equipped to deal with him. Without means of monitoring him, he refused to take his medication thereby making him delusional and unpredictable – a loaded weapon.

On the outside, no one could have known or predicted that he was capable of killing anyone, but in his mind none of it was real – it was all a fantasy to him.

He was smart and charismatic. He gave his victims, imagined or real, a chance to walk away, but they chose their plight.

Is he to blame? When the definitions of right and wrong are blurred, can we blame him?

Now, he sits looking out of his bedroom window, counting each day…thinking.

Who will watch him? Who will protect us from him? I guess we will have to wait and see.

# *W*HO IS *I*ZRAEL?

Look around you. Look at all of the faces around you.

Can you see it? Sometimes you can, but by that time it is too late.

Mental illness has a lot of faces...young, old, white, black, rich, poor, etc.

Mental illness is a subject often not discussed within our community; along with AIDS, poverty, teenage pregnancies, black on black crime, and everything else for that matter. Common traditions, myths, stigma, misinformation, and fear unjustifiably influence many of our families and their decisions to take ownership for the things that ultimately destroy us and everything around us. Consequently, while our families experience these things in amounts that are the same or in some cases more than the rest of the population, they are more likely to put off seeking treatment or answers – believing that "if it isn't broke don't fix it." As a result, ignorance and fear becomes a cancer that eats away at everything we are or could be.

We tend to rely on family, religion and friends for emotional support, rather than turning to the professionals, even though this may at times be necessary.

Often, we are told that ignorance is bliss, and that knowledge is power, but you wouldn't know it based on our actions. So a majority of us avoid responsibility for ourselves and one another by playing stupid or blaming one another.

We all know someone like Benny…like Izrael…like Ariel. We ignore them, avoid them, or make fun of them. These people are our people and yet, we treat them like sideshow freaks instead of embracing them and telling them that we are here for them.

We avoid the issue because we don't know how to deal with it. We have to stop this and have an honest dialogue about what's killing us mentally, spiritually, economically, and physically. Maybe if we can better understand why we act the way that we do at times – maybe just maybe, we will find solutions to some of those issues affecting us and our communities.

I'm going to get off of my soap box now. I just believe that if we do better, things will get better.

Thanks for allowing me to vent.

Available Now

# REVIEWS FROM
# READERS LIKE YOU

Excellent & Bravo! The title *[Autumn Leaves]* made me pick it up. Meeting you made me read it. Finishing it made me glad for both. Your message was tremendous!!

**- Floria Christine**

Thank you for being such an inspiration. I read the entire book yesterday. As you stated *Autumn Leaves* was a very "adult" book. I thought you had a powerful introduction; it pulled me in. I found the story line and character development to be interesting. I like your straight to the point, down to earth writing style. I found myself smiling at some of the phrases you used. I think you have a wonderful gift of storytelling and there are unlimited possibilities before you.

**- Sharon J. Kendall**

Just like *Never What it Seems* (Diane's first novel), *Autumn Leaves* had me on the edge of my seat from beginning to end. The subject matter is shocking, to say the least, but I completely understand why the author included it. The story is about cause and effect...right and wrong. It is a story that makes you take inventory of yourself. The author put together a story so compelling that I couldn't stop reading it...I couldn't put it down. I enjoyed it...a lot. I can't wait for the next one.

**- Tonya Flowers**

*Autumn Leaves* took my interest from the first two chapters, I remember reading it in the car at night with the lights on because I couldn't put it down. I thought I knew what was going to happen next, but the author has a way of putting you into the story and then shocking you as though you were right there as another character in the story watching it all unfold.

Wow, this was awesome and won't be disappointing to anyone who reads it. I need more. I cannot wait for the next novel. These awesome novels can't come fast enough. Diane Martin has an amazing talent. I am hooked!

**- LaKessa Murphy**

If you are an outsider looking in you would never know what is going on with Claire. This is why you have to read Autumn Leaves. This book is going to take you on a mission with Claire, Mimi, and Autumn. The three ladies put you in a world spin of twists and turns that is going to make you take a look in the mirror at yourself and say Awww...

This is my first book that I read of Diane Martin and she has a new fan to add to her list. The author leaves you with a deep message at the end that leaves you saying to yourself, what if Claire...?

**- Claudia Mosley, author of**
**_I Can Have My Cake And Eat It Too_**

I just finished reading *Autumn Leaves* at 2:30 a.m. this morning. I could not put the book down until I finished it. Oh my God, I was so surprised at the out come at the end. You must do a sequel and tell us what happened to Wayne. Claire was a very interesting character that wasn't sure who she was. Keep me posted when *Falling Angel* comes out. Be blessed and keep on inspiring me to take the time to write.

**- Emma Johnson**

I started reading *Autumn Leaves* yesterday around 11 am while I was out taking [care] of business. Girl, I was so into the book that I was on Chapter 30 before I knew it. So, I said when I get home I have to finish up this book, because I want to know what the he** is happening to Claire. So, I began again around 9 pm and finished at 2 am in the morning. Yes, your book was a page turner. I was laughing out loud at the end when Claire told Mimi what was going on and how Mimi responded. I said that sounds just how a friend responds to a situation like that.

Omgosh.....your book was EXCELLENT! After talking to you at the library and you told me how you dream of the events and the book...you are truly gifted. *Autumn Leaves* is another well written book. I could relate to the situations presented in the book as well. Girl, you are so talented and all I can say is that I am happy I know you. It's truly a pleasure to read the novels you write. So, you say there is talk about making "Never What it Seems," into a movie, "Autumn Leaves," should be a movie as well. I wish you tons of prosperity in all your future endeavors.

**-Michelle Moorer (Author of Shhh...Don't Tell)**

It *[Autumn Leaves]* kept my attention that's for sure. Very suspenseful! This is what I would look for in a novel. Keep up the good work.

**- Otilla Stokes**

Making Choices and Keeping Secrets Can Be Deadly

In *Autumn Leaves,* author Diane Martin, introduced readers to a unique and interesting story of forbidden love, secrets, revenge, and choices. Claire thought she had everything she wanted – she was in love with the man of her dreams and she had a great best friend. Yet, there was still something missing. After being introduced to Autumn, a high school friend of her boyfriend, Claire began to experience desires that she never felt before. Claire began to make choices that affected her relationship with her boyfriend. She also began to keep secrets and tell lies that became deadly to them all.

Martin has written a very sensitive story. Readers will become involved in the lives of the characters as they made choices that affect everyone. Many of the topics discussed are considered taboo despite being considered mainstream by others. Martin discusses the consequences and options that character Claire had to face and the impact her choices had on her everyday life. I found the book to be very entertaining and I literally dropped my jaw when I got to the end. This book is a must read for anyone that likes drama mixed with some mystery.

**- Priscilla C. Johnson**

Available Now

# REVIEWS FROM READERS LIKE YOU

I purchased your book and once I completed it…WOW! This was a great book and I couldn't put it down until I was finished. I passed the book on to my daughter-in-law and she thought the same thing. Keep up the good work. I'll be looking for more to come.

**- Beverly Price**

I'm reading *Never What it Seems*. It's a page turner. I found myself wanting to find out what happened next as I ended each chapter. I'm on chapter 48 (pretty good for a day an a half)…Where the girls former loves have now re-enter their lives. The story line is impeccable, well written, and I am suggesting this book to all my friends and family who loves to read. I'm going to read this book again.

**- JoMonique Whiteside**

You won't remember me but I met you at the [Black Women's Expo] on Sunday afternoon. My sister and I were together and she brought your book *Never What it Seems*. She let me read it first since I read faster than she (smile). Remember she was telling you how she would be sixty-nine on her birthday which is today. Anyway, I just wanted to let you know that I have just finished your book and enjoyed it very much. If your second [book] is as good (and I'm sure it will be) as this, I will be waiting for the third. Just wanted you to know you have a fan that was happy to meet the Author. May your success continue.

**- Anita Williams**

I have already started *Never What It Seems* and I am thoroughly enjoying it. Your characters are so believable; I can't wait to see what happens next with AJ and Dee. You are very talented and I am looking forward to reading *Autumn Leaves.*

**- Yvonne Whaley**

I finished your book *Never What It Seems* a few days ago. Wow! It was a page turner. AJ, as the kids [would] say, was no punk. It was an interesting story about two friends and how they managed to overcome some tough obstacles in their lives. So, I could relate very well to it. Just wanted to let you know I look forward to reading your next book, *Autumn Leaves.* Keep up the great work.

**- Angela Powell**

It was truly a pleasure meeting you and sharing time with you. I started reading your book and I must have read the first chapter 3 times. It is so easy to read and it flows so well. I guess you are wondering, why did I have to read this chapter 3 times? Well, because it was like reading a portion of my life. I couldn't get over seeing this before me. It is part of my past, but I just kept reflecting on it. (It was kind of therapeutic.) I also decided to let my daughter read it first to see how she reacts. Actually, I'm in the middle of a book and I can see I'm going to [really] enjoy your book girl!

We laugh often about where God has delivered us from.
Stay encouraged and be blessed.

**- Ms. Sheila**

I think this book *[Never What it Seems]* is phenomenal. It takes us into the lives of two young women that basically go through what all women experience growing up in this day and age from childhood to adulthood. It also points out not all men are deceiving, but are willing to take chances when it comes to true love. It was wonderfully written, and I look forward to the next novel written by Diane Martin.

**- Marjorie Billinger**

I've just gotten back to Chicago and while I was away I completed *Never What It Seems*. All I can say is Superb, Excellent, and Outstanding! That book was one of the best books I've ever read and I'm encouraging everyone I know to get a copy. Let me tell you it had me on the edge of my seat from beginning to end. This is definitely a book for everyone, so check it out!!! That being said, I have got to get a copy of *Autumn Leaves* if it is anything like *Never What it Secms*...I just can't wait!

**- Ana Mar'e (Pink Diamond Inc.)**

Diane Martin's vividly, entertaining tale of friendship between two women was a true testimony of trial and triumph. An anthem for every woman who has ever loved, lost, and regained the true meaning of an unedifying spirit of hope. For every page read, I was drawn deeper and deeper until I was left wanting more.

**- Elise Burks**

I just had to let you know that I read *Never What It Seems* over the weekend. It was really a fast read. I was very involved and hated to put it down for even a moment. The story allowed me to take a break from my reality.

**- Danielle L. Broadwater**

*Never What it Seems* is truly never what it seems. I found myself drawn into the story. I couldn't put it down! The chain of events continued to grab me. The author is very consistent about several things, but what warms you most is that the two main characters, Dee & AJ, are amazingly strong. I love and admire their courage. The author displays a relationship of real unconditional friendship between these ladies. Such a relationship is rarely seen or experienced today; the one that ultimately facilitates their success. This was an awesome start for a first novel. I so look forward to the next!

**- LaKessa Murphy**

I really enjoyed your first book, *(Never What it Seems)*. When I started reading the book, I could not put it down. It captivated me to the point where I did not want to see or do anything, but find out what was happening on the next page and in the next chapter. Your book was truly a "Calgon Moment", it took me away. It forced me to relax, smile, laugh, and take my mind off of the small stuff. Throughout the entire book there was never a dull moment. Your book took me back to when I was a young girl reading Judy Blum's novels; sweet, innocent, and down to earth.

**- Virnita Martin**

Girl, let me tell you! I finished reading your book earlier today and it was excellent! Your book was a trip. Let me just say that the ending was not what I expected. I was out done! Your novel [Never What it Seems] was a well written and a very intriguing piece of work [written] by a vivid and creative mind! Congratulations and much success on all your endeavors to come!

**- Michelle Moorer (Author of Shhh...Don't Tell)**

# $\mathscr{A}$CKNOWLEDGMENTS

To all of the people who purchased my novels entitled, *Never What it Seems* and *Autumn Leaves,* I appreciate all of your support and thank you for all of the wonderful reviews and feedback.

To all of the African-American bookstores in Chicago, thank you so much for taking a chance on me and placing my novels on your shelves.

Much appreciation goes out to all of the libraries who have allowed me the opportunity to place my novels among all of the literary minds that came before me.

A special thank you goes out to Denise Billups of Borel Graphics of Chicago. She is the creative mind, the genius, behind the design of my novels from cover to text.

A heartfelt thank you goes out to the ladies of the Jus' Sisthas book club, Ms. Burgest, and Kelley Nichols for inviting me out to speak and break bread with them. I had such a wonderful time. I am also grateful to all of the online book clubs. I have developed some wonderful relationships with readers here and abroad. Thanks for all of the encouragement, the pats on the back, and the jokes. You guys keep me laughing (you know who you are).

A special shout-out goes out to all of the readers, professors, and friends at Chicago State University.

Thank you goes out to the nurses and doctors at my clinic, friends at the local stores, post office, my neighbors, and my best friends – old and new.

Hugs and kisses goes out to my Mama, Tonya, Oriel, Janice [Scoop], Sharmonique, Simone, Otilla, and Beverly. To all of my pretend sisters, I haven't forgotten about you – thank you for always being there and forgiving me even when I couldn't call, visit, write, or email. I love you guys so much.

Please note that initially everyone's name was listed here, but to avoid accidentally overlooking someone, I've kept it "generic". I love and appreciate all of you.

To all of you, thank you for believing in me and for your continued support. I'm extremely grateful to you for your guidance, patience, and understanding.

Diane Martin

Email: dimartin01@yahoo.com | Website: http://dimartin01.books.officelive.com